BUTTERFLIES
IN NOVEMBER

AUÐUR AVA ÓLAFSDÓTTIR

BUTTERFLIES
IN
NOVEMBER

Translated from the Icelandic by
Brian FitzGibbon

PUSHKIN PRESS
LONDON

Pushkin Press
71–75 Shelton Street
London WC2H 9JQ

Original text © 2004 Auður Ava Ólafsdóttir
English translation © 2013 Brian FitzGibbon

Butterflies in November was first published in Iceland as
Rigning í nóvember by Salka

This edition first published by Pushkin Press in 2013

ISBN 978 1 782270 10 2

 MIÐSTÖÐ ÍSLENSKRA BÓKMENNTA
ICELANDIC LITERATURE CENTER

*We thank the Icelandic Literature Center for their generous
support of this translation.*

Set in Monotype Baskerville by Tetragon, London
and printed by CPI Group (UK) Ltd, Croydon, CR0 4YY

www.pushkinpress.com

Dedicated to Melkorka Sigríður

Where are there towns but no houses,
roads but no cars, forests but no trees?

Answer: on a map.

(Riddle on children's breakfast TV)

ZERO

This is how it appears to me now, as I look back, without perhaps fully adhering to the chronology of events. In any case, there we are, pressed against each other in the middle of the photograph. I've got my arm draped over his shoulder and he is holding onto me somewhere—lower, inevitably—a dark brown lock of hair dangles over my very pale forehead, and he smiles from ear to ear, clutching something in his outstretched clenched hand.

His protruding ears sit low on his large head and his hearing aid, which seems unusually big and antiquated, looks like a receiver for picking up messages from outer space. Unnaturally magnified by the thick lenses of his spectacles, his eyes seem to almost fill the glass, giving him a slightly peculiar air. In fact, people turn on the street to gawk at him, staring first at him, then at me, and then pin their eyes back on him again for as long as he stays in view, as we walk across the playground, for example, and I close the iron gate behind us. As I help him into the seat of the car and fasten his safety belt, I notice we are still being watched from other cars.

In the background of the photograph, there is a four-year-old manual car. The three goldfish are writhing in the boot—he doesn't know that yet—and the double blue sleeping bag is soaking wet. Soon I'll be buying two new down duvets at the Co-op, because it's not proper for a thirty-three-year-old woman to be sharing a sleeping bag with an unrelated child, it's simply not done. It shouldn't be any bother to buy them because the glove compartment is crammed with notes, straight from the bank. No crime has been committed, though, unless it's a crime to have slept with three men within a 300-kilometre stretch of the Ring Road, in that mostly untarmacked zone, where the coastal strip is at its narrowest, wedged between glaciers and the shore, and there is an abundance of single-lane bridges.

Nothing is as it should be. It's the last day of November, the island is engulfed in darkness and we are both wearing sweaters. I'm in a white polo-neck and he is in a newly knit mint-green hoodie with a cabled pattern. The temperature is similar to what it was in Lisbon the day before, according to the man on the radio, and the forecast is for rain and warmer weather ahead. This is the reason why a woman shouldn't be venturing into the dark wilderness alone with a child, without good reason, least of all in the vicinity of those single-lane bridges, where the roads are frequently flooded.

I'm not presumptuous enough to expect a new lover to appear at every single-lane bridge, without wanting, however, to preclude such a possibility.

When I look at the picture in greater detail, I see a young man, a few steps behind us, about seventeen years old I would guess, between me and the boy, although his face is slightly out of focus. I discern delicate facial features under his cap and get the feeling he has bad skin, which is beginning to improve. He seems sleepy and leans against the petrol pump with his eyes half closed.

If one were to examine the photo in extreme close-up, I wouldn't be surprised if there were traces of feathers on the tyres or bloodstains on the hubcaps, even though three weeks had passed since my husband walked out with the orthopaedic mattress from the double bed, all the camping equipment and ten boxes of books—that's just how it went. But one needs to bear in mind that things are not always what they seem and, contrary to the dead stillness of a photograph, reality is in a state of perpetual flux.

ONE

Thank God it wasn't a child.

I unfasten my safety belt and leap out of the car to examine the animal. It seems to be pretty much in one piece, totally unconscious, with a dangling neck and bleeding chest. I suspect a crushed goose heart under its oil-soiled plumage.

Papers flew out of their folders as I screeched to a halt, translations in various languages are scattered on the floor, although an entire pile of documents has remained intact on the crammed back seat.

The good thing about my job—and one of the perks that I never hesitate to remind my clients of—is that I deliver everything to them in person, drive over to them with proof-read articles, theses and translations, as if they were Thai noodle salads and spring rolls. It might seem old-fashioned, but it works. People like the tangibility of paper and, for one brief moment, to glimpse into the eyes of the stranger who has, in some cases, peered into the essence of their souls. It's best to deliver right before dinner, I find, just as the pasta is reaching cooking point and cannot be left a second longer, or when the onion has been fried and the fish lies waiting on a bed of breadcrumbs, and the master of the house hasn't had the good sense to turn off the heat under the frying pan before answering the door. In my experience that's the quickest way to get through it. People don't like inviting guests into a house smelling of food or to get sucked into a discussion with a stranger when they're standing there in their socks or even bare-footed, in the middle of a narrow hallway crammed with shoes and surrounded by squabbling children. In my experience these are the ideal circumstances in which to settle a bill with the least likelihood of people trying to persuade me to knock off the VAT. As soon as I tell them I don't take credit cards, they put up no resistance and swiftly write me a cheque and grab their delivery.

When people come to me in the small office space I rent down by the harbour, they normally give themselves plenty of time to ponder on my remarks and convince me of their good intentions, of their in-depth knowledge of the subject matter, and precisely why they decided to word things in the way they did. It's not my job to rewrite their articles, they tell me, pointing out that in such and such a paragraph I skipped nine words, but simply to correct typos, as one of my customers put it, as he was adjusting his glasses and tie in the mirror in the hallway and flattening his kiss curls.

The idea wasn't to oversimplify complex concepts, he says, the article is geared to experts in the field. Even though I had refrained from making any comments on his dubious use of the dative case in his *Dam Project Report*, I did wonder whether the word *beneficial*, which cropped up more than fourteen times on one page, might not occasionally be replaced by alternative and slightly more exotic adjectives, such as *propitious* or *advantageous*. This wasn't something I said out loud, but simply a thought I entertained to perk myself up. Once these issues have been settled, some men like to say a little bit about themselves and also to ask some questions about me, whether I'm married, for example, and that kind of thing. On two or three occasions I've even toasted bread for them. I have to confess, though, that I didn't write my ad. It was my friend Auður, who obviously got a bit carried away. Overkill isn't my style:

I provide proof-reading services and revise BA theses and articles for specialized magazines and publications on any subject. I also revise electoral speeches, irrespective of party affiliations, and correct any revealing errors in anonymous complaints and/or secret letters of admiration, and remove any inept or inaccurate philosophical or poetic references from congratulatory speeches and elevate obituaries to a higher (almost divine) level. I am fully versed in all the quotations of our departed national poets.

I translate from eleven languages both into and out of Icelandic, including Russian, Polish and Hungarian. Fast and accurate translations. Home delivery service. All projects are treated as confidential.

I pick up the lukewarm bird I've just run over and assume it's a male. By a cruel twist of fate, I recently proof-read an article about the love lives of geese and their unique and lifelong fidelity to their mates. I scan the flock in search of his widowed companion. The very last members are still waddling across the slippery icy road, towards the sidewalk on the other side, spreading their big orange webbed feet on the tarmac. As far as I can make out, none of them has stepped out of the flock to look for her partner and I can't see any likely match for the bird I'm holding in my arms. I have, however, recently developed the knack for distinguishing black cats on the street from each other on the basis of their responses to caresses and sudden emotional reactions. The thing that surprises me the most, as I stand there in the middle of the road, still holding the fairly plump animal by the neck, is that I feel neither repulsion nor guilt. I like to think of myself as a reasonably compassionate human being; I try to avoid confrontation, find it difficult to reject requests delicately put to me by sensitive males, and buy every lottery ticket that any charity slips through my letterbox. And yet, when I go to the supermarket later on and stand there in front of the butcher's slab, I'll feel the same rush of excitement I get before Christmas, as I muse on the spices and trimmings, and wonder whether the pattern of the Goodyear tyre will be visible under the thick wild game sauce.

"Well then, good year to you in advance," is what I'll say to my guests at the surprise dinner party I'll throw on a dark November night, without any further explanations.

I rip out several pages of a painfully tedious article about thermal conductors to place under the bird, before carefully lowering the carcass into the boot. It's obviously ages since I opened it, because I discover that it is almost completely full of kitchen rolls that I bought to sponsor some sports excursion for disabled kids—a good job I didn't opt for the prawns.

The goose won't suffer the same fate, because I'm about to spring a fun culinary surprise on my husband, the great chef himself. First, though, I was planning on taking one last detour to an apartment block in the Melar district to do something I'd told myself I would never do again.

TWO

I park my car close to the block and rush up the threadbare carpet of the lily-blue staircase, tackling two steps at a time. I don't allow myself to be bothered by the two or three doors that open during my ascent, ever so slightly, to the width of the vertical slit of a letter box, releasing the odours of well-kept homes. I don't care if anyone can retrace my steps, because what I am about to do for the third time in three weeks is not a habit of mine, but a total exception in my marriage. When I rush out later on, I'll be able to tell myself that I won't be coming back here any more, which is why I can afford to be indifferent to those gaps in the doorways and prying eyes. I'm in a hurry to wrap my hands around my lover's neck, standing on his newly laid parquet, and to run my fingers down the hollow of his neck, leaving a red streak in their wake, and then to get it over with, as soon as possible, so that I can buy the trimmings for the goose before the shops close. The most time-consuming task turns out to be the removal of my boots; he stretches to hold onto the door frame as I offer him one foot. He has removed his glasses and his eyes are glued to me throughout. The faint October sun, which is sinking over the tip of Seltjarnarnes, filters through the semi-closed slats of the venetian blinds, corrugating our bodies in stripes, like two zebras meeting furtively by a pool of water. I can sense from the waft of washing powder emanating from the bedclothes that he has changed the sheets. Everything is very tidy; this is the kind of apartment I could easily abandon in a fire or war, without taking anything with me, without any regrets. The only incongruous detail in the decor is the patterned curtain valances, concealing the top of the blinds.

"Mum made those and gave them to me when I divorced," he says, clearing his throat.

Naturally, the environment is bound to change according to one's moods and feelings, although I don't want to get into a discussion on the notion of beauty and well-being right now. One can't exactly say that there's anything premeditated about the fact that I'm sitting here naked on the edge of this bed, nothing planned as such, it's just the way my life is at the moment. I'm indifferent to the drabness or even perhaps ugliness of this apartment and I don't mind that he sometimes spells *hyper* with an *i* or writes *hidrodinamic fluid*, and if he can be a bit vulgar in the way he talks or even inappropriate sometimes, it is because he has a firm and secure touch. Although I can't really boast of any extensive experience in this field, I know there is no correlation between sex and linguistics, I've learnt that much.

A small feather has stuck to the bloodstain on the first page, but I don't have to ponder on whether I should give him the article before or afterwards. I know from experience that it's best to wait, business and pleasure shouldn't be mixed. After we had slept together for the first time, he looked surprised when I handed him the bill with the VAT clearly highlighted.

After the deed, I help him smooth out the sheet, while he squeezes the goose-down quilt back into the stripy blue cover, which has slipped off the foot of the bed into a ball. He confides in me, sharing something a woman should never divulge. It is only then that I first notice the bizarre tattoo on his lower back. It vaguely resembles a spider's web, which seems incongruous for a man of his social status. Skimming it, I feel the protuberance of a scar. When I quiz him about it, he tells me it was an accident, but I don't know whether he is referring to the scar or the tattoo. He holds out his hand, clutching a pair of white lace panties between his thumb and index.

"Aren't these yours?" he asks, as if they could be someone else's.

I'm in a hurry to get home, but when I've finished washing my hands with his pink floating scented soap and step out of the bathroom, I see he has set the table, boiled eggs, buttered two slices of toast with salmon and made some tea for me. He is still topless and bare-footed and stands there, watching me eating, as he slips his shirt back on.

"I saw your car in town in the middle of the week and parked right beside it, didn't you notice?" he asks.

Can't say that I did.

"So you didn't notice that someone had scraped the ice off your windscreen either?"

No, I didn't, but thanks anyway.

"I noticed your car is due for an MOT..."

When I've finished both slices of toast and am about to say thanks and kiss him goodbye because I won't be coming back again, he asks me how often I think about him.

Every three or four days, I say.

"That makes 5.6 times over the past three weeks," says the newly divorced expert, who has only fastened one of the buttons on his gaping shirt. "I obviously think of you a lot more than you think of me, about sixty times a day and also when I wake up at night. I wonder what you're up to, and watch you putting on your cream after the bath, trying to figure out what it must be like to be you. Then, in the evenings, I imagine you don't slip into bed until your husband is asleep."

My husband isn't home much in the evenings these days.

Then he asks me if I intend to divorce him.

"No, that hasn't entered my mind," I say.

Because I probably love my husband. But I don't say that. Then he bluntly tells me that this will be the last time.

"The last time that what?"

"That we sleep together. It's too painful saying goodbye to you every time, I feel like I'm standing on the edge of a cliff and I'm scared of heights."

It has grown eerily dark by the time I dash down the stairs of the apartment block for the third time in as many weeks. This time I'm gone for good and I will never again do what I've just done, I'm in a hurry to get home. Even if it is unlikely that anyone is waiting for me there. Driving, I listen to Mendelssohn's "Summer Song" on the car radio. It's an old crackly recording, but the presenter doesn't seem to notice, not that I'm really listening to it.

THREE

Although no woman can ever fully map out her life, there is, nonetheless, a 99.9 per cent chance that I will end this day at home in bed with my husband. And yet, to my surprise and precisely when I'm in a hurry to get back home, I find myself reversing my four-year-old manual car, with some difficulty, into a parking space close to my old house on the street I lived on two years ago. The curtains look unfamiliar to me and I suddenly remember I no longer have a key to this front door, that I've moved twice since I lived here, without, however, moving very far. As I'm about to drive away from the house, I see they've hung a crib mobile in the room that once hosted my computer. To be absolutely sure of it, I wait until I see a man walk past the window with a little baby on his shoulders. At least I know it's not my husband, nor my child. Because I don't have a child.

I'm still in the car when the phone rings. It's the music teacher and pianist, my friend, Auður. She is a single mother, and has a four-year-old deaf son and is now six months pregnant again. In the evenings she sits up on her bed playing her accordion and rarely says no to a glass of brandy, if the opportunity presents itself.

She tells me she can't talk long, because she's busy dealing with a difficult pupil and an even more difficult parent, but it so happens, she adds, almost lowering her voice to a whisper in the receiver, that she has booked but can't go to an appointment with a fortune-teller, although not exactly a fortune-teller, she says, more of a medium, and would I like to go instead of her? I hear someone crying behind her, but can't make out whether it's a child or an adult.

She stumbled on this medium on a whim two years ago and since then has been firmly entangled in the web of her own destiny; nothing that happens to her catches her unprepared any more. At least the child came as no surprise.

I'm still waiting for the baby to disappear. I don't think about it. That's how I make it disappear, by not thinking about it. Until it stops existing. I can't say I never think of it, though. I've looked it up in a book and know that it is no longer a 2.5-centimetre creature with webbed feet and that it has started to take on a human form, that it has developed toes. Soon I won't be able to fit into my flower-embroidered jeans. I hide it under my woollen cardigan with brass buttons so that no one will notice it, so that no one will know. Soon I will be going out into the world. When I've finished school. It's all still purely imaginary.

Auður knows my scepticism regarding fate.

"What do you mean you'd rather not? There's a two-year waiting list," she blabs on, as if she were trying to firmly and rationally deal with a capricious child. "They say she's the absolute best in the northern hemisphere, they've been doing tests on her in America with brain scans and electrodes and stuff and they just can't figure it out, can't find any pattern, no thread, you've got to be there in twenty minutes on the dot, so you need to get going right now. It'll cost you 3,500 krónur, no credit cards, no receipts. If you let an opportunity like this slip by, you'll never get a chance again."

She has to stop talking now, but will call me later to hear how it went, she whispers in a hoarse voice, before hanging up.

FOUR

Twenty minutes later, here I am out in the middle of a new estate on the outskirts of the city, once more on my way to the house of a stranger. The neighbourhood is in mid-construction and stretches out flatly in all directions under a high sky, with patches of marshland here and there, and little to shelter the houses. It takes me a good while to find the half-finished house. The streets are barely discernible and devoid of lamp-posts, house numbers or names, chaos seems to reign with all the randomness of the first day. But at least construction seems to have started on a church. What finally draws my attention to the right house is a pile of small pieces of wood in the driveway, tidily arranged to form a bizarre pattern, some kind of broken spider's web that must have required some thought. Scaffolding still covers the façade and the lawn is strewn with stones and, no doubt, berries in the summer.

She is nothing like the image I've built up of a fortune-teller and reminds me of an Italian sex bomb from the sixties. It's Gina Lollobrigida in the flesh who greets me at the door, without me remembering having knocked, looking stunning and of an indeterminate age, wearing a close-cut dress and high heels. What distinguishes her from the common fold, though, are her piercing eyes and tiny pupils, pinheads in an ocean of shimmering blue.

Inside, the house is almost empty. Naked light bulbs dangle here and there, a few plastic flowers, an image of Christ with pretty curly locks and big blue eyes welling with tears. On one wall there is a pencil drawing of a tall Icelandic turf house with four gables. Despite the mounting darkness outside, the house seems full of light. The woman's voice is as charming as she is:

"I was expecting you earlier," is the first thing she says to me, "months ago."

Her spell works on me and my thoughts immediately become transparent. Pinned to the sofa, I feel the muscles relaxing around my neck. I rest my head on the embroidered cushion and ask whether she minds if I lie down, instead of sitting opposite her at the table.

She constantly shuffles an old deck of cards and arranges them on the table, counting and pairing numbers and suits, my past and future. She can obviously read me like an open book. I find it quite uncomfortable to be browsed through in that way. But she makes no mention of adultery or the dead goose in my boot, and doesn't talk about what must be written all over my forehead, that I'm still carrying alien liquid inside me that I fear could leak onto the velvet sofa.

Instead she focuses on my childhood and other things I've no memory of and know nothing about. She mentions mounds of manure and the broken elastic of some skin-coloured breeches, and keeps on coming back to the torn thread, they could be underpants, she says, cream-coloured, or they could be a pyjama bottom. I don't know where she's going with this.

"I'm just telling you what the cards show me, hang on to it."

Then, in the same breath, she turns to my future.

"It's all threes here," she says, "three men in your life over a distance of 300 kilometres, three dead animals, three minor accidents or mishaps, although you aren't necessarily directly involved in them, animals will be maimed, but the men and women will survive. However, it is clear that three animals will die before you meet the man of your life."

I wearily try to point out from the depths of the sofa that I am a married woman and, by way of proof, feebly raise my right arm to stroke the simple wedding ring between my thumb and index. She pays no heed to this information, I'm not even sure she heard what I said.

"Things that no one will be expecting will happen, people will experience a lot of wetness, short-sightedness, greed, isolation, more wetness."

"How do you mean wetness?"

"It'll wet more than your ankles, that's all I can say, impossible to know anything more than that today. I do, however, see a large marine mammal on dry land."

She pauses briefly, there is a dead stillness in the room.

"There is a triple conception," she continues, "one of them may be a trinity."

What does the woman mean?

"My brother had test-tube triplets, they're two years old now," I awkwardly interject.

"I'm not talking about them," the woman snaps, "I'm talking about three pregnant women, three babies on the way, three women who will give birth to babies over the coming months."

"Well, there's my friend Auður…"

Fortunately, she clearly has no interest in my input and shuts me up with a dismissive wave of the hand, as if I were an irksome teenager interrupting her private dialogue with some invisible being.

"And then there's a big boy here, an adolescent, a narrow fjord, black sand, dwarf fireweed, the mouth of a river, seals nearby."

Another one of her pauses.

"There's a lottery prize here, money and a journey. I see a circular road, and I also see another ring that will fit on a finger, later. You'll never be the same again, but it's all done, you'll be standing with the light in your arms."

Those were her words, to the letter, "with the light in my arms", whatever that was supposed to mean.

"To summarize it all," she concludes in the manner of an experienced lecturer, "there is a journey here, money and love, even though you can expect some odd twists along the way. But I can't see which of these three men it will be."

When I finally stand up, I notice that she has placed all the cards on the table and arranged them in a strange pattern that is not unlike the one formed by the pile of wood outside, some kind of spider's web with broken threads.

I suddenly feel the urge to ask:

"Did you make that wooden structure outside?"

She fixes her gaze on me, her pupils piercing through an ocean of shimmering blue:

"Keep an eye on the patterns, but don't allow them to distort your vision, it takes a while to develop a good eye for patterns. Nevertheless, if I were in your shoes, I wouldn't allow myself to be led into marshland in the fog. Remember that not everything is what it seems."

As I'm about to hold out my hand to say goodbye, she suddenly embraces me and says:

"It wouldn't be a bad idea to buy a lottery ticket."

Her two adolescent sons offer to escort me back to the car, which I've forgotten where I parked, seemingly quite far away. Marching on either side of me, they look on with determined airs, as if they'd taken on a mission that had to be accomplished at all costs. We walk for what seems like a very long time, I even get the impression we're travelling in circles and can't remember ever coming this way. Then, just as I'm beginning to feel totally lost, the car materializes in front of me, close to a sea wall, in a place I don't remember leaving it. It is unlocked, as usual, but all the papers are in their proper place, although I couldn't vouch that every single sheet is in its pile. I see no point in checking on the goose in the boot. As I say goodbye, I realize for the first time that the brothers are twins and notice how they both always seem to shift their weight to their right legs as they walk. There is something odd in their gazes, pupils like black pins in an ocean of shimmering blue. As soon as I turn the key in the ignition and am about to wave them goodbye, I realize they've evaporated into thin air.

FIVE

He's home. I linger on the frozen lawn before entering, looking in at the light of my own home, and shilly-shally by the redcurrant bush with the goose in my hands, wondering whether he can see it on me, whether he's noticed. From here I can see him wandering from room to room for no apparent reason, shifting random objects and alternately flicking light switches on and off. I move from window to window around the illuminated home, as if it were a doll's house with no façade, trying to piece together the fragments of my husband's life.

Then he has suddenly emptied the washing machine and is standing in the bedroom with all the laundry in his arms, something he doesn't normally do. He's not much of a handyman either, but for some odd reason he seems to have changed the bulb under the porch and fixed a cupboard door in the kitchen. All of a sudden he is staring out the window into the darkness and I feel as if he were looking straight at me, scrutinizing me at length, as if he were pondering on how we might be connected or whether I'm going to come in or remain in the garden. He is naked above the waist, which must be quite chilly for him with that wet laundry in his arms, unless he is insulated by his body hair. When he bends over the bed, for a brief moment, I get the feeling there is someone lying on the bed, below my line of vision, and that he is about to lie down beside the person, but then he suddenly springs up again with my light blue damp panties in his hands, which he carefully stretches and presses in his big hands. He hangs them on the drying rack he has set up by the bed. I now see four pegs tugging at the extremities of my underwear. He may not spend much time at home and we may not talk much, but I have a good husband and I know I'm the one to blame, I never went to the shops.

SIX

He has obviously cleared up the kitchen and left a plate on the table for me, complete with knife, fork, glass and napkin. He has put on a shirt and tie, as if he were on his way out to an urgent meeting, and slips on the thick blue oven gloves, before stooping over the stove to pull out the lasagne.

He doesn't sit with me, but tells me that he needs to talk, that we need to talk, that it's vital, which is why he is pacing the chequered kitchen floor, in straight lines from the table to the refrigerator and then from the refrigerator to the stove, without any discernible purpose. His hands are burrowed in his pockets and he doesn't look at me. I sink onto the kitchen stool, with my back upright, still wearing my scarf.

"This can't go on."

"What can't go on?"

"I mean you've had your past abroad, which I'm not a part of. Initially, I found all the mystery that surrounds you exciting, but now it just gets on my nerves, I feel I can't reach you properly, you're so lost in your own world, always think-ing about something other than me. It's all right to hold some things to yourself, maybe fifteen per cent, but I get the strong feeling you're holding on to seventy-five per cent. Living with you is like being stuck in a misty swamp. All I can do is grope forward, without ever knowing what's going to come next. And what do I know about those nine years you spent abroad? You never talk about your life prior to me and therefore I don't feel a part of it."

I note that he refers to a swamp and mist, just like the medium had.

"You never asked."

"I never get to know anything about you. You're like a closed book."

I feel nauseous.

When I was seven years old, I was sent on a coach to the countryside in the east on my own for the first time, with a picnic, a thirteen-hour drive along a road full of holes and dust, which the passengers ground between their teeth, in the coldness of the early June sun. The novelty that summer was that the bus companies had started to employ coach hostesses for the first time. There was a great demand for these jobs because the girls got to dress almost like air hostesses, in suits, nylon stockings and round hats fastened under their chins. The main function of the hostesses, apart from sitting prettily on a nicely upholstered cushion over the gearbox and chatting to the driver, was to distribute sick-bags to the passengers. When I had finished vomiting into the brown paper bag, I put up my hand the way I did in school whenever I needed to sharpen my pencil, and then the hostess came, sealed the bag and took it away. I saw the pedal on the floor right beside the entrance that she pressed with the tip of her high-heeled shoe to open the doors, which released a sound like the steam press in the laundry room, and how, with an elegant swing of the arm, she slowly cast the paper bag into an Icelandic ditch. The driver kept driving at fifty-five kilometres an hour and seemed relieved to be able to carry on chatting to the lady on the cushion once the problem had been solved. Looking back on it, I think it more likely that the hostess was not wearing a hat but a scarf. I'd assumed they were a couple and engaged, she and the driver, but now realize she must have been two years out of the Commercial College whereas he had been driving the coach for decades.

He paces the floor again and loosens his new green tie, as if the stale air of the muggy late-summer heat were smothering him. He has also just had a haircut and he is wearing a shirt I've never seen before.

"Let's take the way you dress, for example."

"How do you mean?"

"The guys all tell me their wives buy their lingerie at *Chez toi et moi*."

"I'm just me and you're you and we are us, I'm not the guys' wives and you're not the guys."

"That's exactly what I mean, the way you twist everything, I can never talk to you."

"Sorry."

"Men are more attentive to these things than you think. We mightn't say everything, but we think it."

"I can well imagine."

He looks offended.

"And there's something else. All you've got to do is touch a light switch and the bulb blows. It's not natural to be pushing a trolley-load of light bulbs every time I go shopping, minced meat and light bulbs, lamb and light bulbs, now I'm known as the man with the bulbs at the checkout."

"Maybe we need to have the electricity checked."

He paces the floor again.

"It's as if you just didn't want to grow up, behaving like a child, even though you're thirty-three years old, doing your weird and careless things, taking short cuts over the gardens and fences of perfect strangers or clambering over their bushes. Whenever we're invited somewhere, you enter through the back door or even the balcony, like you did that time at Sverrir's; it would be excusable if you were at least drunk."

"The balcony door opened onto the garden and half the guests were outside."

"You're always forgetting things, arriving the last at everything, you don't wear a watch. And to top it all, you always seem to choose the longest routes everywhere."

"I don't get where you're going with this."

"Like that time you climbed halfway up that flagpole with the Icelandic flag in your arms…"

"Big deal, we were at a party, there was a knot in the rope, everyone looked helpless and the flag was drooping pathetically at half mast, like a bad omen for the asthma attack Sverrir was about to have later on, on the evening of his own birthday."

"That's the only time I was grateful that you were wearing trousers and not a skirt. The amount of times I've prayed to God to ask him to make you buy a skirt suit."

"Wouldn't it have been simpler to just ask me?"

"And would you have done that for me?"

"I'm not sure, I thought you were just happy to know that I was well."

"There, you see?"

"I realize I can be impulsive sometimes."

"Impulsive, yeah, you always have the right word for things."

He rushes into the living room and returns with two volumes

of the Icelandic dictionary in his arms, frantically skimming through the first tome.

"Words, words, words, exactly, your entire life revolves around the definition of words. Well, here you go, impulsive: abrupt, hasty, headlong and impetuous. Wouldn't you like to tell me how they say it in Hungarian?"

His anger seems way out of proportion to the argument. Still sitting on the stool by the table, I notice a butterfly hovering close to the toaster, which is unusual for this time of the year. It is settling on the wall now, close to me, and perches there motionless, without flapping its silver wings. If you gently blow some warm air on it, it is clearly still alive. I swallow twice and remain silent.

"Those were my colleagues and Nína Lind was there too, she remembers it vividly. How do you suppose I felt?"

"Who's Nína Lind?"

"Your hair is shorter than mine," he says wearily, stroking his thick mane. He has taken one of his hands out of his pocket.

"And?"

"And then there are those friends of yours."

"What about them?"

"Like that Auður girl, fun in some ways but a total crackpot. And with another fatherless child on the way."

"That's her business."

"Yes and no, it's been one year since we moved in here and we haven't emptied all your boxes yet. I get the impression this home doesn't really mean that much to you."

"We need to find time to do that together."

"You have a pretty weird idea of marriage, to say the least, you go out jogging in the middle of the night, dinner is never at the same time. Who else—apart from Sicilians—do you think would eat Wiener Schnitzel at eleven? Then when I get home on Tuesday you've cooked a four-course meal on a total whim, a Christmas dinner in October. And there's me clambering over your runners in the hall holding a pizza with some awful topping in my arms, just to have something to eat. And who did the shopping again this evening? There's no organization in your life, you can't be sure of anything. It's very difficult to live with these endless fluctuations and extremes."

"You yourself often work nights or are abroad, you've only been at home for four nights this month."

"I mean you speak eleven languages that you practically learnt in your sleep, if your mother is to be believed, and what do you do with your talents?"

"Use them in my work."

"Having a child might have changed you, smoothed your edges a bit. But still, what kind of a mother would behave the way you do?"

It was bound to reach this point, the baby issue. But I'm a realist so I agree with him, I wasn't made to be a mother, to bring up new humans, I haven't the faintest clue about children, nor the skills required to rear them. The sight of a small child doesn't trigger off a wave of soft maternal feelings in me. All I get is that sour smell, imagining their endless tantrums, swollen gums, wet bibs, sticky cheeks, red chins, the cold dribble on their chins. Anyway, it isn't motherly warmth that men come looking for in me and they're not particularly drawn to my breasts either. Besides, there are plenty of children in the world, our national highway is full of cars crammed with children, I should know. Three or four pre-school toddlers escaping from their young parents' cars to raid every petrol station shop along the way. They need hot dogs and ice creams, after which they're packed into the cars again, reeking of mustard, their faces plastered in chocolate. The parents look tired and don't even talk to each other, don't communicate, don't notice the dwarf fireweed or glacier because of their carsick children. Your kids vanish into the bushes of camping sites, without ever giving you a chance to browse through a thesaurus in peace by the entrance to the tent, because you're always on watch duty, I imagine. Some of our friends haven't had a full night's sleep for years and no longer make love, except for the very occasional little quickie. These are people who don't even kiss any more, when they collect each other from work they just turn their heads and gaze out of the windows of their cars. I know that much, I've seen it. The relationships that survive having children are few and far between.

"You should at least organize yourself better, otherwise you'll never be able to cope with having a child," I hear him say to the broom cupboard.

If one really put one's mind to it, it might be possible to develop the ability to read two pages of a book in a row. The child has grown suspiciously silent, the cookie is probably stuck in its throat, which is why you have to check on it every four lines, you're always either putting a child into a sweater or pulling it out of one, shoving Barbie into her stockings and high heels, groping for your keys outside the front door with a sleeping child in your arms. No, it's not my style. I try to regurgitate an entire paragraph from a manuscript I once proof-read:

"One of the things that characterizes a bad relationship is when people start feeling an obligation to have a child together."

I have to confess that's something I read somewhere, because we can't experience everything in the first person. Nevertheless, I throw in an extra bit of my own.

"But maybe we could adopt, in a few years' time, a girl from China, for example, there are millions of surplus baby girls in China."

"That's exactly it, when you're not talking like a self-help manual, you behave as if you were living in a novel, as if you weren't even speaking for yourself, as if you weren't there."

"At least I'm not Anna Karenina in a railway station."

"What's that supposed to mean?"

"I don't necessarily absorb the content of all the text that I proof-read, you know, nor do I emulate it."

"But just remember this: not all men are bright and chirpy in the morning, and you can't expect them to appreciate the nuances of linguistics over their morning porridge."

He has straightened his back and randomly presses his thumb against the window pane, just beside one of the butterfly's wings.

"What do you mean?"

"It isn't always easy to figure out what you're on about. Other people just chat when the bread pops out of the toaster. Maybe, for example, they say things like: the toast is ready, would you like me to pass it to you? Would you like jam or cheese? They talk about cosy, homely things like washing powder, for example, things that mean something in a relationship. Have you ever asked yourself if I might like to talk about washing powder? Somehow you're never willing to talk about washing powder. Last time you washed my shirts it was with your red underwear. It's true that I was the one who gave it to you, but I don't remember ever seeing you wear it. And that's not the only thing."

"No?"

"No, I just want to let you know that I've spoken to a marriage counsellor and he agrees with me."

"About what?"

"About you. He had a similar experience. With his first wife."

As I'm calmly sitting there on the stool and sip on the glass of water, I realize that he is now about to say something that I've somehow sensed he would say, something that has crossed my mind before. And the thought is accompanied by a feeling that I've also experienced before, although I cannot for the moment remember where it will lead, to something good or bad. I know what he's going to say next.

"And then there's Nína Lind."

"Who's she?"

"She works at the office, handles the switchboard and takes care of the photocopying for now. She's planning on studying law."

His voice vanishes into the collar of his shirt. Some hairs protrude through his buttonholes.

"She's actually expecting… a baby."

"And?"

"Yeah, and so am I, with her."

"Isn't she the one you said was coming on to all the guys at that Christmas punch party in your office last year?"

"Not any more. You should also know, with all your vaster knowledge," he says with a touch of sarcasm, "that when a man is unjustifiably critical of someone, it's often to conceal a secret admiration. Men quite like women to have a bit of experience. I have to confess I've sometimes wished you had vaster experience in that area yourself."

I note that he's using the word vaster for the second time. If I were proof-reading this, I would instinctively cross out the second occurrence, without necessarily pondering too much on the substance of the text.

"You don't even know how to flirt, don't even notice when men are looking at you. It's not much fun when the signal that a man's wife gives out to the world is that she is completely indifferent to the attention the world gives her."

I can't control myself and note that this is the second time he has called upon the world as his witness in a single sentence.

"Besides, she's changed, pregnancy changes a woman."

"When is the baby due?"

He hawks twice.

"In about eight weeks' time."

"Isn't that a rather short pregnancy, like a guinea pig?"

"This is something that has evolved between us over a period of time, not just an accident. I just want you to know that this wasn't a decision on the spur of the moment, or just a whim, even if you think it is."

His face has turned crimson, with his hands dug deep into his pockets.

"How did you get to know each other?"

"In the photocopy room or around there."

"When?"

"You could say the relationship turned serious sometime after the Christmas party."

He fumbles around the refrigerator, takes out a carton of milk and pours himself a full glass. I didn't know he drank milk.

"Christ, how old is this milk? It's the 25th of October today and this is from September."

"What does she have that I don't have?"

"It's not necessarily that she has something you don't have, although in many ways she's more feminine, has breasts and stuff."

"Don't I have breasts?"

"It's not that you don't have breasts, but she'd never been to Copenhagen, for example, I had the feeling I could teach her something."

"Did she go to Copenhagen with you the other day?"

"Yes, she did, as it happens. Like I said, it's been evolving."

"And Boston too?"

"She was visiting a cousin there as well."

He has started to nurse the plant on the window sill, and fetches a glass to water it, and then massages the soil around the stem with his fingers. I've never seen him care so much for a plant.

"Do you love her?"

He gives himself plenty of time to readjust the plant and wash his hands in the kitchen sink, after his labour in the soil, before answering.

"Yeah. She says she loves me and can't live without me."

In retrospect there had been a number of signs in the air. He had suddenly started to plant clues in various parts of the apartment and wrote "I will never forget you" on the back of an unpaid electricity bill, knowing that I was the only person in the house who ever does chores like paying bills. I actually didn't notice the inscription until I got to the bank and the cashier blushed and double-stamped the bill. And then there were the home-made crosswords he left by the phone: love, nine down, longing six across, coward seven down. Affection, desire and chicken.

"I want you to know I'm very disappointed things didn't work out between us," he says.

I've shovelled down two mouthfuls of the spinach lasagne and am preparing to stab the third morsel with my fork. Once I've swallowed it, I adjust my garter-stitch scarf, wrapping it around my throat.

"Thanks for the dinner. When are you leaving?"

"Nína and I are looking for an apartment and we're going to see one tomorrow. In the meanwhile I'll stay at Mum's."

In light of all the things that can happen in a day, coincidences clearly have a tendency to come in bunches. Two men have given me my marching orders today, dumped me. I feel like a prisoner who has helped a cellmate escape by lending him my back. But I'm still capable of surprising myself. I can do better.

"I was going to cook some goose this weekend."

"Goose, where did you get goose?"

"In Mum's freezer."

"Unfortunately I'm really busy."

"Come on, everyone has to eat, it's not as if I was asking you to tidy up the garage or something."

It would be OK to eat together. We can make it our last supper, our Christmas feast.

He is unable to resist.

"I'll come for the dinner at any rate, no point in letting a goose go to waste."

SEVEN

I can't say that I particularly enjoy cooking, but anyone who can read can cook. That's all there is to it. You can even browse through recipe books in their original language alone in bed at night. I find a tolerable radio station, have the music quite loud, fetch the bird from the balcony and roll up my sleeves.

I got the soul of every rapper in me, love me or hate me.

A post-pubescent rapper starts to curse his mother. This is the kind of ingratitude you can expect from an offspring.

Fuck your mother.

I'm increasingly starting to feel the enormous benefits of not having a child. Kids of his age have bad skin, you have to book appointments for them at the dermatologist's half a year in advance, and buy them steroid creams that will only make them more hostile towards you. They grow too fast, just one segment of the body at a time, wake up in foul moods, never open the window and, if they make their beds, they feel like they've done enough housework for a whole month. They sit at birthday parties in their anoraks and refuse to take down the blinking Christmas lights that were put up in their rooms, even after Easter has passed, and collect dirty socks under their beds.

I just found out my mum does more dope than I do.

Cooking is educating yourself through reading. I never commit recipes to memory, but conscientiously follow the written instructions, thus managing to produce the most laborious and time-consuming dishes with music in my ears. When I cook lemon chicken with olives it is to the accompaniment of my Khaled Sahra CD, when I make pumpkin soup it's Pinetop Perkins, for grilled corn on the cob it's Rubén González, and when I make Osso buco or Baccalà alla livornese it's Gianmaria Testa. Dvořák or Liszt are in my ears when I make Diós palacsinta pancakes with a nut filling and, even though I'm not a big Strauss fan, I put up with him when I make Pustertaler Kassuppe. When it comes to Icelandic meat soup, it's got to be something out of the Bjarni Thorsteinsson collection and with Borsch or Moscow beetroot soup it has to be Prokofiev's orchestral suites. It may not be particularly original, but I'm not the first person in the world to make meat-stuffed cabbage rolls.

If anyone asks me how I did it, I answer: I looked up goose in the index, read the recipe and followed it. It even had photos of secure, well-manicured male hands demonstrating the whole procedure, step by step. There is no connection between culinary talents and other talents in life. People don't need to, for example, be child-friendly or of a particularly benevolent nature to be able to cook good food.

I've just plonked the bird on the draining board when the doorbell rings. It's my neighbour from downstairs with a cat in her arms.

"I know how you feel," she says, "that makes two divorcees in the building now."

I ask her how she heard the news, since I've barely heard it myself and I haven't told anyone about it.

"I've known about it since the spring," she says, fondling her cat, stroking and scratching it all over so that its fur soon looks like it has been blasted by a hairdryer.

"It's a good job it's out in the open now," she says, holding out her empty sherry glass to me for the fourth time.

"Apart from anything else, she's pretty plain-looking. So what if men find her beautiful?"

The liquid level of the bottle has dropped considerably by the time she takes her leave and I can fully devote myself to the bird on the draining board again. You obviously need to start at the right end, the book says, and to pluck the bird's feathers from the outer layer in. How are you supposed to do that? I call Mum, who tells me she was just about to call me, had the phone in her hand, because she has just found my old skates.

"They'll be as good as new," she says, "once I've finished polishing them."

As for the plucking of the goose, her conclusion is that the method used is just a matter of personal taste, feather by feather or by the handful, it all comes to the same, the main thing is to ensure that once it has been plucked its skin has a greyish-blue colour, with a pretty diamond pattern. Then run a blowtorch over the rest, the remaining down, to make it presentable. Mum sends her regards to Thorsteinn.

"I got him to move a cupboard for me the other day and he seems to have lost weight lately," she says as she rings off.

I can't say she's wrong and hang up too.

Naked there on the draining board, the bird reveals its vulnerable nature more than ever before. Because I don't have any proper tools, like a welding or a primus blowtorch, I assemble my entire collection of candlesticks, aligning and lighting all the candles on the table—gilded, red, tea light and scented candles—and start the operation.

The butterfly doesn't stir on the wall, not even as the match approaches, not a single twitch, its wings sill calmly folded.

I could also surprise him and invite some other people. I draw up a guest list in my mind. I randomly include two of his colleagues from work, who on second thoughts, however, wouldn't really be appropriate for this occasion, a female equestrian friend of his and a Middle East expert, who happens to be a childhood friend of mine, then another one of his acquaintances, an actress, who is currently between men, and my trusted friend, Auður, a pianist. Neither of the widows, i.e. neither my mother nor his, since this isn't a bonding exercise, but a last supper, at which both women would only be backing and defending their thirty-something offspring.

The neck dangles over the table. This is no ordinary goose, having been felled in this very special manner, slightly maimed perhaps, certainly with a dislocated shoulder, but not blatantly battered, or at least no worse than if it had been machine-gunned with pellets. You won't lose any fillings eating this bird, there is no lead in this flesh, which will be exceptionally tender, since it didn't have to flee a vast distance from snipers, felt no adrenaline rush when I hit the brakes, couldn't have known what was coming.

Whatever is lacking can be compensated for by the stuffing, good stuffing can always save you, nice and spicy, so long as you don't go over the top, something few men understand. I don't go over the limit, although I may come pretty close to it. I'm hardly going to poison my husband, turn an unborn child into an orphan, am I? No, a child needs a father, a boy needs a dad.

The doctor laughed. No father, eh? So it happened all by itself, did it? Just like the Virgin Mary in the olden days? You're such a smart girl, you'll turn into an incredibly attractive woman given a few years. If you could only stay still a moment, instead of wriggling like a worm all the time.

It's at this moment, however, that I ask myself: does my husband have good taste when it comes to flesh? Was it a man of taste who chose me?

One of the principal advantages of being married to a man who is often abroad on business is that there's always plenty of booze in the wine cupboard to fix a slightly dodgy dish or save a sauce, liqueur aperitifs to blunt the guests' sense of judgement and boost the confidence of the chef, although I probably shouldn't drink too many more glasses of this yellow lemony liquid.

The goose has not been hung for long enough, that's clear. I scan its skin in search of any brown blotches that might indicate the animal had been ill. Not that it could actually kill either of us—at worst give us a nasty tummy bug.

On second thoughts, it's probably best to cut the breasts off and make a thick, creamy wild sauce to camouflage the tread marks of the tyres. But later, when he scrapes the sauce slightly off the bare meat, he is bound to see the imprint of the wheels, like finding the hidden almond in the Christmas rice pudding. Then I'll grab his attention and get him to look up, not necessarily into my eyes, and I'll say:

"Well then, Happy New Year in advance and thanks for the four years of marriage, plus the 285 days and seven hours."

I finally break her open and rip out her bleeding heart, surprised by the appearance of the creature's innermost entrails. The heart is so small it would fit into the palm of the hand of a newborn child.

I kiss the small bleeding palm and his hand, smearing my lips in red. That's what my classmate Bergsveinn was like in the eighth grade, with blood-red lips. I, on the other hand, had long brown hair with a fringe. Our religion teacher once told him that he had kissable lips. Bergsveinn blushed, increasing the blood flow to his lips even more. But the religion teacher was a married man, so it was clear that he was teasing him for the sake of us girls in the class. After that, all we girls in the class learnt that not all lips are equally suited to all tasks. This is how a woman can suddenly learn what she can expect from life.

Detach the tiny fingers protruding from the heart, by pulling them out one by one, like a midwife retrieving the bloody newborn child from the arms of a fifteen-year-old girl to deliver it for adoption. There is no way of discerning from the cry, as it is being carried away, whether it is a boy or a girl. Some say the cry of a boy is more delicate, fragile and feeble than the cry of a girl, boys who have no natural fluff on their heads and wear light blue hoods. He, however, has a big mass of dark hair. The woman is from the east of the country, not very young. I only catch a brief glimpse of her and say nothing, buried under the pillow. I'm not sure the crying can be heard for long because the corridor stretches far away, the coffee percolator is brewing and the singing of the plover that has recently returned from the southern hemisphere can be heard through the window. Because it is spring, one can smell the perfume of the woman who is driven away with the baby in the car. She is sitting in the back with the child enveloped in a small down quilt, her husband alone in the front.

I could, of course, delve into all kinds of regional variations of chicken, pigeon or duck recipes, marinated goose, sautéed in butter and sprinkled with ground pepper and thyme or roasted very slowly for a long time in the oven, while I nip off for a swim and steam bath in the meantime and pop into the bookshop to see if my order has arrived. I also consider following an Irish recipe, which consists in letting the bird simmer in a pot for four hours with onion and stuffing, while the evidence erodes away, and then fry it. The solution comes to me in a flash; I try to merge several recipes, mixing unrelated flavours in an unexpected way.

In fact, the major challenge and biggest obstacle I have to face in any of my cooking is the cutting of the onion. My vulnerability to the onion isn't comparable to my vulnerability to any other aspect of my life. It is standing unpeeled on the table and I've already started to cry. I take off my wedding ring and place it at the top of the draining board, behind the bird's gutted entrails. I brandish a knife and my eyes immediately well with tears. I can't see a thing, but nevertheless blindly stick to the task at hand, groping for the second onion and then the third and have ceased being able to see the book ages ago. I fumble and zigzag into the dining room, searching for the balcony door where the chives are still steadily growing in their pot, even though we're in October.

"You're far too sensitive for this world," my neighbour from downstairs said to me once, when she saw my violent reaction to onions one day as I was staggering outside to try to focus on the world again. These are the kind of things women say to other women. Even women who sleep with your husbands. After some time they phone you and say: "He isn't exactly the way I thought he'd be, sorry," and they even want to meet up with you in a café and form a book club.

EIGHT

When my husband opens the door with yet another new tie around his neck, I've already opened both of the bottles of wine that were being kept for the next special occasion. He immediately mentions the peculiar smell in the apartment, which the well-seasoned bird in the oven fails to mask. It's true that there are some feathers in the kitchen and bathroom, and even one feather on the bed, as I discover later that evening, as well as several bloodstains sprinkled on the parquet.

It had been a difficult operation.

We normally sit face to face to feel each other's proximity, but we now sit at the far extremities, each occupying their own end, since I've extended the table by two leaves, both because we're separating and also because it gives the occasion a festive air. There is a huge gap between us, the vast distance between conciliation and separation. On the white tablecloth there are new candles in tall brass candlesticks and six side dishes with all the things he likes: baked potato wedges, home-cooked red cabbage, French beans, carrot mousse, salad and succulent redcurrant jelly, made from berries out of Auður's garden.

It occurs to me that this may be my last chance to ask him about things I haven't asked him up until now.

"How is your mother?"

"Fine, thanks. And yours?"

"Good."

"Thanks for everything," he says, visibly moved.

As soon as he wants to speak, I will allow him to, because I'm a woman and know how to remain silent. He hasn't prepared a speech.

"You're welcome."

"I just want you to know that I'll never forget you."

He doesn't say that he will cherish me in the depths of the blood-red chambers of his heart, because he would never put it that way.

"Thank you." I refrain from replying likewise, at moments like this one doesn't necessarily say what one is thinking.

"I won't say it was exactly the way Mum does it, but there was something special about it, something personal."

"Thank you."

"It was wonderful to meet you... I mean marry you... and live with you... but sometimes things don't turn out the way you expected... but differently... you've also been quite busy lately... we haven't seen much of each other..."

He has stood up and I realize how tall he is, he is literally towering over the table. He hands me a parcel wrapped in gilded paper, after fishing it out of the inside pocket of his jacket. I finish the remains of two glasses before opening it, exhausting my annual ration of alcohol in a single day.

It's a wristwatch.

"Thank you, you shouldn't have, I don't have anything for you."

"It has a calendar, so you'll be able to see both the time and the date. Forewarned is forearmed," he says with a smile.

In addition to the calendar, the watch has two dials, a bigger one that says HOME and a smaller one that says LOCAL, the local one presumably indicating the time of the place where one happens to be at that moment. They both therefore follow their own time.

"A bit like you," he says with a touch of warmth.

It is true that I didn't actually have a watch, but I do have a compass in the car that has always enabled me to find my way, even though I may not always know the precise time in terms of minutes.

He stands behind me at the table and loosely places his hand on my shoulder, as he explains the watch to me. I sense a creeping weakness in my body and suddenly feel that this relationship still stands a chance that entirely hinges on me being able to dissimulate the fact that I know how to read the time, that's my trump card right now. Because I'm a woman and he's a man.

"So you can set whatever time you want on one dial, free time, your own personal time, whereas the home dial will show you the time we other ordinary, boring, mortals live on," he says in a soft voice. "Do you have any plans?"

"I'm thinking of taking a late-summer holiday and travelling," I say, even though the thought hadn't even crossed my mind until I heard myself say it. "At least I'll know what time it is," I add, flashing the golden watch.

"I see you've already removed your ring."

He's right, I'm not wearing the wedding ring because I took it off when I was cleaning the insides out of the bird. But I only have to glance at the glistening draining board to realize that it actually isn't there any more; it has vanished with the innards of the goose and vegetable peels. Tomorrow, when I'm in a more lucid state, I'll rummage through the garbage and go through the bird's entrails again, digging for gold.

He doesn't seem to be taking the ring issue too personally and is already thinking of something else.

"Shall we lie down for a bit?"

NINE

I follow him into the bedroom with the two-timing watch on my wrist for one final exchange of bodily fluids.

It's a double bed, the bed of a woman and man who were close, of a woman who has kissed his tummy and a man who has tightly wrapped himself around her and kissed her breasts and more besides. Here, as I blow fluff off his navel, I peruse the familiar territory one last time.

I wouldn't call it a guilty conscience, but I can't deny that Nína Lind has briefly entered my mind. Even though this could be looked upon as a repeat performance or an action replay, my husband is nevertheless being unfaithful to the future mother of his child and I am his new mistress.

Afterwards we spend some time chatting about our childhood scratches and mutual scars, but despite our four years and 288 days of marriage, I had never noticed that scar under his shoulder blade.

No matter how often or cunningly I try to put the question to him, he won't give anything away about what might have happened to him, other than:

"Doesn't matter now, good night."

"Good night."

He turns over on his side. I wonder if there is some way of prolonging the moment, of finding something that will grab his attention.

"Good night."

"Yes, you've already said good night."

"Yeah, I just wanted to say it again, I wasn't sure if you'd heard me."

"Yes, I heard you, I said good night too."

"Good night."

He is half buried under the quilt, his head under the pillow, one of his legs protruding over the end of the bed, hairy all over, except for the soles of his feet. His clothes are in a pile on the floor. His mum has started to do his laundry; I notice the pleat of the iron on his underpants. He obviously isn't troubled by his conscience, this man lying beside me with his hairy arm draped over my stomach. Once he has drifted into sleep, I move his arm to be able to readjust my viewing position: now that we're divorcing it's about time I got to know my husband. I watch the way his expression dissolves and his facial features revert to their original formless state, his mouth half gaping. I scrutinize the remaining traces of the little boy in him, which are in themselves more than sufficient to satisfy any need I might have for a child. I watch his hairy chest, who knows if it is the heart of a child beating underneath it? Seems such a short while since those first sounds were stuttered, before he could master words and use them to his advantage. A little pout suddenly forms on his mouth and I sense he may be having a bad dream, although his deep breathing betrays no emotion. I try to remember what we might have done over the course of the past five years, but am unable to fill in all the little time lapses. Vague as the recollections may be, I can categorically say that he never vacuum-cleaned. And neither did I, because we don't have any carpets, most of the memories end in the bed. A relationship to me is all about the right body and the right smell, the home is a shell for the body, not a place for exchanging existential views and having discussions. Even though you still have to load the washing machine and cook for the body.

But I do have a flashback of him solicitously carrying me some tea, taking slow, cautious steps out of the kitchen with a bright yellow liquid in a rattling porcelain cup, his big body looming over the delicate vessel with its pattern of blue flowers, flexing his knees and hunching his shoulders, as he carefully places one foot in front of the other, as if he were carrying the egg of life in his hands, as if he were holding the slippery body of a newborn child, his entire being focused on the task at hand. Apart from that, it's mostly mornings I recall; we're saying goodbye to each other, then a short moment later we're saying goodnight to each other; there are vast gaps in between, I could perhaps resuscitate some extra quarters of an hour here and there, but other than that can remember nothing else. If I were forced to, if I were to be locked up between the walls of an old classroom and compelled to produce an account of our four years and 288 days of cohabitation, I could maybe dig up enough events and words to fill a blackboard totalling thirty days. How many pages would that be in a double-spaced manuscript? The same words frequently recur over and over again. You can't really say that conjugal life does much to advance the evolution of language.

I gently lift the quilt, as if uncovering a newborn child in a cradle to peep at its curled-up body and baby crochet socks. I place the palm of my hand flatly on his warm stomach. He heaves a faint sigh and turns over on his back, and then on his stomach again, exhaling heavily and producing a deep, faint sound, like the foghorn of a ship as it pulls out of harbour to sail off to another land.

And now I commit him all to memory, since he is about to leave. I scan his throat, shoulder blades, back, ribs, buttocks, thighs, the crease of his knees, calves and the soles of his feet, all unbeknown to him, without waking him, secretly shifting my gaze from place to place, studying his body like a relief map, exploring him, surveying him from vertebra to vertebra, recording everything I see, capturing him in the minutest detail, storing every single hair of his body so that I will be able to conjure them up at will again, until the day comes when I lose the longing to do so and no longer remember the feel of his skin, because he has been replaced by another body perhaps.

A new sound has penetrated the bedroom, at first almost imperceptibly, then growing and switching tone until it turns into a distinctly intrusive buzz. There can no longer be any doubt: at least two bluebottles are hovering in the vicinity of the bed. At that same moment, I spot one of the flies landing on the man's face, plunging its legs into the lake of his chin and strolling around the undergrowth of his stubble. I wave it away, but it lands again on his forehead, cheek, nose, chin; I blow on it and try to dust it off my husband's face without waking him. Then I stretch out to grab the poetry book on the bedside table: *The Head of a Woman.* I use it as a fan to banish the fly, ever so delicately, like a diva who has grown weary of a suitor in an operetta. The fly then doubles its efforts, so I roll up the book and strike it on my husband's upper lip, squashing it in a single blow and turning it into a shapeless black blotch just under his nose. Thorsteinn wakes with a start, springs up and grabs his head the way air passengers are instructed to do when bracing themselves for a crash landing.

"You hit me?"

"Sorry, there was a fly on your upper lip so I killed it."

"A fly, at the end of October?"

He looks at me incredulously, with a wavering and unfathomable expression, but still relaxed and soft, his facial features still unformed, a little boy with no pyjamas and a hairy chest. He is already getting over it, lies down and quickly drifts into sleep again. Then I carefully lie over his warm body, flat out, stretching all over him, trying to cover him in his entirety as he lies there; but no matter how hard I try, parts of him seem to protrude from everywhere. He doesn't stir, but breathes deeply and regularly. Then a part of him suddenly wakes up, I feel a movement against my tummy, his breathing halts a moment and I hold my breath with him. Nothing happens until he locks his arms around me.

Once he has fallen asleep again, I audaciously set the time on the second dial—the free one that can be set according to my own conscience. It has got to be said to my conscience's credit, though, that on this October night it is proving to be more steadfast than my heart, which is why I set the same time on both dials and they both read seventeen minutes past three, as I lay down in the hollow of my husband's elbow, nestling into him as if nothing had happened, with one arm over his chest, which heaves and sinks, causing the alarm clock on the bedside table to flash in and out of view. Then, as usual, I tire of the twisted position of my shoulder and slip my arm away as I turn from him and he follows my movement with a heavy arm.

All things considered, you can't really say that he ever treated me badly.

TEN

I wake up beside the close body of a stranger and move cautiously in the bed, groping through the ominous crack of dawn. I had almost forgotten under the quilt that we are no longer lovers. His eyes are open and for the next three-quarters of an hour he too looks as if he has forgotten. By the time I wriggle myself out of bed, he has drifted back to sleep again. I stretch my hand out to my new watch and see that the dial indicates my conscience's time stopped at 7:05. Which is the exact time of my birth, some thirty-three years and three weeks ago to the day. I stare at my watch, as if it were the heart of the goose that had ceased to beat.

There is a time for everything, a time for sleeping, a time for loving, a time for breaking up, for running—everything has its time. Abandoning the warmth of the conjugal bed, I tiptoe to open the door out into the cold darkness of dawn, holding my runners until I reach the steps. My neighbour from the basement is standing in the driveway, holding a child in one arm and a boiled kettle in the other. I see her pouring water over the lock of the car and windscreen to melt a porthole that is just about big enough for her to be able to peer through on her way to the kindergarten. The hot steam from the kettle oozes into the darkness in breathy puffs that colour the air in a milky grey hue that then fuses with it.

"I don't know what I was thinking when I locked the car in the driveway," she says, waving at me. The kettle is now resting on the bonnet of the car.

"They're forecasting rising temperatures and rain," I say, trying to restore my neighbour's faith in a better future.

As soon as I step onto the pavement, the dog from the floor above gives me a warm welcome. Brandishing the handle of a leash in his mouth, he thrusts it at me and is so beside himself with excitement and joy that he barely seems to know which leg to stand on. I pat him, but don't touch the leash—this time I'll run alone. He whines after me and runs in confused circles by the garden gate.

I start to trot along the traffic island that separates the opposing lanes of traffic. Mute and weary faces populate the cars. The blinking of their red indicators is reflected in the thin film of frost that covers the traffic bollards at the crossroads.

I trot past eleven stationary cars in a row at the traffic lights and no one is kissing in the frozen air, not even those who kept their cars parked in their heated garages overnight. Nevertheless people are, generally speaking, well disposed to the world when they wake up and start off on their journeys, their eyes still glistening with dreams. So few of them would have the energy to start quarrelling or two-timing their partners before eight in the morning, I would imagine, or at least not until they've had a child together. Most people are travelling by car, but those who are on foot drag their feet along the ice, all round-shouldered, without lifting their heels or the tips of their shoes, as if they were wearing tiny cross-country skis, sliding forward by three to six centimetres with each thrust.

The front gate is closed, but I don't bother looking for any other entrances. Even though the wall carries a CCTV surveillance sign, it's a piece of cake to climb over it, as I always do, and sneak into the garden of the dead. I land close to the grave of the City Council Treasurer and his widow. This is something my ex would never do; he isn't the kind of guy who climbs over walls. I have the whole graveyard to myself; I'm at peace and safe in here, in good company, many of these people must have been feeling lonely. Taking a closer look at the tombstone of the couple, I calculate that she had been a widow for sixty years. I would guess that must have left them with four years of married life and three children.

Everything is veiled by a thin coat of snow, but I still feel a good grip under the soles of my shoes and start running on the gravel path, under the beam of the spotlights, like a convict taking his daily jog around a guarded yard, surrounded by insurmountable walls topped with barbed wire, and I picture guards brandishing machine guns on the multicoloured corrugated iron rooftops. The city centre is still sunk in darkness, but a faint violet glow is beginning to spread across the sky.

Whenever I give directions to foreigners who happen to be standing by the cemetery, unfolding maps and scanning the horizon for some sign of a city centre, and spotting neither souvenir shops nor cafés, nor the faintest hint of an urban axis as they are being blasted by the rust-brown northern wind, I say: "Yes, if you want to go to the centre of the town, you've got to go through the cemetery first. Then you go to the lake. Everybody has to go through a cemetery in life. Yes, you turn to the right and then to the right again and then you turn to the left—but only after you've passed the cemetery. Yes, that's right. This is Reykjavík. You need a cemetery to go through life."

Then the foreigners carry on their way and, as I watch them, I see that they all bypass the graveyard, without exception, as if they had no interest in death but were content enough to simply peer through those little slits for their eyes and nostrils in the hoods of their parkas, looking in all directions, over the heads of the rest of us who live below, as if they thought there was something worth seeing up there.

I can cover a few hundred metres in a straight line down the path if I run over one or two overgrown graves that have long fallen into a state of disrepair. I then turn around on the edge of a tiny freshly dug grave between the resting places of two elderly brothers. A premature baby was buried there during the week beside his great grand-uncles. I zigzag back between the trees, and then pace a stretch over my footprints, running back and forth sixteen times, without pausing, faster and faster each time, until I can barely catch my breath any more, the path has been completely trampled and I feel my heartbeat pounding in my head and ears. Then I truly feel like a living being in the middle of this garden of the dead, I'm most definitely alive in here.

I sense I'm no longer alone; there is a crunching sound in the snow behind me and a twig snaps with still no sign of daylight. I feel heavy excited breathing close by, first right behind me and then beside me, we run side by side, he and I. A moment later his hot and muscular body is rubbing against me, his wet tongue in the palm of my hand. In his eagerness and passion he fawns all over me, pressing me against a granite pillar under which a mother and son repose.

It's my friend from the top floor, Max the mastiff, a mongrel between innocent Icelandic gullibility and foreign rigour, neither a sheepdog nor a watchdog.

He has taken the dog with him and set him loose on me, while he himself snugly rests his back against the statue of our national poet. The tip of his cigarette is glowing.

"Stop a second, I need to talk to you."

My ex is wearing a yellow-patterned Mickey Mouse tie. I speed up; what could he possibly want here among the dead?

"Just one more lap."

He grabs the sleeve of my sweater as I come running out of the darkness.

My breathing is swift and hot and there is a taste of blood

in my mouth and blood in the slime I spit out between the impeccably polished shoes of the man who is standing there.

I bend over in front of the national poet, allowing my arms to dangle, as my dark hair almost touches the white earth. Then I straighten and stretch up to touch his forehead with the flat palm of my hand, running my fingers down his wet face in the morning frost, over his nose down to his chin, passing his chest, feeling his knee, thigh, and stroking him all the way down. He is wearing a long coat that is open at the front and pressed trousers. The features of his face are sharply sculpted and a faint smile chiselled on the edge of his lips seems to lose itself in the cheek. Finally I knock on him to see what stuff he is made of. It's bronze; our national poet is hollow on the inside, cold and stiff. Could this poet really have loved his sweetheart as warmly as he swore in the complex internal rhymes of those quatrains?

Then my husband stretches out his hand as if to caress my cheek and I recoil.

"You seem to wake up with a blank face that doesn't take on any fixed expression until lunchtime, sometimes not until the afternoon. In some ways it's quite charming to live with a woman like that."

"But?…"

"On the other hand there are too many uncertain factors for an ordinary man like me."

I don't say anything, but gaze at the dawn spreading over the rooftops.

"I forgot to ask you, is it OK if I take the mattress and the bedstead with me? Because of my back."

"That's OK."

"I'll confess to adultery, that should speed up the divorce proceedings."

"OK," I say, dropping onto the white cracking grass. Big decisions are made swiftly, whereas in about five years of married life we never managed to decide on the colour of the walls in the hallway.

"I'll put the apartment on sale."

"OK."

He shilly-shallies on the snow-sprinkled gravel.

"Don't suppose you could take my coat to the dry-cleaner's, it's hanging in the hall?"

ELEVEN

My ex-lover phones me in the middle of the night to tell me he's heard the news and wants to come over to give me his personal support.

"What news?"

"About the divorce."

"So you probably heard it before I did then, like everyone else?"

He calls me three times on his mobile. The third time he tells me he's pressing my bell with his elbow and wants to know if I intend to leave him locked outside. I point out that I haven't locked him out and remind him that he was the one who told me that it was all over between us a week ago. In any case I wasn't going to open the door to him. If he wanted to meet me, it would have to be sober and in broad daylight. On skates on the lake, for example, I say rashly, without quite knowing where the idea came from. Probably because of the skates Mum had mentioned over the phone. It's our last chance to go skating, because they're forecasting a big thaw after the weekend. A lot of things will undoubtedly change after that. I actually bought myself some new skates ages ago, keep them at work, and sometimes go down to the lake for a spin when I can't think of a word in a translation.

And then to make matters worse I say:

"I'll be there tomorrow at 17:00 hours."

"I'd do anything for you," he says, even go skating stone sober, you know I love you."

"You can tell me that tomorrow then, sober as a judge, in front of the islet."

When my mother delivered the skates to me, she included a pair of folded old trousers with a flowery strip embroidered at the bottom that belonged to me when I was fourteen.

I haven't told her about the split-up yet. She's right, though, when she says I don't have the build to be a mother, I still fit into the trousers I wore when I was fourteen years old.

"I went skating the night before I gave birth to you," she tells me, "took three or four rounds with a friend, arm in arm. I was in a red woollen coat with my hair pinned up."

She is probably confusing it with the ball they went to a few months earlier, but I don't say anything.

"Then I had this sudden pang of hunger, because I'd only had rice pudding for dinner. By the end of the fourth round, my hunger had turned into me feeling totally famished so I decided to walk home alone to eat some yogurt and drink a glass of milk. If I'd decided to take an extra three rounds, you would have been born on the frozen lake bang in the middle of town."

Chatting with my mum, I seem to vanish from the burden of the present and travel back to my origins. I feel squashed in amniotic fluid and my eyes are swollen.

"I suffered terribly when I gave birth to you, thirty-six hours of labour, five giving birth to your brother. Took me four months to recover, just physically I mean, after having you. I have to admit, in some ways I feel closer to your brother, he also calls me more often."

TWELVE

In five minutes' time I will have written him off, not that I ever really thought he would actually come. There's no one on the ice in the mounting thaw; the kids have all gone to the indoor ice rink and are listening to FM 97.7, licking green and violet ice pops. The circle in which the ducks are squabbling is growing larger and with every round I take I'm drawn slightly closer to the water.

There I am standing on the glistening ice, with the steel dents of the skates pressed into the surface to steady myself, when I see the man nonchalantly walking towards me in his long woollen coat and a pair of skates slung over his shoulder, like some image from a century-old Alpine postcard. Complete with a red and white striped fringe scarf. Under his coat he is in a suit and tie. Darkness has long descended on the islet in the middle of the lake, but the lamp-posts from the surrounding residential streets shed some light on the surroundings. He has left the engine of his car running on the edge of the lake to allow the headlights to illuminate his path on the ice, because he intends to be brief, just a moment. He simply wants to collect me and take me home to console me.

He isn't very tall, seen from a distance, in his socks just a few feet from his car. He now sits on the wall by the lake to put on his skates. Then he advances cautiously on the ice. He is not as ill-experienced as I imagined, or he is skilled enough to be able to follow me at any rate, although the skates are clearly as new as his blue car on the edge of the lake.

I wasn't prepared for this. The perseverance and determination my ex-lover displays on the ice triggers off mixed feelings in me. I'm not sure I can cope with anything at the moment. When all is said and done, this is my first experience as a woman on the brink of a divorce. But if people mean well and show some masculine and persuasive sensitivity, it won't be easy for me to remain indifferent.

The ice in front of us is silvery blue and I'm about to launch myself into a figure, drawing intricate patterns under the beams of the car headlights. That should give me some technical one-upmanship, although I feel him coming eerily close to my back, like a waxing moon over a frozen sea.

He is trying to sidle up to me; I can hear he is out of breath and feel him panting in the dark, but can't really think of anything to say to him. I don't know if I'll go home with him or not yet, because I don't know if I love my ex-husband, so I just try to keep a step ahead. If I had it all written down on a sheet of paper, my options I mean, in a manuscript, in front of me in black and white, I could simply cross out one of the possibilities.

When I glance over my shoulder, scanning over the white-streaked ice, I see that I'm drawing a pattern that looks like the intersection of the lifeline and fate line in the palm of my hand. I could probably carry on writing important messages with my skates, or even perform a pirouette and allow myself to glide towards him, etching the shape of a curved heart in the cold grey ice.

Instead I dash towards the hole in the ice, with headphones pressed to my ears and the volume pumped up high. The circle steadily grows bigger as I near its edge. He is trying to phone me now; I can feel my mobile vibrating in the lower side pocket of my trousers.

Personally, I can easily avoid that hole in the lake. The question is whether I might not be putting him in peril by coming so dangerously close, creating unnecessary suspense just to buy some time, simply because I don't know what to say to him yet. Despite my mastery of many languages, I've never been particularly apt with words, at least not eye to eye, woman to man. Even though I know a regular sentence will require a subject, object and verb and, if it is to achieve any level of complexity, at least three prepositions, my power over words doesn't stretch that far. I'm not particularly good at conjuring up words, the right words I mean, or saying them, what really counts. I can't even spurt out the most important bits like "be warned" and "I love you". In that order.

Now that there is nothing in front of us but the black hole and a decision urgently needs to be made, I can suddenly clearly see the difference between me and my ex-lover. I slow down and prepare to sway to the side, drawing a semicircle close to the edge, while he skids to a halt in a straight line, almost crashing into me, but I manage to swing away, taking a long curve that almost takes me to the bridge.

He catches up with me as I'm flexing my knees and about to shoot under the bridge, and envelops me in his turn-of-the-century scarf. I feel his hot breath on my eyelids. Everything is suffused in a reddish glow and I am, in spite of everything, a woman with a beating heart. I could just as well go home with him.

"Don't you want to see me any more?" he gasps.

"No, I haven't stopped wanting, but this is a difficult patch for me so I'm going away for a while, on a journey," I say, because it is only at that precise moment that it dawns on me that I should perhaps take a trip somewhere.

He wants to know if he can come with me. I tell him that's not possible.

"Can I visit you then?"

"It's so far away, halfway across the planet," I add, coming up with the kind of stratagem that always surprises me just as much as it does the men in my life. "I'll be away for a long time," I say to add further weight to my words and make sure there can be no turning back.

"But I'll send you some postcards anyway," I add.

He asks if he can make some Spaghetti carbonara for me.

"We could catch a movie afterwards."

I tell him I feel it's too soon to be going to the cinema with him.

"We could catch the ten o'clock screening instead."

THIRTEEN

He is standing on the steps with a pile of cardboard boxes. I count ten, all the same size, and most of them carrying the logo of the company he works for, solid boxes with strong bottoms. This man never tackles any task unprepared, always so organized, precise. If it had been left to me, I would have turned up with three discarded boxes grabbed from the shop on the corner, smelling of bananas and cream biscuits, and totally unsuited to carrying books.

I help him pack, standing behind him, as he picks the books off the shelves and arranges them in the boxes.

Occasionally, we glance at the title page to see if a book is marked in either of our names; the ones we gave each other are mostly unread. I would have sworn that some of them were his, but I discover from inscriptions in his handwriting inside that they are mine, from him.

The travel books are on the lower shelf, an entire row. Childless couples are always travel agencies' best clients. It is only now that I can discern some pattern in our purchases: *Journeys to the Poles*, *The Arctic Trail*, *Adventures in Greenland*, *A Year in Siberia*, *Hidden Alaska*—the entire northern hemisphere disappears into the boxes. I've got nothing against the purity of the white universe, but I prefer to be bare-footed in sandals and to travel as light as possible. Geographically speaking, he has always favoured the cold and I the heat.

As he examines a series of green icebergs, I skim through a book on the wildlife of a small island in the southern seas that he has left on the shelf. We're the opposite in the bathroom: I like my showers lukewarm, he likes his steaming hot. That on its own could have explained the absence of children, if I had not systematically taken measures to prevent their conception. One of the best things about being a woman is you can at least have some control over the unforeseeable.

He occasionally browses through a book or opens one at random and silently reads, moving his lips.

I've never seen him do that before.

"Listen to this," he says, reading some account of a struggle with a polar bear from some old memoir of an exploration to Greenland. This is something he has never done either, read out to me. He's changing, is a changed man, he's expecting a child.

I pretend not to see him when he packs away some books I received as prizes for being equally good at everything, for not being particularly good at anything more than anything else, for finding it difficult to prefer one thing more than another, for not knowing exactly what it was that I wanted at that point in my life. Which probably hasn't changed much.

Mum and Dad chatted in Danish in the evenings, if there was something that wasn't for me or my brother's ears. They had met at a Danish Folk High School in Denmark. "Han må da være en god elsker, der er i hver fald noget hun ser ved ham,"* was the first sentence I remember learning in Danish. When I was five and a half I could wade my way through the Bo Bedre *magazine.*

When I was six years old, I mowed a lawn with an old manual lawnmower for a neighbour of ours who was a German teacher and sometimes gave private tuition in the summer to pupils who had failed their spring exams. Instead of being paid in money to buy candy at the shop, I would ask him for two German lessons instead because I had already mown both his front and back lawns. He then said he would offer me two extra classes, forty-five minutes each, at the end of the day on Tuesdays and Thursdays, when the other kids had gone home. The teaching took place at the kitchen table and, when I arrived for my first lesson, he had put on some potatoes to boil. He lived alone and knew he could expect to receive some fish balls through me from my mother.

---

* "He must be a good lover, she obviously sees something in him."

Once, as I was sitting on the cushion on the chair beside him and the book was open on the vinyl tablecloth, he pointed at the picture of a boy with golden hair in short lederhosen who was raking a field. "Das ist ein Kind," was the first sentence I learnt in German. I remember thinking how extraordinary it was that the same word, "Kind", could mean different things in two different languages, since it meant child in German and sheep in Icelandic. This meant that people could be discussing the same word at cross-purposes, without being able to establish the legitimacy of what was being said. Since the same word could mean two things, two individuals could be both right and wrong, simultaneously on the same subject; that is something I learnt when I was barely seven years old.

The lesson was almost drawing to an end and the potatoes were over-boiling in the pot and fogging up all the windows, when the language teacher pointed at a picture of a naked woman bathing in a stream. She was not in the school book, but in a magazine, but I nevertheless had no difficulty grasping the connection between the text and the image. "Das ist eine Frau," he said. And then added: "Eine heisse Puppe."*

I would have thought the ten boxes he came with would have been sufficient to contain our entire collection of books, but apparently not, there are plenty left, almost half, in fact.

"Do you mind if I have this one? It's out of print."

I do mind, but say "You're welcome."

"There are some pages missing from this one," he says.

"Yes, I ripped them out."

"You ripped them out?"

"Yeah, I ripped them out."

---

* Literally "a hot doll".

"Hang on, did I hear you right?"

"Yes, I own that book, I bought it and I ripped out the pages as I read them. I was going to give them to someone, but then didn't bother."

"Why didn't you rip them all out while you were at it?"

"I didn't read all of it, just enough."

"Who were you going to give them to?"

"Doesn't matter now," I say.

He looks annoyed.

I can't remember exactly how it happened, whether I inadvertently hit him as I was stretching out for the foreign thesaurus I had recently bought and which he was accidentally packing, but was clearly too specialized to be of any interest or use to him, or whether he got hit as he was trying to dodge me with a box.

"Sorry," I say.

"No, I'm sorry," he says at the same moment as a siren is heard outside. It's a well-known fact that certain extraneous circumstances, such as the sound of an ambulance siren or the blinking of fire brigade lights, can create an unexpected intimacy between two people in the face of a common external unknown, giving rise to questions such as who, how, why, how much, how old, inside, outside? The shudder provoked by the prospect of an unknown crime or accident can push people closer to each other. Empathy with a victim can even lead an estranged couple back into each other's arms again. At this dark hour of the day, there is barely a child playing outside. Let us imagine instead that it was an old-age pensioner, who forgot how to open his door from the inside, couldn't undo the safety latch to get outside or slipped on the wet tiles of his bathroom after the help had left him.

Whatever it was, we suddenly found ourselves naked on the leather sofa and were swiftly done with it, after which I helped him sellotape the boxes. I was right, ten boxes represent half of the house's books; my husband is so precise and meticulous. Then we order a Thai takeaway, which we eat with the plastic forks it came with, straight out of the boxes.

"Is it OK if I take the sofa?"

"Sure, by all means."

This means that Nína Lind will be sitting on this leather with her crisps to watch the latest Danish series on TV, unaware of the sofa's history and its contribution to the multiple pleasures of conjugal life. She probably won't even realize that I translated the series' subtitles. He is more than welcome to take away this bachelor set, with its downtrodden cushions and over-upholstered armrests. I prefer something more spartan.

"And the coffee table?"

"Yes, go ahead, they go together."

"And is it OK if I take the sideboard?"

"Yeah, I've no use for it."

"Did you hear the weather forecast for the weekend?"

"No, why?"

"Nína Lind and I were thinking of driving out of town, our last chance to see the autumn colours," says the man who up until now has never particularly vented any thoughts on the seasonal colours of the earth.

"I think they're forecasting warmer weather and rain," I say, suddenly realizing that my conversations with other people have now been reduced to passing on meteorological information.

"Is it OK if I take the sleeping bags?"

"We forgot to air them this summer."

The sleeping bags are still zipped to each other since our camping trip in the summer. The giant bag will resuscitate my scent for him, traces and odours of moss, traces of me.

"So can I take the bags?"

"Won't you be staying at a hotel?"

"We could end up having to kip out somewhere."

I can't imagine guest houses being overbooked in November, even the migrating birds have left the country by now.

After we've taken ten trips with the boxes out to his company van, he stretches out his hand and I take it, wishing him a nice journey.

"Thank you," he says, "I'll never forget you."

This is the third time he's said this to me in as many days. Someone ought to tell him he is starting to repeat himself.

"I'll pick up the rest after the weekend."

He leaves his wedding ring on the shelf on top of a pile of unpaid bills and turns towards the doorway.

"I left the aftershave you gave me in the bathroom so that you won't totally forget me; odours are what we remember the longest. Even on the deathbed, when everything else has vanished, the smell remains. And one other thing: would you mind throwing what's left of mine in the laundry basket into the washing machine?

FOURTEEN

After this final wash, it will just be a matter of conscience whether I do his laundry in the future or not.

It's relatively simple to sort clean laundry in a wardrobe, four shelves for him, four shelves for her. But it's another kettle of fish when it comes to the laundry basket—my panties tangled in his shirts, his underpants in my blouses, odd socks here and there—all those things that just got chucked in together, both because they were of the same colour and because we were married, formed a unit. But there are also grey areas. What, for example, should be done with duvet covers that have been embroidered with our initials, cross-stitched under the figures of two white doves? Should I ask Mum to undo the labour she poured her soul into?

I'm feeling peckish and peep into the fridge. There is the cold goose and trimming inside. It feels somehow inappropriate for a single woman like me, at this new juncture in my life, so I decide to go out to the shop.

It's not my style to be crying in public or, more ludicrous still, in the vegetable section of a supermarket, shoving peppers into a bag, far from the crate of onions. I'm standing there, weighing and evaluating two peppers in the palms of my hands, one yellow, one red. I let one hand sink and the other rise, counterpoising the vegetables in my palms a brief moment, like that naked goddess balancing her scales in search of truth. The idea was to bung them into the oven with some olive oil and salt. A man looks up from the mushrooms to fix his gaze on me, as if I were that very same goddess, weeping behind her reading glasses. An old woman gropes some very ripe bananas with her bony hands and finally chooses two spotted ones, and places them in the basket beside a tub of buttermilk.

By the time I tie a knot in the bag of peppers I've made two important decisions. One, to get contact lenses that will enable me to discreetly eye up the men scattered around the store and, two, to take some time off to go on a distant journey, as I've already declared to two men I would. Actually, I've never really ever taken a summer holiday. There is nothing to stop me from going away for as long as I like. I can take my work with me, change lifestyle, stop printing things out, stop delivering by car. I realize now that my workspace by the harbour was nothing but a pretext to be able to stare out at the shipyard.

FIFTEEN

I've decided what I'm going to do when the removal van backs out of the driveway and I'm left alone in the virtually empty apartment. I'm going to take a bath.

I wait another five minutes before turning on the tap and undressing. The top bathroom cupboard is open and empty. His shaving gear, cream and deodorants have been cleared away, although he has left his toothbrush and aftershave. Now that I have all the time in the world to myself I can do as I please. I feel perfectly fine on my own and, in a few moments, the bath will be ready. I add some hot water and sprinkle it with a cocktail of elements coming from a variety of bottles my friends—mainly Auður—have given me on different occasions: relaxing oils, soothing drops, energy-giving bath salts, rosemary oil, camomile, lavender, jasmine. I fetch a glass of cognac and place it on the edge of the bath.

A relaxing bath feels like a fitting way to start this first hour in the first square of my new life, allowing the water to run down my neck, over my face, down my throat, all over me, as the salts froth all over my pale body. I just wallow there in the middle of the bath, banishing every thought and image. How many mothers get a chance to stretch out in a hot bubbly bath like this? With drooping eyelids, enveloped in water, to just lie there in peace in neutral territory, while most kindergartens are closing their doors? A fifteen-centimetre buffer separates me from the world of warfare and potential domestic strife.

From that point of view, I'm a woman with no distinctive features, no visible scars, just one tiny beauty spot on my pale skin, dark hair and green eyes, as specified in my passport. And because I don't have to help a child to brush its teeth and get into its pyjamas and read the same story to it for the seventy-ninth time, I could very easily run another bath in two hours' time. Or stay lying in this one. The question I have to ask myself, however, is who would miss me if I never resurface again? And also can a young woman drown, out of the blue, in her bath? Is it possible to die from an overdose of serenity in a bubble bath? Would he mourn me? Am I missing out on something?

And then I remember seeing the duck sail past and counting as many ducklings on its trail as I could count up to—four. I know today what I didn't know back then, that ducks look after each other's ducklings. Therefore she might have been the mother of the first two, and her friend the mother of the other two.

But I didn't think like that back then, because I was only two years old, so young, in fact, that my age was still only measured in months. It wasn't long after I had heard my mother say that I was twenty-two months old. My brother, on the other hand, is six and supposed to mind me, but he is busy doing something else that is more important, fishing for tiddlers. Which is why I'm alone, milling about on the banks of the lake in the city centre in size 23 boots that are, in fact, far too big for me, because they belong to my brother, as do the blue trousers I'm wearing. Then I lie down on my stomach and stretch out my hand to stroke the soft down. I'm so small that, when I watch these yellow ducklings swim past me, we look each other in the eye and they don't seem at all small to me, although they are perhaps smaller than I am. They embody all of the natural features of my own family: they are tiny like me, soft like my mum and hairy like my dad. I feel a deep empathy for them, even though I won't know the meaning of such words until many years later. I may be my brother's sister, but I also don't feel it is unlikely that I may be one of them. We're all in the same family, me and the ducks and ducklings. Because I'm a girl I can understand other living beings, identify with them and merge with my surroundings. I'm not separate from this world, nor is this world separate from me; time had not taken hold of me yet and distances are nothing but ripples on the water. That is why I can quack like a duck. It is also why I follow my friends' trail and step into the depths after them. For an instant I can walk on the muddy green water but then sink just as fast. On the surface of the water I can see the orange feet wriggling in a state of commotion.

It is only when I start to drown and to experience what dying is like for the first time, only when my cloth nappy and trousers have been engulfed by a mass of light green lake sediment, that I realize that I am not a duck, that I belong to another species.

From here on in, I'm on my own and, once more, it is up to me to attract the attention of the boy who is trying to catch tiddlers in his jar; my fate as a woman lies in my brother's hands.

Even though my age is still only measured in months, it is at that moment that I grasp what lies at the core of the interplay of opposites in the relationship between men and women. Number one: I have to attract the fisherman's attention; number two: win his admiration; number three: trigger off the desired response. As I'm swallowing the gallons of sediment in the lake, knowing perfectly well that it is pointless to try to use the few words I have officially mastered, another key element in human communication springs to mind, and that is the abyss that lies between interest and action, that admiration can, in fact, in some cases, result in a lack of initiative and even inertia. The vain expectations of the other can end in disappointment and ultimately destruction and death. Unthinkable as it may seem today, I knew back then, barely two years old, that I was a woman in the making, a future woman.

"He quacks like a real duck," says the policeman who finally pulls me out of the water.

The moment he takes me in his arms, green spew gushes out of me, all over him and his colleague.

"He's swallowed gallons of water, the car will be flooded."

And it is there, draped over his shoulder like a spineless wimp, that I realize there is a world behind the colourful rooftops of the surrounding wooden houses and that this is where my future lies; that the world is not shapeless chaos, but structured in many layers, like the rings rippling across the surface of the water, and that I am now standing very close to the innermost ring. I had yet to travel far and take many rounds.

"That's not a boy, it's a girl," says his colleague when he takes off my soaking trousers.

He wraps me in a brown woollen blanket before escorting me to the warm inside of the police car. Meanwhile my only brother in the front gets to play with the handcuffs and truncheon.

I linger there, semi-submerged, feeling little or no pain. I've settled all my affairs and am about to take my summer holiday in November, what more could a woman ask for?

It is precisely at that moment, as I'm lying there with my hands planted on my foaming knees protruding from the surface, like two islets somewhere in the southern seas, and trying to think of some way of simplifying my life and making it more accessible—precisely as I'm beginning to feel that I'm finally catching my bearings out there in the open ocean—that the phone rings.

I can't be bothered to drag my body out of the Caribbean Sea until it rings for the eighth time; only Mum could be that persistent.

"You could have been downstairs in the laundry room, hanging up your washing," she would say.

It's not Mum but some man from the Association of the Deaf, who obviously isn't deaf since he tells me his name and then asks me if I am me.

"We have a new policy of directly contacting the winners of our lottery," he says. For the first time the numbers of the autumn lottery are now traceable to the people who bought them, he explains, since the ticket numbers are made up of a combination of the holders' social security numbers, phone numbers and car registrations. He is therefore very happy to inform me that I've just won the first prize in the Association of the Deaf's lottery: a ready-made mobile summer bungalow with an American kitchen, deck and grill, that was built by deaf builders and can be taken apart and transported to any part of the country. Could I collect it as soon as possible and in any case no later than the 15th of the month?

I'm on my knees with the receiver in my hand and a trail of water that has followed me down the corridor. The telephone table vanished in the move. It's quite possible that I have this

77

ticket, since I buy practically every lottery ticket that is offered to me. I do this primarily for three reasons. One: the person standing on my doorstep is blue from the cold. Two: too young to be out alone in the dark. Three: he or she is in difficulty for some reason, either because he or she is blind or deaf, for example, or in a wheelchair outside a store. Then I always forget about the tickets, without ever bothering to check the winning numbers.

The bath water is lukewarm when I climb back into it, but I can't be bothered adding any hot water, as I try to figure out a possible location for the complete summer bungalow in my new life. Destiny isn't something to be trifled with; in a single day I've lost my home and my neat little past. Instead I've been given a new prefabricated cottage which, for a number of obvious reasons, is more suited to a barren patch of Icelandic land or shrubbery than the tropical forests or coral reefs that featured in my future dreams.

Despite my goose bumps, I linger in the bath tub. My happiness is sinking and my body is beginning to re-emerge through the dissolving foam. Mum is right—I'm too skinny.

I see new possibilities opening up before me, new travel plans in my life. Maybe I should explore this island in the winter instead, make the most of the waning light, stretch out these short days, take little strolls away from the car every now and then, into the barren moors, maybe even go all the way east. It's been seventeen years since I was there last; for some reason or another, my path has never led me back there. Nor have I done much travelling across the island's mossy lava fields and dunes. I limited myself to two nights of camping a year with my former husband, in a double sleeping bag, in places where he felt he could stretch out by the entrance to the tent, facing the low vegetation with a bottle and cooling disposable grill in front of us, waiting for the snipes to shut up for a while in the summer nights so that we could finally catch some sleep. Thinking about it, I never venture any further from the city than the Gufunes cemetery after the beginning of November. But I can imagine how, after several hundred kilometres of driving, things might automatically start to solve themselves in my mind.

There is nothing to disturb my plans here but my ex, who obviously still has a set of keys, since he sticks his head through the doorway while I'm still marinating in the bath.

"I took a few pots and the wok and the mixer, but left the sandwich toaster behind."

"OK."

"See you soon then."

I see him walk by with the folded Santa Claus suit under his arm. He was a big hit in the role at his office's Christmas ball last year. "Me, the only childless employee," he grudgingly remarked as we were driving home that evening.

"They wouldn't have chosen you otherwise," was the best answer I could come up with.

"Maybe I could have a quick shower since I'm here," he says.

SIXTEEN

I just don't get my ex. He's just moved out with most of the contents of the house when he's back again. Always forgetting something, that's the third toothbrush he is collecting, and he even takes mine, which I'd just removed from its wrapping and used maybe once. I keep on buying new ones so that he can come and swipe them, along with a book on the mating of insects and other trifles.

But I don't quite get why he needs to take a shower on every visit. As he is washing himself he slips on our song, loud enough for him to be able to hear it under the jet of water.

As if it were the most natural thing in the world, my ex strolls around the apartment with, at most, a small towel wrapped around his waist that just about covers his crotch or backside, but not both at once. As can be expected from a man in his comfortable position in life, I notice a slight accumulation of flab in the mid-section of his body.

He opens all the cupboards in his journey around the apartment, as if he were checking them for new signs of life. The fact is that most of them are empty, because thankfully he has removed almost everything that was in them. There is actually very little left of him, apart from the black hairs he leaves behind in the shower. By the next time he comes to pick up a toothbrush, I will have unclogged the drain. The question I am confronted with is this: for how long should deserting husbands be allowed to come back to take showers? What if he carries on like this, long into his new relationship? How would I explain these endless repeated clogs of hair in my shower to a new potential partner with perhaps a hairless chest?

SEVENTEEN

On the threshold of a new life, it is important to shed all the things you don't need. Any clothes that can't fit into one case go to a charity, as do any of the furniture or household appliances that have been allocated to me. As I make a list of my belongings, I am greatly relieved to see they only fill half the squared sheet of a copybook. I would never have imagined such a great sense of liberation. I don't even need to call a van; the boxes all fit into my back seat over two trips down to the harbour. Just three floors up and there they are, tidily lining the wall in front of the sofa bed in my studio, until I decide to pick them up again and move once more. I'm left sitting with nothing but the bare essentials, although unfortunately I can't find the cream whisk I was going to use to make *mousse au chocolat* for Auður when she pops by for a visit.

As I'm struggling to open the front door downstairs, with a box balanced on my knees, my neighbour suddenly appears on the landing of the second floor and rushes in his black socks down the newly washed lino, which reeks of ammoniac, to open the door for me. He then offers to help me carry the box up to the third floor. He looks like he could be in his fifties and smells of alcohol and aftershave. He gives me a brief summary of himself on our way up the stairs:

"The boy was three when we split up, he'll be seventeen in nineteen days' time, then he'll get his driving licence and the two of us are going off on a hunting trip. He'll be driving the old banger, while his old man takes it easy in the back seat with his flask. We made a deal when I paid for his driving test that he would drive me geese-hunting. It'll give us a chance to get to know each other better, to catch up on things, we've waited such a long time for this."

He has entered the kitchen now and taken out a measuring tape, while I sort out my things.

"If you moved the fridge and got rid of the shower, you could get a small bathtub in here," he says, measuring vertically and then horizontally, before pulling out a little notebook and scribbling into it with a pencil.

"You girls are so much into bubble baths, I know your type," he says roguishly as he expertly strokes the white-varnished doorway with the palm of his hand. If we were slightly more acquainted, he would already be at work.

A short while later my neighbour is back knocking on the door again, with a bottle of Captain Morgan rum in one hand and a gold-framed photo in the other. It's a picture of a drowsy-looking and acned boy with a choppy mop of hair, disproportionate limbs and a headband stretched above his eyes, which fails to fully conceal the bigness of his ears.

I'm in no mood for talking and politely decline his offer of rum. I thank him once more for his help, impatient to see the back of him, so that I can get back to enjoying my solitude again and ponder on my immediate plans for the future.

"Yeah, well I just wanted to reiterate what I said to you earlier, welcome to the building as a fixed resident. It's always nice to know there's a woman up the stairs."

Ten minutes later he is standing in the doorway again, this time with a recipe book under his arm. I give him two eggs from my shopping bag and milk.

On his third and final trip he appears with pancakes and a sugar bowl. I put my papers down to accept the rolled pancakes. He is not going to invite himself in, however, because he is wearing a parka and on his way out to the video store to return a DVD which he pulls out of his pocket to show me.

"Can't say I liked it much," he says, holding up *No Man's Land*.

The film rings a bell, all about a war without winners.

"You just didn't know who to root for, there were no goodies or baddies. You couldn't even tell who the main actor was," he says, pointing at a list of names on the case by way of proof.

Then he sticks the DVD back into his pocket and cracks his knuckles.

"Right then, better get this film back." When I'm on my own I normally just make traditional Icelandic pancakes with rice pudding leftovers.

EIGHTEEN

My current abode is thirty-six square metres and has two walls of a yellow that is not dissimilar to the yellow of I can't remember which South American flag. The other two walls are violet. I didn't change the colours when I originally moved in. The window in the bigger room, where there is a kitchen unit and my computer and desk, faces the harbour, while in the other room there is a sofa bed, table, mirror and a sixteen-inch black and white Blaupunkt TV that once belonged to Mum. I kind of like it here.

He phones three or four times, until I finally answer. He tells me he has recovered from the skating incident and has started cooking, roast beef with potato salad, opened a bottle and set the table for two. I tell him that I'm recovering and need more time on my own to figure out where I'm at in my life, explaining that I'll be quite busy over the next few days and, actually, right up until I leave for an indeterminate time, since there are a number of projects I need to wind up first. I don't tell him that I'm thinking of changing my travel plans. It is then that he asks if he can bring me over some of the food.

After hanging up, I turn back to more serious matters and stretch out for the TV schedule.

Kathleen is pursued by a man. She reverses the roles and starts to follow him. This leads to an accident, which results in him following her again. Meanwhile, she gets into a quarrel with her ex-husband.

I turn the TV off and pull out the sofa bed.

One of the fundamental elements in any woman's life is sleep. I haven't washed the bedclothes; if I sink my nose into them I can still pick up the scent of my old home, the conjugal bed. I don't allow myself to get nostalgic about a piece of furniture and change the duvet cover. Then I shake the pillow and slide it under my cheek. I've got eight hours of freedom in front of me and a pile of translation work in my direct line of vision.

My first night of sleep here is good, considering the lack of blinds and the flickering light of the lamp-post outside. There is nothing familiar about the sounds that travel through the open window. Nothing but the intimate smell of my office.

Some people are chatting three floors below and seem so close that they could be whispering in my ear. One of them is a man, but I can't quite decide whether the other is male or female. The voices hover in the air.

"Like I said, he's probably scared."

"Are you sure you won't come in for tea?"

"No way, thanks."

"I have some Christmas cake to go with it."

I furtively peep out of the window, maybe leaning out too far, balancing like a gymnast on a beam, but see nothing. I can't sleep, so I fetch a nineteenth-century novel, a family drama that spans the lives of three generations and stretches all the way south to the Pyrenees. I finish the first half at half three and wander into the other room to make some tea and toast. I'll buy Christmas cake in the bakery in the morning.

When I finally doze off, I have one of those totally meaningless dreams, in which I'm speaking Gaelic and muttering good morning out of the corner of my mouth to a neighbour on the landing of the stairs. Then I'm suddenly holding an empty glass bottle of Coke I want to sell, but I'm stuck out in some marshland in the middle of nowhere.

I'm suddenly wide awake again, as the first batch of buns come out of the ovens of the bakery below.

NINETEEN

Auður is on the phone.

In celebration of the news that genetic research has now demonstrated that woman played a larger role in the development of humanity than man, she wants to come over and cook me lunch tomorrow. To consecrate the cooker in my studio apartment, she is going to bring some holy water from the baptismal bowl in the church she plays the organ in and sprinkle my home. This is also because, she says, people are always inviting freshly divorced men around to dinner, pampering them and volunteering to scrub their floors for them. Men have such a vast support network behind them: mothers, sisters, friends, friends' wives, ex-wives, the friends of ex-wives, ex-mothers-in-law, sisters of former mothers-in-law. They're told not to think twice about bringing over their dirty laundry, which can be chucked into one or two machines while they're enjoying their meals. What's more, their children get to stay over if their dads are having a night out on the town with their mates. Auður tends to talk a lot, with each clause crammed with multiple digressions and interjections, but apart from that, she's great.

It has started to rain, making the ice treacherously slippery outside, and I rush out before my friend arrives to buy some coffee and Christmas cake. I decide to buy some rock salt to sprinkle over the icy steps, at least for the benefit of the postman with the red hairband, who rings the bell when documents are too big to squeeze through the letterbox in the door and likes to chat about his favourite hobby, pole-vaulting.

As I'm walking up the path with the bag in my arms I see my lovely musical friend is sitting somehow to the side of one of my unswept and unsalted steps, clutching one leg. She has fallen on a patch of ice and her left leg looks unnaturally twisted under her. She nevertheless waves at me with a strained smile. Crouching beside her, my first thought is to fulfil my civic duty and take out the rock salt in my bag to sprinkle it all around her, to mark her territory. Like those chalk lines they draw around corpses in that Scottish crime series I've become the official subtitler of, I trace a white outline around the six-month-pregnant woman on the path in front of my temporary new home.

"It's just a ligament," she says as we peer at the unnaturally big swelling on her left ankle.

I'm filled with a deep sense of guilt and, for some peculiar reason, think of last night's dream. I hear myself telling her that it will be OK and ask her if she can walk. She can't touch the ground with her foot. I try to help her up, but she collapses again with a smothered groan, so I rush inside to call an ambulance.

They've already loaded her onto a stretcher in a woollen blanket, and fastened the straps around her big round tummy, which has suddenly inflated to the size of a huge balloon under the cover, when she turns her head towards a brown paper bag on the steps:

"Sorry, I just brought some takeaways," she says. I promise to cook next. A shot of pain crosses her face as they carry the stretcher away. I follow her to the ambulance and she squeezes my hand as we say goodbye.

"Can you collect Tumi from the kindergarten for me and keep him over the weekend, I don't want to involve Mum in any of this, not yet at least, her blood pressure is far too high. The only thing you need to watch out for is his sleepwalking, he's been known to open doors and vanish behind corners, and even to put himself in danger. Once I found him down by the lake. Just make sure you don't startle him when he's in that state."

"OK," I say.

"He also likes to feel a lock of hair brushing across his face when he's falling asleep. I find it also reduces the likelihood of him sleepwalking," says my friend with the long ponytail.

"I'll bear that in mind."

"*Hakúna matata!*" she cries out to me. That's Swahili for "don't worry", by the way, from *The Lion King*, his favourite movie. She waves me goodbye, beaming from ear to ear.

I'm left standing in the unsalted slush, in the pale grey light of noon, with a bag containing brown rice, an organic vegetarian dish and apricot mousse in little paper boxes. For the sake of making some token gesture, I sprinkle the steps with salt.

TWENTY

Although I wouldn't want to add to Auður's worries in her current state, it's got to be said: I haven't a clue when it comes to children. There were no younger siblings in my house. The neighbourhood I grew up in as a kid was mainly populated by old people. No one ever came to pick me up to babysit a little cousin and, in the countryside in the east, all the other kids were around my age, and there were no smaller children there to interfere with our plans in the attic of the barn.

I walk off to collect him, with the sky above me and, hopefully, the Almighty himself. An entire weekend is a very long time to have to spend alone with a child, a non-stop forty-eight-hour watch to be exact, under my constant responsibility. That makes at least eight meals, four of which would have to be hot, and brushing his teeth five to six times. In fact, the only way to plan this is from one half-hour to the next. Children's games last for about five minutes, after which you've already got to think of something new. It must slow everything down; one would have to put everything else on hold, I imagine.

Gnome House certainly lives up to its name; its low multi-coloured wooden structure, wedged between higher buildings, seems oddly incongruous in this district. Inside everything has been dwarfed down to scale in a nannified universe. As you step in, you turn into a Gulliver in Lilliput and have to watch you don't tread on any of the small folk that live their minuscule lives here from eight to five, five days a week.

I spot him immediately. He stands out in the crowd, with his unusually big head for such a short trunk, slightly drooping shoulder blades and a rather old-fashioned hearing aid for such a young child. His big ears protrude through his hair. His mother had told me he wants to keep his hair long, to cover those ears. Having been premature by two and a half months, he is considerably smaller than his peers. His torso also seems oddly proportioned, an old man locked in the body of a child.

"I normally buy clothes for him that are twice or three times below the size of his age, mostly French children's sizes," Auður told me.

What's more, the boy wears glasses that are attached to the hearing aid behind his ears with springs and his eyes seem to almost completely fill the lenses. He has a look that often attracts attention, frequently evoking pity, Auður says, particularly from old women, who sometimes pull sweets out of their pockets.

He instantly recognizes me and seems visibly happy to see me. Wrapping his arms around my waist for a brief moment, he looks up at me intently as he speaks and then patiently waits for me to give him some sign of understanding and recognition. Because I don't know sign language, he strives to speak as clearly as possible, exaggerating his lip movements and equally stressing every syllable as he forms the sounds that he himself can only barely hear. Nevertheless, his voice sounds strange and I have problems grasping what he is saying. I squat so that we can at least look each other in the eye when he's talking.

"We had a special mushroom day today, the kindergarten teacher interprets," although I'm convinced he was trying to say something else to me. "Few of the kids wanted to eat the mushrooms we were offering today, one of them retched and threw up on the table. This week we're focusing on the sense of taste," she continues to explain, "in connection with the globalization theme and in collaboration with the Intercultural Centre."

"We offer a mixture of national and international foods, now that all the borders are opening up to investment. We had a buffet with all kinds of delicacies on cocktail sticks for these little fingers to taste: black olives, fermented whale, mozzarella, feta cheese, French goat's cheese, blood pudding, dried fish and mushrooms."

The boy dutifully hands over several drawings of mushrooms, sketched both from the side and above, as if to illustrate the woman's speech. In addition to this, he is holding in a plastic bag two mushrooms, which have been dissected in two to examine their interior.

Questions requiring immediate answers spring to mind. Are two mushrooms enough for the dinner of a four-year-old? Should I put him into his overalls or will he be offended? Does he want to do it himself? Is what he wants also what is best for him? Do the two go hand in hand? If not, how am I to distinguish between the two?

Auður has phoned the school in advance and the woman decides to spell it out for me:

"The guiding principle we work under here at Dwarf House is that each individual is unique and different," says the kindergarten teacher. We believe in the strength of those who are weak and have had to overcome obstacles and are therefore, in a certain way, stronger than the others. If one sense is defective, another sense will often compensate by becoming super-sensitive, like the hearing of the blind, for example, or the sight of the deaf."

I resist the temptation to mention Tumi's glasses and hearing aid in the same breath.

"If a person is different, that can also make them a little bit special," interjects some proper little madam who is slipping into some woollen socks.

"Exactly, Geirthrúdur," says the kindergarten teacher emphatically, "that's what we're focusing on in our group work."

"I've got freckles and my grandad has cancer," the little girl continues.

"Exactly, that's the idea."

The child is then given a sign to let her know that her contribution to the conversation must now end and the woman turns back to me.

"We have a child here with a Senegalese father, obviously Tumi, who has serious hearing difficulties, hyperactive and development-impaired children, children way over the ideal weight, children with same-sex parents..."

I finally pluck up the courage to dress Tumi in his blue winter overalls and to put on the balaclava he hands me, at least I can do that much. Temperatures have risen by eight degrees since yesterday.

"If the weather forecast is anything to go by, it'll be puddle gear after the weekend," says the woman, "we love our puddles, don't we, Tumi?" Then she turns back to me again and says in a warm confidential tone:

"Some hate fighting, others love splashing. To be honest, we're concerned about how little communication he has with the other children. Above all, he prefers to be left alone or to play with the girls in the doll corner. We're trying to build up his self-esteem, but he categorically refuses to fight, there's no hunting instinct in him, no conquering. He always stands at the back of the group, avoiding conflict. If he were a sea lion he'd be the first one to be slaughtered by the males and he'd never get to reproduce. Aggression needs a healthy outlet if it is to be channelled into creativity and we've tried different methods to toughen him up. Even though we don't allow weapons, we turn a blind eye to the kids that use sticks as guns. Tumi, on the other hand, engages the sticks in a sign language conversation, one as granny and the other as grandad."

"Bang, I'm dead," the teacher exclaims to the boy as she falls to the ground, or rather feigns to, crouching down on her knees but then deciding to go no further. Then she swiftly springs to her feet again, dusting her knees and smiles warmly:

"The kids like playing cops and robbers."

The boy slips behind me.

"Not Elísabeta and me."

"Not you and Elísabeta," she interprets for me, "isn't that right?" She looks me straight in the eye as she speaks to the boy. "But Illuga Már, he likes being shot, doesn't he? He likes playing dead, isn't that right?"

TWENTY-ONE

Auður phones as we are on our way to the store for a basic weekend shop, stocking up for the kid. She tells me she is undergoing some tests and that they've put a pressure bandage on her foot and are now examining other parts of her body, the mid-section, for example, which is actually the job of another department and belongs to another area of expertise. She can't talk long, she says, but just wants to know if the boy is OK.

"And another thing," she says, lowering her voice. "Could

you buy me a bottle of red wine? The only beverage they offer you with your food in ward 22b is milk."

One can spot the weekend dads a mile away. Even though they haven't bought any food for dinner yet, at 7:30 on a Friday night, and they've yet to go home to cook for their exhausted children, they still find the time to ogle me and cast meaningful glances over the stacks of kitchen roll. I've got my eyes on them too, but purely for practical reasons, to see what they buy and how they go about it—which is why I pick one out of the herd and decide to follow him, some guy with two timid children sitting in his trolley in overalls. I study the manner in which he arranges items in the trolley, how he first chucks them to the sides of the children and then piles the merchandise under their knees: whey, Superman yogurt, bananas, hopping sausages, children's cheese, Little Rascal bread, milk, kindergarten pâté, letter pasta and Cutie cookies. He wedges some packets of cold cuts between the children, and stacks kitchen rolls over their wellies.

When I try to recall what it was like to be a child, nothing significant comes to mind. It does, however, occur to me to buy some oats, since Dad always used to make porridge for my brother and me in the mornings; it was about the only thing he could cook. I then add some roasted chicken drumsticks, simply because the boy indicates to me that he wants them. Then he points at a jar of olives, he wants olives with the chicken. Once we're in line for the checkout, I add a Ken doll in a swimsuit with a child in his arms, because I notice Tumi staring at it at length. If memory serves, childhood was all about yearning for the things one couldn't have. I'm not about to let that happen to my protégé for just one weekend. It's not nearly as complicated

93

as I imagined, shopping for a child. I simply buy the things the kid wants; he either shakes his head or nods.

On the way home, I pop into the video store around the corner. I was lucky I got to keep the DVD player, Nína Lind has a new one of her own. While I'm torn between two films, which the transvestite serving behind the counter emphatically recommends—both for singles or divorcees, he says—the boy is quick to choose his own.

I step into the adjacent shop where a young man with a lot of gel in his hair, shaped into a cone, sells me a lottery ticket. Tumi chooses the numbers. I hoist him up to the height of the counter where he skilfully ticks five boxes with a badly sharpened pencil.

"We'll go fifty-fifty on the winnings," I tell him, "you'll get your half," but he's too busy concentrating on his writing and doesn't even seem to realize that I'm talking to him.

"The winnings are sevenfold this week and a chance is always a chance, no matter how slim it may be," says the young man behind the counter, who seems to be more mature than his pimples might suggest. We walk out with *The Lion King* and *La Pianiste*, the sadomasochistic masterpiece that isn't suitable for sensitive viewers, but will remain indelibly imprinted on the minds of those who are not, according to the blurb on the case.

TWENTY-TWO

I take the boy out of his shoes. He seems content and, in almost no time at all, finds two hiding places in the minute apartment, one in the shower and one inside the cupboard. His focus immediately shifts to the boxes and I give him a signal to let him know he's welcome to take a look inside. Then he suddenly appears in front of me, clutching with both hands a glass of water that is full to the brim, and puts it down on the table. He vacillates and strokes his earlobe before sliding his hand up the sleeve of my sweater, searching for my elbow, and finally caressing my hair with the palm of his little hand. Vanishing for a moment, he swiftly returns with a comb and pair of scissors, standing motionless in front of me with a questioning air. I understand this much.

"You can comb my hair," I say, "but not cut it. I'm letting it grow."

So far our communication has greatly exceeded all expectations. I sense a growing communion and understanding between us. Strictly speaking, a woman with a child requires no other company.

After watching *The Lion King* one and a half times, I place him on the couch, which I can't be bothered to pull out into a double bed. We share the same quilt. He chews on a corner of the pillow and sucks on the duvet cover. Once he has fallen asleep, I leave the room to double-lock the front door to ensure he doesn't escape on me. The books from the boxes have been stacked into tall twin towers on the floor.

It's raining and windy. A window someone seems to have forgotten to shut is banging somewhere. It occurs to me that the owner might be off working on a night shift. My balcony, which under normal circumstances can just about hold a kitchen stool and a book, is inundated. The drainpipe is cluttered and the electricity flickers. It's a huge responsibility, being with a child. After checking that he is still asleep, I slip outside to try to free the balcony of some of the slush and ice to prevent my

95

temporary home from flooding. A woman armed with a dustpan is attempting a similar kind of operation in a building across the way. On every floor, in fact, some sleepless woman seems to be wrestling against the elements and potential flooding.

The child is restless and kicks the duvet off every time I try to tuck him in. I'm worried he'll catch cold, which is why I stay awake and pace the floor, monitoring his sleep. His breathing is making me anxious; it seems to have slowed down, abnormally, as if he were holding his breath or simply not breathing at all. I gauge his breathing in relation to the normal rhythm of my own, there's no comparison. But then, just as I'm about to intervene, the boy suddenly sucks in a very deep breath and his chest begins to heave. I gently pull the duvet back, ever so slightly, to be able to follow the contractions of my protégé's ribcage, although I can detect no breathing from his nostrils and mouth. It takes me half the night to become acquainted with the child's breathing patterns, until I finally fall asleep with a cushion and chequered woollen blanket on the floor.

When I wake up again I feel I only dozed off for a moment, but the dark morning has dawned outside and I'm still in charge of this unrelated child. I get up and brush my teeth, without turning on the light, and unscrew the tap under the shower. Finally, I fetch the sleeping child and pull him out of his pyjamas. He shivers, naked on the cold floor, even after I swiftly throw my sweater over him. Then I take the pale child under the shower with me and soap him from head to toe. After some initial protest, he soon wakes up and starts to stamp his feet in the water, clapping his hand. Then I lift him onto the stool and wipe the mist off the mirror so that he can see me parting and combing his hair. Water trickles down my throat. I clearly know nothing about kids, but try to execute the task I've been entrusted with as efficiently as possible. It's the same with my mother and cats. Being allergic to them, you couldn't exactly call her cat-friendly, but she'd never be bad to one, and always pats and strokes the ones that happen to rub up against her and serves them creamy milk on the doorstep.

"He seemed to be in such a bad way, poor thing," she would say, plucking off the cat's hairs.

Abandoning his wet towel on the floor, I fetch his clothes and draw the sign of the Cross over him, even though I'd never try to invoke a divine blessing of this kind on myself. After rubbing cream into him, I dab the back of his ears with a drop from the bottle of male cologne that has been left in my possession. Then I dress him in stockings and a sweater and sit him in front of me in the narrow corner of the kitchen.

Winter mornings are dark and silent. The weather has grown calmer, as if a kind of numbness had descended on mankind, bringing all activity to a halt, after the sharp depression that had swept its way across the island, as if everyone had fallen under some sleeping beauty spell. I make some porridge and coffee. The boy is shoving the fourth spoonful into his mouth when he points at the clock above the fridge, showing me four fingers with his left hand and then three with his right hand and then one with his left hand again. Finally, he holds up both thumbs and vigorously shakes his head towards the clock. There are no two ways about it: the kitchen clock reads four zero seven and it is still indisputably night outside.

I take him under the duvet with me in his stockings. There is no point lying there awake, so I turn on the TV and slip the DVD into the machine. The lottery ticket is in the same bag as the disc. Sometime later, I freeze the drama in mid-action, precisely at the point when the heroine is about to slash her wrists with a razor blade on the edge of the bathtub, because it occurs to me to dial the number on the back of the lottery ticket. I get an answering machine.

"Only one person got all the numbers right and is therefore entitled to the full undivided prize," chirps an air hostess voice at the other end of the line, "44,000,523 krónur." I draw a circle around the third row of numbers on my ticket and redial. I get the same voice as before and the same numbers. I feel an urge to check that all the slush has disappeared from the balcony, to tidy up the kitchen, drink a glass of milk, see if any lights have come on in the surrounding houses and finally settle down to watch the end of the DVD. This time the person, who bought the ticket just five minutes before closing time and hit the big-gest jackpot in the history of the Icelandic lottery, isn't some father of five on disability benefit who'd gone bankrupt after underwriting a loan taken out by his ex-brother-in-law, nor is it some good-hearted old granny from Selfoss with eleven grand-children, who are mostly just starting off on their own in life and need a helping hand, but instead it is a relatively young woman who will be pocketing the whole prize—she and her fellow in good fortune, a deaf four-year-old clairvoyant boy with poor eyesight and one leg three centimetres shorter than the other, which makes him limp when he is only wearing his socks. One can't really say that this woman is hard off in the strictest sense of the term, even though she has just become single again, nor that she particularly needed to win a prize of this kind.

Looking purely at the laws of probability, it can be assumed that, since it is possible to be unlucky twice in a row, it must be possible to be lucky twice in a row as well. Bad luck can trigger off a chain of bad luck in the same way that good luck can trigger good luck, luck brings luck.

"The chances of a woman, who masters eleven languages, several of which are Slavonic, winning two lotteries simultaneously are nevertheless pretty remote," says my friend Auður, and about as likely as you meeting an elf on a rockslide on the national Ring Road. But, she adds, under certain circumstances and for the chosen few, a remote possibility can become a concrete reality.

TWENTY-THREE

My guilty conscience hasn't been appeased by the time I drive to visit her in hospital, which is why there is a huge bouquet of white roses in the front seat from the boy, along with a drawing he's done for her, of a trumpet. It turns out, however, as Auður herself is quick to point out, that the spraining of her ankle on my doorstep was a stroke of luck. If she hadn't, they would never have realized she has a deformed pelvis, as well as contraction pains, the beginning of a cervical dilation, and far too high blood pressure. The bottom line is she won't be leaving the hospital any time soon.

She vacillates in the doorway, wearing some kind of garment that is clearly marked as State Hospital property, and I see that she has put on a thick sweater under her white gown, as if she were going off on a weekend trip to a summer bungalow. She is wearing a thick woollen sock on her right foot and bandages on the other. Judging by her behaviour, you would think she was being pursued by a gang of merciless thugs, on the run in some American mob movie. She's keen on me playing a role in this getaway drama with her and wants me to skid off with the door open before she is even fully inside the car. It takes a good while to get her into a comfortable position. Spreading her knees wide apart like an old sailor, her navel protrudes through her hand-knit sweater and the pattern stretches over her inflated belly, which seems to reach the dashboard, even though she is still only six months pregnant. This is the best way for her to sit in the car, she feels, with her belly drooping between her legs, between her knees.

"There are two of them," she bluntly spurts out before swallowing. "It's like having a belly full of kittens. I can't lie on my stomach any more or wrap my arms around the pillow."

I try to work out what consequences this new information will have on the fate of my friend and my protégé of three nights. Meanwhile, I try to ask some sensible questions:

"Did you get their permission to come out?"

"Nobody will notice if I vanish for a short while, did you bring the bottle?"

I drive on, while my friend tells me where to turn next. By the time we have passed the church for the fourth time and are moving down Skólavörðustígur, she is already halfway through the bottle of red wine. I justify this in my mind by reasoning that for centuries women in France and Italy have given birth to perfectly healthy babies, probably without suffering from anaemia as much as Nordic women.

Tumi sits still in the back seat with a box of chocolate raisins, watching his mother knock back the wine. The accordion she requested lies on the seat beside him.

"I want to ask you a big favour."

I already know what it is. I have experience in these matters, like that time she went off on a five-week music course to Amsterdam. She's about to ask me to pay the bills that lie on the shelf in her hall, to fetch all kinds of creams and things from her apartment, to water her plants, the yucca in the corner by the TV, two full cups, and to then let it dry completely for a whole week before watering it again. The plants on the living room window sill are another story, she'll tell me, they have to be watered daily, half a cup each, mustn't be too moist or too dry, otherwise the one in the middle won't produce its purple flowers in February. Last but not least, she will ask me to bring over her Discman and CDs, and not to forget Clara Haskil, who has the same interpretive sensitivity she has, although she doesn't actually say that.

"I wanted to ask you to mind Tumi for me while I'm in hospital."

This catches me totally unprepared and I can think of nothing better to do than turn into Bergthórugata.

"But that's another three months."

"Maybe and maybe not. I've got a hunch it won't be that long, two and a half months at the most. He'll be in the kindergarten while you're at work."

"I can't handle children, you know me, I haven't a clue about kids."

"You were a child once. Isn't your ex always saying you're still a wretched child?"

I clutch at every thought that springs to mind and spurt it all out. He could die in my arms, I even end up saying. Auður glances at the windows of the fashion boutiques as we crawl down Laugavegur.

"I just don't have that maternal gene, I've never considered having kids. I don't even look like a mother."

"The only thing mothers have in common with each other is the fact that they slept with a man while they were ovulating without the appropriate protection. They don't even have to repeat the deed. Not with the same man at any rate."

"I'd neglect him, he wouldn't get enough to eat, enough sleep, I'm in the middle of a divorce right now and moving."

"Being a mother is about waking up and doing one's best and then going to bed again and hoping for the best. I heard that in an American movie once."

"But what about his dad?"

"Last I heard he'd moved to Hveragerði."

"Besides, I'm about to go off on a trip—on a long holiday—and I'll be away for at least six weeks, maybe even for Christmas. I'm going to try to find a spot for the chalet in the east. In fact, they're about to load it onto the truck as we speak—all disassembled," I say to add weight and credibility to my information. I'm trying to think as fast as I can, although it sounds false to tell her I need to be on my own, that I'm preparing this voyage into the unknown precisely to find myself again.

"You can just take him with you, he's the easiest kid in the world, he doesn't need any entertaining. He just sits in the back seat, you'll barely notice him, he won't nag or pester you, doesn't even sing the way other kids do, all you've got to do is give him something to drink every now and then, hand him a banana every hundred kilometres or so, and stick a straw into his cocoa milk."

"I don't know sign language."

"He hears a bit, lip-reads, and gesticulates when he speaks

to people who don't understand sign language. He's a linguistic genius, just like you, four years old and he speaks three languages. You'll just have to learn his language, add another one to your collection. Seriously, you could understand a camel."

I don't bother telling her I sometimes have enough problems trying to express myself to people with perfectly good hearing and speech. Maybe it'll be no worse with a hearing-impaired child with a speech impediment.

"Hasn't the time come for the linguistic expert to examine the appearance and shape of words? To see what concepts look like in three dimensions and learn how to make words with your body, without your voice?"

At least I have a weekend's experience of what it's like to have a child in one's care; it's quite similar to being alone with one's self. You don't even have to cook, just buy something ready-made and split it in two. He has no idea of when regular mealtimes are, has nothing to say about their preparation and just eats what he's given, pretty much like a monkey at the zoo.

By this stage of the conversation, my friend has moved closer to me and is almost sitting on the handbrake with her arm around my shoulders.

"But what about you? Don't you think you'd miss him?" I ask.

"I have enough on my plate, I wouldn't be able to take good care of him, it'll be another two and a half months before the twins are born and I'm supposed to lie still until then. Otherwise, there's the danger of Tumi's history repeating itself—respirators, oxygen tents, kidney problems and all that. He didn't cry until he was six weeks old, and even then it was more like the meowing of a kitten."

"But what about him? Can he be without you for that long?"

"The only thing I'm allowed to do in the ward is watch American soaps and wildlife documentaries until I'm driven daft. And kill everyone around me because I get so depressed when I can't play. I've nothing to give the child."

By now she has drunk over half the bottle.

"It'll do you good to have some company. Mark my words, he'll change you."

"In what way then?"

She chooses to ignore the question.

"Besides, he likes your smell."

"Huh?"

"He's told me he wants to be like you when he grows up; he's very fond of you."

Guilt isn't an easy thing to swallow, which is why a woman ceases to think rationally and starts to see only one side of the issue: Auður is a close friend of mine, who has chosen an unconventional lifestyle, a single mum with two more father-less children on the way, highly educated, a music teacher with a fondness for wine, who slipped on the unsalted steps of my house one lunchtime, with a vegetarian Indian takeaway with rice for two in her bag, a broken ankle and six months pregnant.

She was the one who had come over to comfort me. I could, of course, turn this on its head, the same way Auður did, and say that it was a stroke of luck that she fell on my steps and got a thorough medical examination. "If one looks at the big picture," as the article I'm currently proof-reading keeps on repeating (and I don't know whether I should edit it or not), "If one looks at the big picture," all of these factors will help to ensure that my friend has children just like any others, and not children for whose survival she will have to struggle and who will then have to prove that they were worth struggling for, even though they might just be the way they are. It therefore falls directly on me, the friend she was coming to comfort when she slipped on my steps, to take care of the boy who loves my smell. Females can tend to each other's offspring, just like those ducks do at the lake.

I glance over my shoulder; he seems apprehensive. All he can see is the backs of our heads and he doesn't realize we are deciding his fate. I probably have no other choice but to take the child with me on the trip.

"You're my best friend, the best person I've ever met."

"Do you really think you should drink any more?"

"I won't get many other chances over the next months, it's good for the blood."

I give it one more shot:

"I won't even be able to sleep with anyone."

"Join the club. It's no big deal in my experience. You don't have to have him in bed with you. Besides, I thought you were divorcing and going off on a trip to have a change, to be alone, into the Christmas darkness of the east, however refreshing that may be."

I make no comment, but that is precisely what's on my mind. Who knows if there's a man waiting for me on the Ring Road? Who knows if he won't suddenly appear, somewhere within my grasp, by a waterfall or a mound of fallen rocks on the side of a mountain that plunges straight into the sea, or perhaps I'll find him leaning nonchalantly on the fragment of an iceberg in the middle of the black sand, a man one could talk to. He would suddenly appear, freshly divorced, a responsible father of two who wants no more children, dressed in full hunting gear with a rifle slung over his shoulder. But instead of blasting the

meat with lead, over his hunting companions' heads, or shooting himself in the foot, he would look straight at the goose and
shoot it right between the eyes. A good part of the excitement
would lie in tracking such a man down.

"Did you let Thorsteinn take everything?"

"No, just the things he wanted, some stuff."

She is obviously drunk. The boy is growing restless in the
back seat, despite the strawberry ice cream I bought in the
petrol station on the way.

"You're my best friend, the only person who doesn't try to
change me. No one else would have brought me a bottle."

"You asked me to."

"It's our progeny that makes us immortal."

She steps out of the car in front of the hospital with a white
woollen sock on one foot, a bandage on the other and an accordion in her arms, and sticks her head back into the car again:

"One more thing. I forgot to tell you I picked tons of crowberries this autumn and have them fermenting in two casks.
You're welcome to them, you just have to shake them every
now and then and take care of them a bit. The hooch should
be ready soon. If you handle it right, it should taste a bit like a
2002 *Montagne Saint Emilion*.

TWENTY-FOUR

We're standing side by side over the little stove, making thick
rice pudding, when she phones from a coin box in the ward.
She spends the first ten minutes apologizing and the next ten
thanking me and telling me that I'm the best person she's ever

met, since she had omitted to mention this before. I try to pour the milk into the pot and stir it, with the receiver stuck to my ear, as Tumi sprinkles the pudding with raisins from a bag.

"Loads of raisins," I hear him say.

He helps me mix the cinnamon and sugar, which screeches in the glass and echoes down the phone.

"And then blow on it."

"There's just one other thing," she yells down the phone, because she feels there is a poor connection at her end of the line; "I promised Tumi a family pet as a consolation prize, nothing too big, but at least furry; it could be a hamster, guinea pig or even a mouse, although personally I'm not too fond of mice."

I'm frank and tell her that, as things are now, I wouldn't be able to face any hairy creature smaller than a man, even temporarily. She tells me that there's a long story behind this, that she and her son have been through the entire process together:

"At first, the animal had to be furry and big enough to be able to pat or even sit on the back of and comb. Then, bit by bit, he mellowed his demands, but it still had to be furry, with hairs that would stick to the green sofa and our clothes." She tells me this isn't the case with hamsters and mice, and that you can even buy hairless mice now, the only problem being that they can easily vanish behind washing machines, never to be seen again. They had negotiated for weeks, reviewing every single furry creature, big or small, under the sun.

"I'd be extremely grateful if you'd take him to a pet shop to buy him something you can easily take on your travels with you."

She apologizes even more.

Once we've finished eating the rice and liver pudding bought from the store, I explain to Tumi that we're going on a journey, speaking to him with slow, clear, exaggerated lip movements, and tell him that we can't take a hamster with us because he would get lost at the first petrol station. I draw a mouse, put it in a traffic sign and draw a line across it: not possible.

He responds by drawing a picture of a four-footed animal that could be a dog, but has the tail of a horse and fills up the whole page.

"We can go horse-riding on our trip," I suggest, "there are bound to be horse-riding farms on the way," but I'm not sure he's understood me correctly. The next two and a half hours are spent drawing animals, alternately presenting our offers to each other, like two hagglers at a market in Marrakesh. His drawings are more or less variations of the same quadruped in various colours, patterns, spots, stripes and waves. He spends considerably more time on his creations and is reluctant to deliver any unfinished sketch.

We reach the store half an hour before closing time. I go through the motions of looking through a series of miserable-looking hairy animals with him and then point at an aquarium, trying to turn the boy's focus to the scaly creatures swimming inside them, but he pulls me elsewhere, encouraged by the shopkeepers.

The turtle is currently seven centimetres long but can grow to one metre and seventy kilos with the right treatment, tem-perature, compresses, diet and, above all, a lot of time, the shopkeeper explains conscientiously.

He's quite hairy himself, as it happens; not only does he have hair sprouting out of his collar and between the buttons of his shirt and beyond his sleeves, but also out of his nose and ears.

"For the whole of a woman's life," I interject.

Long after the child has grown up, the turtle will still be lying in its mother's bathtub.

"People are increasingly discovering the soothing qualities of turtles as family pets. Another advantage is that you can keep it in your fridge for up to three weeks when you go away on holiday—while it's still small. Families can rarely stand being together for longer periods than that."

"We'll be away for longer than that," I say. Besides, it is not, as yet, clear whether there will be a fridge in the summer bungalow, let alone electricity.

"With every purchase of two guinea pigs we give away some blow bubbles, and every purchase of two hamsters comes with a voucher for a McDonald's kid's Happy Meal box. With a dog you get two free hamburgers and two tickets for a dinosaur movie that's for over-tens only. If you buy a dog, two hamsters and two guinea pigs, we'll throw in a balloon-making machine, tickets to the dinosaur movie and two free alcoholic drinks in town."

I point out to the boy that the store is about to close and, once more, in a gentle but determined manner, direct his focus to the aquariums. Compromises are often humiliating for both parties and rarely live up to either's expectations. The man in the fish department has small and extraordinarily round aquamarine eyes, with virtually no eyelids.

The fish don't come with any extras.

"Choose," I say, lifting the boy up to offer him a view of the submarine life in the aquarium on the top shelf. "That means you can have any fish you like, we'll put a lid on the aquarium and take it on our journey. There's guppy fish, discus fish, vacuum cleaner fish who eat all the others, electric pumps, fluorescent lighting, plants, treasure chests, stones, sand and fish toys. We'll fill the aquariums with submarine caves to give the fish some seclusion and family life, and allow them to spawn in peace and bring up their offspring. Instead of just one animal, there'll be loads and we'll buy ourselves some hamburgers and go to see the dinosaur movie afterwards."

I could have added that we won't need a babysitter for the fish while we're at the movie, but instead I say something else:

"We can look into the possibility of a puppy later on."

We walk out of the shop with three goldfish in a plastic bag, an aquarium without a lid, sand, three artificial plants and a box of fish food. The man with the fish eyes slips me a voucher at the door.

"This voucher entitles you to a free drink at the bar" is printed on one side of it, and "Meet me tonight if you want" has been handwritten in ornate cursive blue letters on the other.

The following day, I phone the kindergarten to inform them that the boy will be away for an indeterminate length of time. Auður has already informed them that I am her next of kin and that I'll be taking care of Tumi.

TWENTY-FIVE

You bid your husband farewell for ever with a vigorous handshake and then meet him next morning buying sesame seed bread rolls in the local bakery, queuing in the bank at lunchtime, swimming in the pool in the afternoon, or at the registry office later in the week, and then, the weekend after that, at the theatre with his new significant other—always inevitably bumping into each other.

We haven't completely renewed our wardrobes yet. Generally speaking, it's underwear that people renew first after a divorce, both the person who leaves and the person who is left behind. Of course, I don't know how far his imagination can stretch and whether it can reach under my clothes, but he can see that my hair has grown over my ears; pretty soon it'll be longer than his. We've indulged ourselves a bit, both the one who left and the one who was left behind. It's a gross misconception to assume that the one who is left behind doesn't binge out on food any more than the other, eating out in restaurants, savouring an entire fillet of lamb on a Monday, drinking cognac straight out of a bottle and downing half a kilo of vanilla ice cream with hot chocolate sauce, sprinkled with a packet of almond flakes.

While we are queuing in the bank, he examines me for any external signs of change. Even though everything may seem identical on the surface, I am no longer the person he knew and once owned, and pretty soon I'll be even more different and newer, so new and transformed, in fact, that it may even take me some time to get used to the new me staring back at me in the mirror. He is looking extremely well, it seems to me, rested, energetic. He's put on a kilo and a half, by the look of him. I can see now what a good couple we made. We exchange mutual questions about each mother's health.

"Hi, how's your mum?"

"Hi, fine, thanks, and how's your mum?"

"Fine, last I heard. Are you paying bills?"

I can't tell him that I'm opening two new accounts to deposit my millions and those of my child in care, 22,261,000 krónur each, so I just say:

"No, buying some currency."

"Are you going on a journey?"

"Yes, you could say that, taking a late summer holiday."

"Where to?"

I suddenly feel an irrepressible urge to conceal the bungalow from him, the fact that I now have a summer house all to myself, in the same way that he has a woman all to himself. They seem to be of equal value to me at that moment.

In the line in front of me there is a small Asian woman with shiny jet-black hair, holding the hand of a little mixed-race girl.

"South-east Asia probably, Thailand, Burma, Vietnam, Cambodia, Malaysia, Singapore."

"Wow, will you be gone long?"

"At least six weeks, maybe longer, six months, maybe longer."

"Wow…"

To be able to settle my business in peace, I allow a few people to skip me in the queue until he has left the building, climbed into his car and turned the key in the ignition. He looks tired to me now, stressed. He seems to have lost weight. He has bags under his eyes, as if he weren't sleeping properly. I see now what a poor match we made.

Cashier no. 4 looks at me with a puzzled air when I place the cheque on the counter in front of her and ask her to split it, by depositing it into two separate bank accounts: 44,523,622 krónur. Then I ask for two million in cash, preferably in thousand-krónur notes. I see no need to leave a trail. Her colleagues at the neighbouring desks slow down their counting.

"That would be 2,000 thousand-krónur notes," she says reluctantly, twenty wads.

"Yes," I say, without bothering to recalculate, "that's right."

"Just one moment," she says, because she has to leave her desk, probably to nip into the coffee room at the back to discuss this with her colleagues, after which she'll have to nip down to the basement to get the wads of cash from the safe. Four of her co-workers check me out with surreptitious glances during her absence.

"It's best to keep large amounts of cash in nondescript plastic bags, not in a Gucci handbag at any rate," says the cashier when she returns to me. "It'll draw less attention, a used supermarket bag, for example, or library bag," she says.

As she passes the bag stuffed with notes through the hole in the glass to me, she says:

"The branch manager sends you his regards and apologizes for the breadcrumbs, he kept his lunch in that bag."

TWENTY-SIX

I'm not taking much with me. The main thing is to hold onto as little of the old clutter as possible. It's not that I'm fleeing anything, just exploring my most intimate and uncharted territories in a quest for fresh feelings in a new prefabricated summer cottage planted on the edge of a muddy ravine with my hearing and sight-impaired four-year-old travelling companion. The most important thing is to never look back, to only ever sleep once in the same bed and to solely use the rear-view mirror out of technical necessity and not to gaze into one's own reflection. Then, when I eventually return, I will have become a new and changed person, by which time my hair will have grown down to my shoulders.

I chuck my things into a bag, but can't show the same casualness when it comes to packing the boy's outfits and clothes. Even though I may not be an expert in children or their clothing, I can see quite clearly that he is outgrowing his winter overalls. I buy him a two-piece winter outfit instead, the dearest money can buy, and two pairs of trousers, as well as two new blue eiderdown sleeping bags, one for me and one for my travelling companion. I fetch my flower-embroidered jeans and slip into them.

There's no point in cramming the car with things; we'll take a picnic, two bottles of water, some books, two favourite fluffy animals, two favourite pairs of pyjamas and some toys that we choose together, as well as optimism, enthusiasm for travel, several CDs and—last but not least—a glove compartment stuffed with thousand-krónur banknotes. This is the best way to travel without leaving any trail behind us. I guess you could call it a trip without promises, but not without cash—there's more than plenty of that.

But first I've got to return the aftershave to my ex, along with the wedding ring and the sandwich toaster he forgot.

I park my car beside Nína Lind's Subaru and ring the bell. Their names are already engraved on a plaque beside the bell, his on top of hers, which is more than we ever achieved in our four years, 288 days of marriage.

The boy's spectacles glisten from the back seat and he watches me intently as I stand on the porch steps in my sweater, holding a co-op carrier bag. It's Sunday and almost noon when my ex-husband comes to the door in his striped pyjamas. I'd never seen him in pyjamas before. The smell of the apartment also catches me by surprise, a totally new and alien odour.

"Thank you, there was no need to," he says without looking

into the bag, but gazing stiffly into the mid-distance towards the car. The boy's chin doesn't reach the window; the only thing that is visible is the top of his woollen hood and eyes.

When I've reversed out of the parking space again, my ex is still standing in the doorway in his striped pyjamas watching me, as if he couldn't quite bring himself to close the door straight away.

Without having any precise idea of exactly where I'm going, I start heading east, moving towards an increasingly lower sun and shorter days, and soon find myself driving onto the National Highway No.1—the Ring Road—into the darkness and rain. I don't even have to choose a direction because on this island there is only one you can choose: the circular road that follows the coastline. In any case, I'm not the type of person who would venture off the highway down some untarmacked back road. One doesn't come across many crossroads on the Ring Road, and even fewer stop signs.

"Yes, of course we're taking the fish with us."

You can't break a promise you've made to a child.

We place the three goldfish in the biggest jar that can be found with a lid. The orange creatures jigger nervously with every movement, darting furiously from one wall of the jar to the other, in the little space they have to move in. The sand, pebbles and two shells, which the boy had fetched from his private collection at home and which were supposed to give the jar more of a homely feel, only help to agitate the water even further.

We helped each other lower the jar into the boot between the two casks of crowberry schnapps and four plants, which we were going to drop off at Mum's on our way out of town. She had given the plants as gifts to her son-in-law on various occasions, so it seems only natural that she should take care of them now. Everything that dies in my hands always seems to thrive in Mum's. Although I'm not a bad person, as such, I'm totally inept at looking after things or cultivating them. I simply can't find the instinct to help things grow. I either seem to water them too late or too much and always when they are on the brink of collapse, whereas in her house everything seems to flourish all around her.

"Plants thrive best in a thought-free vacuum," she says, as if she were quoting some popular Eastern philosophy.

Since her trip to China last year she has started to study Chinese, her first foreign language after Danish.

"As soon as I saw how many of them there were," she said, "I realized I had no choice. For the future."

TWENTY-SEVEN

She's one big smile, sixty-eight years old and still has all her teeth. With the vestiges of a streak of lipstick across her rosy brown lips, she bursts with vitality and embraces her only daughter and the boy.

"You could have left those behind," she says as we're carrying in the plants, the boy holding the smallest one. "This one's plastic and that's a silk flower and that one's made of tissue."

That explains why they've started to go mouldy. I've been watering plants that aren't even plants and shouldn't be watered. No wonder everything felt so phoney around us, that our relationship was withering; love can't thrive on artificial flowers. I should have copped on; lily-reddish pink and always in bloom, that's no life.

"I'd long stopped giving Thorsteinn living plants, sure you would have just killed them all."

My mother likes to save interesting newspaper clippings for my benefit, because she believes I never give myself the time to read the press; I'm always too busy doing other things. The dining table is covered in clippings that have been sorted according to subject matter: harmful poisonous food additives, the right way to handle raw chicken and avoid salmonella, education, childcare and bullying, the protection of children, animals and nature, reflections on various types of religion, all in double spreads and—last but not least—articles about international aid work.

"Yet another war to guarantee peace," she says, "except that now they've started to calculate the estimated number of wounded and maimed with bar charts and tables divided per age group in advance to enable the pharmaceutical companies to make their projections."

I remember how, when my brother and I were small, my mother used to plant potatoes and sow carrots in the spring, as soon as the earth began to thaw, and how she disinfected our palms and put a plaster on them after she had removed the red playground gravel from them, but I don't remember her ever expressing any opinions on global issues the way she does today. My mother is a woman with a mission in life. She has found a new passion in the autumn of her years, volunteer aid work around the globe; a widow dedicated to the alleviation of suffering. She is a sponsor of Doctors Without Borders, a member of water supply associations in Africa, a fund-raiser for a hospital in Sri Lanka and she is totally immersed in land mine issues and artificial limbs. Her main interest, though, is the education of young girls in the Third World.

"Because woman is the future of man," she likes to say.

She now has seven adoptive daughters in four continents, and has pictures of them and thank-you letters on every shelf and window sill. But she also has one boy. His fly is undone in the photo and two teeth are missing from his upper gum. He is leaning against a tree in the barren garden of some nursery with a beaming smile and oversized jeans that droop over his dark brown bare toes, despite the double turn-ups.

"I'd asked for a girl but they sent me a boy, you can't very well return a child."

The doctor laughed again. Did you really think you could get rid of the baby by running? Did you think it would disappear if you ran fast enough and went around enough times? Tut tut, it's incredible what a young girl's imagination can conjure up. It's growing inside you, whether you like it or not. You've hidden it for too long. There's nothing you can do about it. And then you'll have to get it out when the time comes. Believe me, giving birth turns fantasies into pain.

The big patterned carpet in the living room is covered with old, second-hand sewing machines and spools of thread that need to be inside a container to India before Christmas.

"Over there they will lay the foundations that will enable many girls to be financially independent," she explains to me, for their subsistence and prospects for the future. Tumi wanders between the sewing machines, bewitched.

"Yes, it's amazing how many useful things people keep locked away in their attics."

I had forewarned her of our visit and she has fried some fish balls and insists on us taking the leftovers with us.

"But we're going on a journey."

She pats the boy on the cheek and then me.

"How is he, the poor little thing? They probably would have abandoned him anywhere else."

"Mum, he is a perfectly lucid and intelligent child, he's just hearing-impaired and wears glasses."

"Doesn't he take any calcium tablets, he looks so pale?"

The boy carries the pot of fish balls out to the car and places it beside the goldfish. Mum is going to be taking care of Auður's home-brew, because she's the type of woman who can carry out any task she is entrusted with. If I'd given her a poisonous plant and live lizard, she would have looked after both with the exact same zeal and care. The plant would have sprouted poisonous yellow flowers and the lizard would have multiplied fivefold.

"You can return the pot to me when you come back. Don't travel too far east and make sure you don't…" she suddenly lowers her voice, staring at the ground, "start digging up any old stuff. No point in stirring old memories, you can't change them now."

Thinking back on it afterwards, I'm not sure she said all those things. But one thing I'm sure she did say was:

"Do you have a handkerchief to clean the boy's glasses?"

TWENTY-EIGHT

My happiness could almost be complete. I don't even have to see all that clearly, I just switch on the windscreen wipers, turn on the heating full blast and, bit by bit, the mist vanishes from the windows. There's a great freedom in not knowing exactly where you are heading, to surrender to the security of the Ring Road, where one point leads to another, and you always effortlessly end up back at square one again, almost without realizing it.

Since we're travelling companions, the boy sits in the front seat beside me, barely reaching the dashboard, looking manly with an open packet of raisins on his lap. His safety belt is a bit high, though, even though I've slipped a cushion under him. At the Raudavatn Lake I'm stopped by the police, who check my lights and safety belts and give me some advice.

"There aren't many people out travelling today," says the uniformed officer out in the lashing rain.

The boy willingly climbs into the back seat while I burrow through the bundles of thousand-krónur notes in the glove compartment to find my driving licence. For a moment, I wonder if I should behave as if I were in a B movie and slip the officer a folded wad of cash and then, without a word, drive off into the withered lupin fields ahead of us, vanishing into the mist and darkness, which is eating its way into the day with each kilometre.

Now that the passenger seat to my right has been freed, I use the opportunity to unfold a road map of the island.

"Dog," says the boy quite distinctly, pointing at the map.

It's true, the compressed island looks like a poor vagrant wet puppy dragging its paws. I'm heading towards the tummy, that's the point where my journey begins—our journey—where the lupin fields end.

"We're on our way now."

That's what Dad used to say every time we drove east at the beginning of the summer and had been driving for a while, at least an hour from home and way out of town. I'm inclined to think it was once he'd passed the lupin fields. Then he and Mum would exchange a brief glance and smile, and he would gently pat her hand with a contented air.

As soon as it starts to rain, the outline of the world begins to blur and the horizon is supplanted by vague landmarks. Everything more or less turns to wasteland as soon as you travel beyond the road grid of the city, vast expanses of black sand and black lava fields, with the black ocean not far beyond and the black sky above. At times like this it's good to have objectives. At the moment, mine consist in keeping my foot pressed moderately hard on the pedal, sticking to the right-hand side of the road, and not straying beyond the striped lines dividing my lane to the right and left. No need to make any decisions about what comes next, I just have to stick to the legal speed limit and move into the future that advances towards us as naturally as the next petrol station, as naturally as finding one's future husband leaning nonchalantly against the railings of a bridge—these things happen. It is no small feat for a woman to have to stick to the right-hand side of the road; that's where reason reigns, not the heart.

For the moment, my focus is fixed on the reflecting posts on the side of the road and the glow of the red rear lights of the old jeep towing a horse trailer in front of me, without, however, driving too close, in case some splashes of mud mar my vision. We seem to be the only two vehicles on National Highway One and that creates a kind of solidarity between us. If, for example, we were to continue heading further east and fire were to finally break through the surface of the glacier, and the sandy plains were to be flooded with water, would I and the boy and the man in the jeep, whom I don't know from Adam, end up sharing the half-packet of oaten biscuits I brought along on the same floating iceberg? Other people don't take their summer holidays in November. At this time of the year, normal people have other things to do than renew their bond with the darkness of the land. I switch on the radio, it's the last song before the weather forecast: *If there is a road, there is a way.*

The boy is totally silent in the back seat and refuses to take his hood off, despite the heat in the car. But I can see through the mirror that he is, nevertheless, alert and staring out at the road into the darkness. I mustn't forget that mute children don't attract attention to themselves the same way other kids do and require another kind of care.

The jeep unexpectedly skids to a halt in front of me and the trailer swerves on the drenched tarmac, leaving me no choice but to do the same, to avoid a collision, so I too pull up on the side of the road and kill the engine.

The man leaps out of his jeep. After checking something under his car and giving his horse trailer a kick, I'm not surprised to see him knocking on my streaming window. It's only once his face is right up against the glass and I can see the water trickling down his neckline from his hair that I realize it's the bloke from the pet shop, the man in the fish section, who sent me the handwritten note in cursive blue letters.

"No, there's nothing wrong," I tell him, "I didn't mean to be following you, I just like to know there's a car in front of me, I'm following the rear red lights."

I tell him that, even though I know from experience that I'll soon be able to see the lights of the greenhouses in the village on the other side of the mountain, I find it reassuring to know there is someone else on the road, with a comfortable gap between us, provided he has no objections.

"I don't mean to pry or anything," I repeat.

I feel an urge to speak to him further, to ask him something important, but the best I can come up with is to ask him for the time: what time is it? Absurd as it may seem, I suddenly felt in this precise spot, with no visible landmarks in sight, that I needed to know the time. In the rush of the moment I forget that I have a dual-time watch on the wrist of the hand holding the steering wheel. My divorce watch is blatantly visible to the man looking through the window. He turns back to his jeep without deigning to answer me, slams his door closed and drives off. The time is most definitely a quarter past five.

TWENTY-NINE

Visibility is practically nil and it is precisely here, at the peak of the mountain road, that my travelling companion decides he needs to pee.

He is unwilling to step out into the rain and wind, but doesn't want to wait either. Judging by the map spread out over my lap, there are another twenty-five kilometres of lava fields and sand before we hit the next petrol station, where there will be a toilet. After that we can buy some hot dogs that have been simmering in the boiler since last weekend.

There's no point in me raising my voice, he can't hear me, so every time we need to talk I turn on the indicator and pull into the side of the road, stop the car and turn in my seat to allow him to see the words my lips are forming, my mouth opening and closing. I ponder on whether I should try to convey the information in units of distance or time.

"Hold it in, it's another twenty-five kilometres to the next petrol station, or a fifteen-minute drive in these poor conditions."

But what if he asks me how long twenty-five kilometres is? Or how long it takes for fifteen minutes to pass? Twenty-five kilometres is a long distance to travel with a carsick child, longer than if I were driving a weary old lady to have a hip operation, who would be grateful for the fact that she didn't have to walk to the regional hospital over swampy fields and barbed-wire fences in a skirt and, instead, be able to sit perfectly upright in the passenger seat beside the driver, her bony knuckles wrapped around the handle of a handbag containing the bare essentials: her blood pressure medication, a box of red Opal pastilles and lipstick.

A post-coital silence can seem interminable if the woman no longer loves the man and the man no longer the woman. Time can pass just as slowly if you're travelling with a carsick child. Silences also seem endless when you're fourteen years old in a mixed class of thirty and you've been instructed to observe three minutes of silence in commiseration for some horrific event that has occurred on the other side of the ocean—that's an unbearably long time.

But when you're sitting beside your loved one in the car, twenty kilometres are like the flutter of a butterfly's wings on the wall, the buzz of a fly, the fraction of a moment, no time at all.

I was twenty-nine years old and had been abroad for nine years.
First I stroked his hair, then my hand slid down his shirt.

We hadn't known each other for long. In fact, I think it would have taken very little for me to love some other man instead. But he was giving me a lift down south and I felt good beside him in the car. Then he suddenly said:

"Will you marry me?"

Just like in the movies and without slowing down. I was going to switch topic or say thanks, but unfortunately I couldn't. Maybe it would have been clearest just to say no thanks, but thank you for asking anyway; but the autumn sun was shining in my eyes and blinding my thoughts for a moment, so instead I unhesitatingly said yes. He looked like he was on cloud nine because he'd chanced upon those three minutes in my life in which I actually wanted to get married, and he had obviously expected me to say: "Thank you for asking anyway."

When we drove away again, he had one hand on the steering wheel and the other wrapped tightly around my shoulder. He had to decelerate to forty to be able to kiss me properly, but with his eyes open, since there were cars coming in both directions and here and there dogs that leapt out at us barking and chasing the wheels. At one point we almost drove into a ditch. With the jagged coastline on my right and him at the wheel on the left, I couldn't have been happier with my lot in life. We drove all evening and into the night, and then stopped at a petrol station in the fjord. When I stepped out of the car into the darkness, freshly engaged, and caught the whiff of a pile of dung in the yard in front of a neighbouring shed and faced the fluorescent lights and smell of mustard inside the store, my mood immediately started to change.

Two weeks later the accountant and amateur pilot came to collect me with all my papers and computer and, shortly afterwards, I signed the marriage certificate. It is impossible for me to pinpoint

*exactly when my opinion of him began to change. It was probably
not until our divorce that it occurred to me that I should have got
to know my husband a bit better.*

The boy shakes his head.

"No," he says.

"No, what?"

I don't understand him and he doesn't understand me, so
I get out of the car, open the back door and apprehensively
lead him a few yards away from the edge of the road into the
mist and help him unzip his fly. The car engine is still running
and the lights, windscreen wipers and radio are all on. The
weather forecast is being read: the outlook is for ongoing mild
temperatures and rain. This is now the rainiest November ever
recorded on this island, says a familiar voice that resonates
across the barren heath. At a distance of a few yards, the voice
already begins to sound more flirtatious.

"No, sweetie, there are no lions on the road." He's beside
himself with fear and can't handle the situation, so I hold his
skinny penis to prevent him from sprinkling his new velvet
trousers, and a hair-thin, almost transparent silver thread spurts
into the mist and darkness. This is the first time I've helped a
male to pee. The question now is whether I can pee in front
of him as well.

I think I discern a cairn a short distance away, in the mist.
It seems the ideal place for me to squat like some aboriginal
woman giving birth in the depths of the forest. Can I leave him
behind in the car with his safety belt tightly fastened? What
if I stepped into a hole and got stuck there and never came
back? Can one never let a child out of sight? Never take a few

minutes' break? I would be immediately out of view and he'd be left alone with his huge hearing aids, so terrified that he'd pee in his pants, if he hadn't just relieved himself. He'd cry and produce weird sounds. I imagine he'd try to call out for his mother or grandad. Not that he wouldn't soon be found. The second next lorry driver would hoist him into his cabin.

It occurs to me that he might just as easily wander onto the national highway against the traffic, with no balaclava on, and risk getting hit by a car, because no driver expects to see a child wandering alone in the fog at the top of a mountain road, no mother would ever abandon her child to run in the mist and dark like that. But would a woman who is not related to the child be capable of such a thing? In the end I decide to take him with me and hold his hand, while the car engine is still running on the side of the road. Wrestling against the cold rain, I drag the little man with me onto the moor, moving swiftly in my leather boots, which sink into the soggy earth. After some initial effort to keep up with me he starts to drag his feet and falter, tripping over rocks, as I tow him over clusters of heather that scratch his calves, and stumbling against something every few metres, because the pile of stones that we are heading towards on this forsaken path always seems to remain at the same distance, at least another hundred years away.

The moor is still patched in white, despite the rain, but we manage to avoid the deepest snow-filled hollows. Tinges of November green moss give the surroundings a phosphorescent glow that hovers about half a metre over the ground, like artificial light in a film studio. I'm not at all cold. I can't feel the icy rain running down my neck.

The child's trust in me is beginning to falter, he doesn't

understand where we're going. Neither do I. He starts to whinge, but nevertheless tries to hold back his tears. If he were like other children he would scream, throw himself on the ground and refuse to go any further, want to turn around and go home. And he'd cry and say that he missed his mummy, until he was heeded. But he's not like other children. As if by intuition, it occurs to me to stop trying to walk in a straight line towards my target, but to move in zigzags, like a fox in danger.

And there it is, suddenly standing before us, the beast, dangling its drooling tongue. In the same instant, gunshots resound all around us. Men in green guerrilla overalls spring out of the moss brandishing shotguns. The only animals that kill their own kind stand there pointing their rifles at us; we're completely surrounded.

For a moment I consider putting my hands up over my head, but the boy is so petrified with fear that I take him into my arms and swivel away from the gunmen, like a Jewish mother turning her back on the muzzle of a German lieutenant's revolver, alone out in a field, with a four-year-old child in shorts. I notice some red-pinkish splatters in the snow close to where we are standing, halfway between the cairn and the car, hardly squashed berries—no, it's the blood dripping from the birds hanging on their belts.

The men suddenly lower their weapons and wave us out of the fog, having perhaps mistaken me for a reindeer. We're greeted by a chorus of sombre but friendly voices. Thermos flasks are suddenly produced, cups of boiling, heavily sugared coffee are poured, and we are offered rye bread with pâté straight out of picnic boxes and other goodies that are being unwrapped from foil. I accept the cup of coffee, but say no to the other beverage that is being passed around in a silver flask. The men line up, side by side, and politely introduce themselves, one after another, with a handshake, like a well-groomed football team, or soldiers standing to attention to be reviewed by their head of state on a courtesy visit. I evaluate them each in turn in relation to my ex-husband, starting with their height and build. Wasn't he one metre eighty-three? All of a sudden, I feel I can no longer remember the colour of his hair; it's certainly brown, but was it mossy brown, seaweed-brown, heather-brown or cinnamon-brown? Is the mist on this moor thick enough to veil my former life from me? As I'm finishing the slice of bread I complete the rough comparison in my mind, comparing all the men in view, both with each other and then, broadly speaking, with the other men I've encountered in my life, limiting myself, however, to the past five years. It doesn't take long.

Finally, I notice a ginger-haired boy in the group, hardly over fifteen years old, with big splatters of freckles on his face under his cap.

"He wasn't very big when he killed his first goose," says a man with the same gene of hair that might have been ginger too once, slapping a hand on the lad's shoulder.

"Can't have been more than seven years old, on the garden lawn at home; the bird was wounded and limping, so my boy just grabbed a shovel and rake, but it was his resourcefulness that mattered the most," says the father proudly.

"Soon after that he graduated to clay pigeons and was up to 131 clay pigeons by the time he was fourteen, so it won't be long before your little lad starts showing his mum what he's made of," he says, patting the hooded head of my protégé and winking at me at the same time.

The men escort us back down to the highway, rifles wobbling to and fro on their shoulders like those sticks geography teachers use to point at world maps over blackboards, hopping from Haiti to Palestine and Iraq with the greatest of ease. They're chirpy and content. The boy's cheeks are red after the picnic and he is holding two extra twisted doughnuts in his hands. He hasn't fully recovered from the ordeal, though, and looks pensive and tired.

The feeling I was beginning to get while driving on the mountain road, of the car being somehow unsteady and slightly off-kilter, turned out to be well founded, since it is now blatantly clear that I have a flat front-left tyre.

My escort livens up again. There's a job to be done and there's no need for me to worry, they say. I should just sit the boy inside the warmth of the car, while they happily take care of this for me.

"You can admire us in the meantime," says one of them, jestingly.

I omit to tell them that I have a perfectly good little manual in the car with diagrams and that it would take me as long to learn how to change a tyre as it would to learn how to give my hair a colour rinse; both operations are conducted in four phases, according to the diagrams. I see no reason to memorize knowledge that might never serve me, to prepare for an eventuality that may never happen. We will all most certainly die, and yet there are plenty of people who get through this life without ever having to change a tyre. I therefore strive to focus my preparations with that in mind.

The nine gunmen change the wheel like a well-trained team of surgeons and nurses. Without a word being spoken, they split into those who pass the tools and those who perform the operation on the four-year-old manual patient, who has recently been oiled and sprayed with anti-rust. They find the right monkey wrench, take it in turns to loosen the bolts, effortlessly jack up the car, swiftly pull the spare wheel out of its hidden compartment, without even having to ask me where it is, and then put everything back into its place, professionally, seamlessly.

One of the men even places a comforting hand on the bonnet, as his colleagues wind up the operation. Performing their tasks with warmth and care, they fondle the car with gentle slaps and caresses.

"You poor little thing, you punctured yourself."

"Did you bump into a hole or a stone, old man, is that what you did?"

"All over now, all taken care of, little man."

THIRTY

Here I am, wandering through the rain and darkness with an unrelated child, three pets in a jar, a small pile of documents barely worth mentioning and last, but not least, a glove compartment crammed with banknotes, perfect. I've deliberately left my mobile behind; my sole link to my immediate environment at this moment in time is the weather woman on the car radio, who is saying that the eye of a depression is now pressing all its weight on the centre of another depression.

Who I am is intrinsically linked to *where* I am and *whom* I'm with. Right now all my efforts are centred on making the most out of the fading light, while my travelling companion sleeps in his balaclava, tilted against the window in the back. The only decision that needs to be made now is whether we stop or not and, if so, where. The highway seems almost uninhabited; where are the natives of this island? Apart from the boy and the hunters, the only company we encounter on our way are the shopkeepers inside the petrol stations that punctuate our journey, the woman reading the weather forecast on the radio and, at this very moment, the velvet voice of the host of an afternoon culture show, whose words seem to be streaming into an echo chamber without punctuation.

A giant Pepsi sign shines through the darkness.

Yuletide lights have been hung over the petrol pump; only five weeks to Christmas. We're the only customers and a scrawny, weary-looking girl with big eyes and a dyed ponytail comes running out of the house next door to serve us some petrol. I imagine that must be her brother who comes following her, a little bit younger, taking slow steps, as if he were tackling the strong current of a river. His spotty face and swollen eyelids suggest he's just woken up from a long summer sleep, with a knitted hat pulled over his eyes. He takes over the pump from his sister, petrol is obviously his job. She tells us there was little traffic over the weekend, but that they ran out of hot dogs on Sunday, unfortunately, and they don't have the ice cream machine turned on in the winter. Instead, Tumi gets to choose from a range of multi-coloured wine gums and sweets from last year, displayed in boxes under the glass counter.

Elísabet Marilyn turns out to be a worldly-wise girl, who informs us that she recently came second in a beauty contest at a ball, that she likes reading good books and going to good parties where there is something other to drink than home-brews, that she is currently pregnant, but that she hasn't decided on whether she is going to keep the baby or enter more beauty competitions, and that she has been invited to compete in the Golden Blonde of the World Award. The competition is only open to blondes, she says, because up until now judges have shown a strong bias for brunettes, who always score higher, like the recent Miss India and Miss Brazil, for example; and this is unethical, professionally speaking, particularly since the members of the jury often give the opposite impression in their one-to-one interviews with blonde contestants in the preparatory rounds.

I buy a knitted sweater for the boy with a hood and a jigsaw of two puffins rubbing each other's beaks, as well as a souvenir for myself, a miniature hand-made painted church about the size of my palm, skilfully crafted in wood by a cousin at the farm. I'll put it up on the dashboard. E. Marilyn hands me some glue to ensure it withstands the country's network of notoriously bumpy roads. I wonder whether I should buy the knitted yellow baby trousers on display in the craft corner. That way I could set up a meeting with my ex in some neutral café and, when he sat down at the table in front of me with a wriggling baby in striped stockings in his arms, I could pull out the parcel and hand it to him over the cups of hot chocolate and say:

"Well then, congratulations on the baby."

"Thank you very much, this is the baby we should have had together," he'd say, stroking the light down on the crown of the head of the baby, who would look like neither of us.

But instead I buy two knitted trousers for Auður's unborn twins.

The boy doesn't want me close to him while he's choosing his candy, because he's his own boss in this and is quite proud to be able to buy it on his own. He seems to have a slight crush on the girl in the pink T-shirt and stares at her intently to be able to capture the words being shaped by her pink lips. It's not easy for a deaf boy to decipher the syllables coming out of a mouth that is masticating gum.

I see from the boy's lips that he is doing his best to enunciate his words as clearly as possible, trying to produce sounds that he himself can only barely hear. But she doesn't understand him and looks at him, bewildered, several times before glancing over at me. He suddenly starts to fiddle with his hearing aid, trying to reset it. I can see that he's deeply offended, and by the time he's outside on the gravel by the shop wall again, he's holding in a green cellophane bag something completely different to what he wanted. I walk up to him and tell him he can buy some chocolate as well, but he is unable to choose between the three types that are on display on the glass counter, unable to decide because he's already been distracted once, it's thrown him off-kilter and he's scared of making a dreadful mistake. So I end up buying all three types of chocolate for him—pleasing a child doesn't have to be any more complicated than that.

As we're leaving, the owner and father of the girl steps out into the yard to corroborate all of the main points of his daughter's story about her second place in the beauty contest and her pregnancy, which explains why the girl looks so sickly, poor thing, she can no longer bear the smell of petrol. Recently she even threw up all over a family of four who were sitting in their car.

"But on the other hand, no one understands what she sees in that silly wimp at the pig farm, the guy even plucks his eyebrows," says the father.

Tumi has forgiven Elísabet Marilyn. I think he's in love; he runs around us in circles playing a bird with huge flapping wings to say goodbye. When he's in the car he eats one of his wine gums out of the bag, but then puts them down and doesn't touch them any more. He stores the chocolate in a box with his collection of shells and it's still there under his bed four weeks later.

THIRTY-ONE

One of the advantages of the Ring Road is there is very little danger of losing one's self, even in the drizzle. But it's another matter when it comes to finding things in the dark, like a sign, for example, indicating the turn-off to a farm guest house. We drive back and forth a few times around the spot indicated in the travel guide, moving a few centimetres to the east and a few centimetres to the west of the map. It's difficult to gauge distances in the dark; there are no landmarks here. If there were anyone else around I'd ask for directions. I can see through the rear-view mirror that Tumi is tired and feel such an overwhelming responsibility, it's worse than being alone—I'm responsible for another person's happiness. The area is incredibly black. No echo of life disturbs the silence of this wilderness. I kill the engine of the car in the pitch darkness to look up my farm guest house guide again, and then make out the sound of a bird.

It suddenly dawns on me that no one will be travelling this way before the end of winter. The sun won't rise here until the spring, when once more people will be able to make out the outlines of shapeless things, hear sounds and meet their fellow beings.

I know from experience, though, that there is a landscape out there in the dark, behind those multiple layers of clouds, which the guide commends for its beauty and extraordinarily bright summer days and nights. To conjure up a lava field and valley, I have to summon my imagination, old patriotic poems and memories of foaming streams meandering down the sandy desert. Tomorrow morning I'll wake up and find myself at the foot of a steep mountain, with a slope that descends directly into my bedroom window, so close to the building that I'll have to lean my head back to see the summit between the curtains.

It's the Christmas lights that save me.

On the sign there is a painting of two smiling cucumbers wearing caps and shaking hands over the farm's slogan, which reads "Cucumbers in unexpected places". We walk into the steam of a plate of meat-stuffed cabbage rolls and melted butter in a sauce-boat.

The woman welcomes us and smiles at the boy with a warm and natural air. Maybe she has a disabled relative. She tells me they discovered thermal water in the Hái-Hamar district two summers ago, which is why a small greenhouse has been built to grow cucumbers, their speciality, pride and joy. It's become popular among overnight guests to buy some cucumbers before they set off on their travels again. They can even have them inscribed with names, messages or declarations of love. One of their guests, an accountant from the city, handed his fiancée a cucumber over the breakfast table that said "Will you…" Those were the only two words he managed to carve on it, not that anyone had any problems working out the rest of the sentence. They even got applauded by a group of foreign investors on a team-bonding trip, who happened to be in the room having their breakfast.

"Foreigners seem to like the shadow that hovers over the farm all day and the rain. This is the rainiest place on the island," says the woman. "Because of the shadow from the cliffs we only get to see the sun, when it's around that is, for two hours a day, and then the shadow comes back over the farm again, although it's brighter over in the sheep shelter in the fields facing south, and the sheep can sometimes bask in the sunlight well into the afternoon.

"So far this year it's rained on 295 days out of 320. Not bad, eh? We even wrote it in our brochure; sure, no one comes to Iceland to sunbathe."

We're lucky. One bedroom less and we would have had to sleep in the sheepcote, which they're actually planning on converting into rooms to accommodate thirty more guests. A male choir from Estonia that is touring the country singing German Christmas carols seems to have taken over the entire establishment. It turns out that the guest house has run out of linen to make our beds, so we're given sleeping bag room instead. The lady insists on us having dinner; they've made meat-stuffed cabbage rolls, potato purée and red cabbage. She's just cleared up, but there's plenty left. I watch the child shovelling one meat ball down after another. He hasn't eaten much over the past three days, just a few morsels, like a small bird. But now, on the fourth day, he's eating like a fully grown man or a sailor on a trawler. As we're chatting, he downs three to four glasses of milk with his food.

The woman tells me the sheep keep on getting stuck on the rocks on the cliff and that milk production subsidies have dwindled to a pittance. The summer home for problem kids from Reykjavík has gone up in smoke after two cases of arson, and none of it insured, because the insurance man had only started to appraise the wallpaper and no premium had been decided yet.

"In fact," says the woman, "we'd come full circle and tried the whole lot: traditional farming, breeding poultry, mink, foxes, pisciculture, rearing sea bass, rabbits, and apiculture. We had to keep the beehives warm all winter, only one bee survived the cold and the rain. We're still waiting for an answer to our ostrich-breeding application. That's why we went into the guest farmhouse business. If we get the ostriches we'll just add them to the foreigners."

The food is good, but the coffee is undrinkable, no matter how much I try to sweeten and stir it. For an instant I think I catch a glimpse of the back of a familiar figure in the yard through the window, a mere flash. The imagination runs wild in this drizzle. The farmer's wife offers me a slice of a freshly baked cake called "Conjugal bliss" to go with the coffee. A heavy cloud of rain weighs over everything, but the woman seems content enough.

I dash outside to fetch the sleeping bags in the boot. The pot of fish balls is still firmly in its place, although the same can't be said of the three goldfish. The jar has been knocked over and the lid has come off. Its orange contents are scattered around the boot. Two of the fish lie dead on a dry patch and one of the sleeping bags is drenched. A small puddle has formed in a hollow by the spare wheel, where the third goldfish is still showing some sign of life, judging by the twitching of its tail. After several attempts, I manage to grab him and slip him through the neck of a half-empty bottle of water, but even when I seal the top of the bottle with my thumb and shake it, the fish shows little sign of perking up.

Tumi goes out into the yard after dinner to skip with the little girl of the house, who is around his age, but a head taller. When I come back to fetch him for bed, they're busy saving some worms from drowning in a puddle. I don't mention the fish yet.

On my way up to the bedroom I meet my ex-lover on the staircase and halt at a distance of five, six steps.

"Nice trousers, like the floral pattern, they suit you."

"Thanks."

He looks at the boy, who is in a hurry to get past us.

"I didn't know you had a child."

"No, I'm minding him for a friend."

He smiles and we both move one step closer to be able to shake hands.

He hesitates, reluctant to release his grip.

"I knew you'd left town, but I didn't know where to, this is an incredible coincidence."

"Yes, really incredible." He's still holding my hand.

"I'm not following you, even though I would have wanted to, I arrived here last night," he says. "Ahead of you then."

I offer him a smile.

"Business trip," he adds by way of explanation.

"Actually I'm on the point of leaving. I'm planning to get back to town tonight. Mission accomplished."

Then he strokes me gently on the cheek.

"Unless you need company?"

"I don't know," I say nodding towards the kid, who is standing there perfectly still, watching our lips.

"You're certainly one hell of a skater."

"Thanks, you too."

The boy gets the dry sleeping bag and I a blanket, but as soon as I come across a co-op I intend to buy two new eiderdown quilts, adult size. The boy pours the sand and pebble out of his shoes into the sleeping bag. There are multi-coloured fleece rugs on the floor.

"It smells old in here," he says. Or maybe he's saying that I smell good. He must be already missing kindergarten and his mummy and grandad, who sometimes comes to collect him, but at least he thinks I'm nice and that I still smell good, even though I know I must smell of rain and all the people we've encountered on our journey. After slipping into his sleeping bag he tries to speak in a low voice and wants to whisper something to me in confidence, but his voice comes out as loud and resonant, despite his utmost efforts.

His hand is too small to enclose all the signs of the world in words. But I have three books in the car to teach me how to understand a deaf child; I just need to make time to read them.

Having kicked and tossed under the duvet every night since I collected him from kindergarten over ten days ago, the boy sleeps to dawn without stirring.

I'm also tired. A deep depression looms over the country and I am lying in its eye, while the outside world remains enveloped in a mist.

There is some movement in the corridor; I even think I hear a faint knock on the door. A drowsy numbness starts to spread across my forehead and then descends to my cheeks. Bit by bit, I feel the day fading, odours and sounds evaporate. I sense the world withdrawing behind a thick woollen blanket with brown squares, as the flow of honey-sweetened hot milk trickles through my veins. Someone is holding me tightly. I have a vivid feminine dream and feel the mountain towering over me. When I wake up later to see if the little, dead still body beside me is still breathing, I feel as if someone were quietly closing the bedroom door behind me, but I'm too exhausted to tear myself away from my dream and get out of bed. Although I feel no need to lock the car at night, I do distinctly remember having locked the bedroom door. Granny never locked the little blue house on the seashore when she went south, not even when she spent five months recovering in the geriatric ward of the local clinic one winter. I don't even remember there ever having been a key to the house. It was open to anyone, always full of all kinds of guests, ministers, men out of jail or stone-collectors from around the globe—they sat all together at the kitchen table eating layered tart with jam.

Once, during my last summer in the east, I was kissed on the guest mattress in the attic, without knowing by what cousin. It was almost as if nothing had happened. I barely felt it, but nevertheless knew that it was inappropriate. The following morning I wasn't quite sure and couldn't remember which of the two brothers had slept on the left side. I felt no change except that, for the first time, I asked Grandad to serve me coffee and Icelandic pancakes instead of porridge. After that Granny decided out of the blue that we were too big for the guests' mattress. On the first night I slept alone in the living room, I dreamt I was wearing a half-knit white woollen cardigan with brass buttons.

I wrote this down in my diary: last summer in the east. At the beginning of October I turned fifteen.

When the boy wakes me up next morning, I'm covered in a thick duvet in a blue cover. The blanket has been folded neatly at my feet.

THIRTY-TWO

We have breakfast with the family in the kitchen. The male choir is warming up in the dining hall with a light medley of Estonian melodies. I imagine the lyrics must sound quite exotic to other ears than mine. The woman places a bouquet of red tulips on the table in front of me.

"He asked me to send his regards and hopes to see you again soon."

The tulips obviously grow in the greenhouse between the cucumbers; I should count myself lucky that he didn't send me an autographed one.

Tumi picks the cucumber rings out of the pâté on his bread. Everyone stares at him, children and parents, as he systematically pulls them off, one by one, and places them on the side of his plate, without showing the slightest interest in his audience.

"He's the spitting image of you," says the woman.

"Yeah, definitely a chip off the old block," says the husband.

"Are you travelling alone?" the woman asks.

"Are you going far?" asks the husband.

At the end of the table there is a boy I'm guessing is about sixteen or seventeen years old, stooped over a bowl of Cheerios. His limbs seem strangely disproportionate, as if each body part had grown separately. He has puffy, sleepy eyes and big ears that his hat doesn't quite manage to cover. There can no longer be any doubt as to whom the size 44 runners in the hall belong to. He obviously gets his looks from his mother, who is a pretty woman with fine features. I gaze at him intently, until he finally looks up with his shimmering aquamarine eyes.

"He grew fourteen centimetres last summer," his mother tells me, "barely climbed out of bed in July and August, slept eighteen hours a day and just woke up to eat. He's certainly our prodigal son; we practically had to slaughter a lamb for every meal. He was of little use to us that summer, couldn't even drive the combine harvester he's been driving since the age of eight.

"He was so sluggish in his movements that we thought he'd never get from the sofa to his bed; it was as if he was up to his arms in water."

They talk about their son as if he weren't there and the young man shows no reaction, focusing all his efforts on fishing cereal out of his milk. His father joins in:

"We were on our way home after a ball; everyone was on the coach, which had its engine running and was about to leave. While some people were staring into the dark or kissing, I hopped out to look for my future wife's friend, who I'd been flirting with a little. They both had the same ponytail and I had a few drinks in me."

"We sometimes say that our relationship is based on a case of mistaken ponytails," the woman interjects with a smile. They laugh and I get the feeling that it's a story that's been polished over the years, until it gained its final form.

"Not that he'd ever mistake the tails of two horses."

"She was throwing up behind a building, it was the first time she ever got hammered, and while I was wiping her face you could say that the wheels of our first-born were set in motion.

The best thing of all is that no one on the coach even realized I was absent during those few minutes."

"Yeah, doesn't take Stebbi very long," she says, and they burst into laughter. "We've been inseparable ever since," she adds.

"Yes, you can say that again. I felt I'd reached heaven when I got to know her," says the husband.

His wife's dress has a zip at the waist and she wriggles inside it, like an eel in floral slippers.

The man has dropped out of the conversation and is now staring at the shape of the body that fills out the dress. He peers longingly into her eyes as she's talking, until she finally walks over to him. Could they be completely oblivious to the presence of their morning guests?

Suddenly the door swings open and a little being totters into the room with a bulging nappy swaying behind it, after the night's sleep. The woman turns away from the man and bends over to embrace the child. She picks her up and kisses her and then passes her to her husband while she leaves the room a moment. An instant later she returns with some buttermilk yogurt in a bowl.

"Sugar," says the child, clapping her hands.

"One spoon for the emperor in China," says the woman, "one for Queen Margrethe Thorhild of Denmark, one for King Kristjan the Ninth, who gave us a constitution, one for Ingibjörg, the wife of our national hero Jón Sigurdsson, one for Vigdís Finnbogadóttir, and one for Dorrit Moussaieff."

"Imagine," says the woman, as she is saying goodbye to me with the infant in her arms, "some people in this world have never driven in the rain."

She looks up at the steep climb in her damp sweater. As I'm driving along the back road, it occurs to me that I might have misheard her, that my hearing might be getting worse, and that what she might have actually said was: "Imagine, there are people in this world who've never heard the sound of rain."

And then she pricked up her ears to the sky, her sweater by now drenched.

THIRTY-THREE

We travel at a leisurely pace, slowly crossing the landscape, because we're on holiday and have all the time in the world. Every now and then we stop for a snack and sometimes slip into our rain gear to pick up treasures off the side of the road, precious wet stones, and gradually fill the car with our spoils, pebbles, wet clothes, anoraks, socks, new sleeping bags, hats, gloves, crumbs and tufts of moss. The boy has started to draw pictures and various symbols on his fogged-up window with his index finger. When the weather occasionally clears, we see the landscape suddenly flashing before us through the window in magnificent spectacular waves. We park the car to find a moderately sized crater, close enough to the road, so that we can peer into it and marvel at the chaos of soggy nature. Then we lie down on the moss to see how fast the clouds glide by. The light has a delicate transparent essence that envelops me and the child, like a thin cotton veil.

"Where's left?" he asks in a very clear voice when we're back on the Ring Road again.

To be able to explain what the left is, I have to stop the car again. It is then a good idea to sit on separate wet tussocks.

We're close to a stone sheep pen and I wait for a red van to pass us before opening the door.

"Left is city language, but in the country there aren't two but four directions to choose from. There's north, south, east and west. So left is north, that's out of my window, straight ahead is east, your window is south and the stuff that's behind us and done with is west."

I try to manage as best I can, creating images and signs with my hands, some of which I invent and others which I've seen him use. I talk about before and after, and also what is ahead of us and behind us, what has yet to come and what has already passed. He understands me better than I understand myself.

"In the city there are as many directions as we have hands, here in the country there are as many as the legs of an animal, four."

"Chickens," he says.

"OK, chickens are an exception."

"Back mirror," he says.

"That's right, rear-view mirror."

"Dad lives in the west."

I'm pretty sure that's what he said. Where does the child get these ideas from? Instead of talking about his father, whom, as far as I know, the child has only met a few times, I explain to him what it means to lose one's bearings. The worst thing is to be stuck in a fog out in marshes or in a snowstorm on the moors, I say. Some people never lose themselves in nature, only in cities, and others only abroad. But still, most big cities are built in the same way. Some people get lost no matter where they are, and remain more or less lost for the whole of their lives. I'm speaking the language of the hearing, knowing perfectly well that he doesn't understand it, until he starts crying. Then I stop and take off my divorce watch and hand it to him, saying:

"You can keep it."

"Wet," he says.

I fasten the watch around his wrist.

"We'll stop soon and buy an ice cream and a postcard to send to your mummy in hospital."

"Fly," the boy says distinctly from the back seat as we're about to drive off.

He's right; something is fluttering in the car, not a fly as it happens but a butterfly, in late November. Could this butterfly have travelled with us all the way from the city and might it even be the same insect I touched with the tip of my fingers three weeks ago in my old kitchen? Like a stowaway it finally decides to give itself up and come out of its hiding place, because the ship is too far out at sea by now to be able to turn back.

A red blinking sign suddenly appears in the middle of the sand desert to inform us of our next stop. Hot dog and hamburger joints line the Ring Road at twenty-five-kilometre intervals. When I open the back door for Tumi to unfasten his safety belt, I notice he's written two words on the misty glass: WET FLY.

A coach is parked in the car park and we order hamburgers, after which I push Tumi ahead of me in the queue for the ladies' toilet, undo the buttons on his overalls and he is ready to go. The women accompanying the Estonian choir stand in a single row in knitted sweaters, brandishing hairbrushes in the air and eyeing us through the mirrors, without breaking up the queue.

As soon as he's done, I tell him to wait for me, not to budge, stay by the door.

When I come out, the boy is gone. The coach has driven

off and, in state of panic, I ask the waitresses if they've seen a four-year-old hearing-impaired boy in blue overalls. They look at each other in silence. I run all over the place, thinking of him not being able to express himself, imagining him being taken away in a stranger's car. Finally, I find him behind a shed in the yard where empty petrol tanks are stored. He's holding the hand of a middle-aged man with a red face. They both look happy and timid. I drag the boy away from the man and give him a piece of my mind, telling him that I'll report him for I don't know what. The man hops into his red van and drives off.

"Daddy," says the boy.

That wasn't the boy's father, that's for sure. Both of the fathers of Auður's children are young, handsome, sensitive men, but totally irresponsible.

In my hysteria I fail to catch his number plate.

The boy doesn't want to talk to me and hides under a sleeping bag in the back seat. I rush back in to buy the postcard, my eyes firmly glued to the car and the kid inside. They only sell two postcards and they're both of a waterfall I'm told is somewhere close by. The photos were taken so close to the waterfall that pearls of water can be seen on the lens. When I get back to the vehicle, the boy's head re-emerges from under the sleeping bag. But no matter how hard we look, we can't find the butterfly. It's vanished into thin air.

THIRTY-FOUR

The road suddenly narrows, the tarmac ends and gravel takes over. Visibility is down to about three metres through the windscreen wipers and movie songs are being played on the radio before the death notices and commercials. I pump up the volume when a woman starts to sing about suffering and love. *Piensa en mi cuando sufras*, think of me when you suffer.

There is a river behind us and another one ahead; that makes two single-lane bridges and, as if it were possible, the road is growing even narrower. The number of holes multiplies and cavities deepen. The road meanders on, with a slope and curve ahead of us. Fully focused, I navigate my way between road signs, first warning me of a blind rise and curve ahead and then of a single-lane bridge—that's National Highway One for you.

As far as I can make out, there is no one else out on this Tuesday morning, apart from the sheep, of course. Normally, by this time of the year, the sheep would all already be indoors, being fed on fodder, but because the weather has been so unusually mild they're still rubbing up against the sides of the roads and bridge posts. Sometimes they stand in the middle of the road and stare into the headlights of approaching cars with their bloodshot eyes, looking straight at you without so much as flinching. Family clusters usually spread themselves on either side of the road, with the mother and granny sheep on one side and the smaller ones on the other. But when a car approaches they feel an irresistible urge to reunite, and leap off tussocks, the edges of bridges or other hiding places like foreign soldiers, armed to the teeth, waiting to ambush women and children on their way home from church or the bakery. The same pattern repeats itself forty times a day: sheep dash across the road and I screech to a halt. Then, on the forty-first time, the inevitable happens: the animal catches me off guard, appears out of nowhere in the fog and is hurled up against the bonnet of the car.

When I brake, the animal slides off the bonnet onto the road, into the mud. The windscreen cracks into thin threads, spreading like crocheted lacework or a spider's web, spun by a woman. And then shatters. The windscreen wipers continue to swing to and fro, and the small church, which was only glued to the dashboard with craft glue, stands intact.

It is precisely at that moment that it first dawns on me that I am a woman caught in a finely interwoven pattern of feelings and time, that there are many things going on simultaneously that have a significance to my life, that events don't just simply occur in a linear sequence, but on several plains of thought, dreams and feelings at the same time, that there is a moment at the heart of every moment. It is only much later that a thread through the turmoil that has occurred will emerge. It is precisely in this manner that the destinies of a woman and a beast can intersect. The woman is listening to a Spanish love lament and glances through the rear-view mirror to see how her deaf travelling companion is dealing with his cocoa milk and banana when, at that very same moment, a sheep decides to step onto the road in front of the car, or suddenly panics—how should I know what goes through the mind of a thoroughbred Icelandic sheep? Time is a movie in slow motion.

Maybe I'm ten minutes behind schedule because I lingered under the shower for too long or maybe I'm ten minutes ahead? In any case, if it hadn't occurred to me to take a summer holiday in November, if I hadn't won a prefabricated summer bungalow in the Deaf Association's lottery, if I hadn't met my ex at the time I did, if I hadn't been sent east into the country every summer until I was fourteen years old, and if I hadn't had cultured milk with my muesli for breakfast, I wouldn't be here right now, but somewhere else, I'd be someone else. I'd probably still be on my leather sofa in the old living room, sitting beside my ex, watching a live war somewhere in the world on TV. That precise moment in time—17:11—at which I ran over that sheep on the Ring Road is intrinsically linked to my entire existence, the incidents, decisions I've made, my taste in food, sleeping habits. Because it's impossible to say many words at once, things seem to happen one after another, events get divided into categories of words, which take on the form of horizontal lines in my narrative when I phone Auður to tell her the news. In practice, though, the connection between words and incidents is of a completely different nature. I don't say any of this to her over the phone, however. She's got enough to deal with as it is. No, no one was hurt, except for the sheep that is, who is no longer of this world. Yes, it's true what she's saying: at least I slaughtered the sheep faster than the nomadic shepherds in Siberia do; they shove their arm into the beast and grope inside it until they find its aorta and rip it out. Moreover, it's a skill that commands respect. She's worried about Tumi—but not because he is in my care—and worried about me, worried about her mum and worried about her unborn children, the health system, her students, and the bad roads on the island, worried about the wars and greed of the world, worried that she's not allowed to play the accordion—her only outlet in all this waiting—in the bed of the room she shares with four women. Instead, she's forced to listen to the Bible on tapes. In fact, she'd reached the Book of Job 14:7 when I call.

"So I'm getting my fair share of suffering here," she says.

I scan the horizon, not a car in sight; the road is deserted, the whole area is deserted, the island seems uninhabited. It figures; I'm driving through a constituency that distinguished itself in the last local elections for its exceptionally good turnout at the polls. Ninety-seven per cent of the electorate, both men and women, voted, that is to say thirty-three individuals. I picked up that titbit from the local newspaper.

I leap out of the car and first check the boot. It's full, so I drag the beast into the passenger seat. It's a lot heavier than the child. The boy has thrown up and his vomit is quivering on the dashboard. The whole car is in a mess, might as well sell it and buy a new one, as soon as I get a chance.

Black with white rings around its eyes, it makes an odd-looking sheep. It almost looks like a unicorn, since it only has one fully formed horn and the other is little more than a stump. Her extended family bleats in protest before dispersing in the November rain. The bloody carcass rattles in the passenger seat, but I have no choice but to drive it to the next farm, and slip a CD into the player: *O mio babbino caro*, an aria by Puccini. It's getting dark again. I open two gates and drive towards a cluster of houses at the foot of the mountain, with wet soiled fingers.

I'm seven years old and my friend Sigurður knocks on the door to tell me that Brandur has been run over, that he's dead in a cardboard box under the apples in the locked guest toilet and that it will cost me five krónur to see him through the window. I join the queue with five krónur in my hand. The line shortens and I'm wearing new plimsolls because the first day of summer was two days ago. It's my turn now. I hand Sigurður the coin and climb onto the wooden box outside the window of the guest toilet, where Brandur lies dead. Standing on the tip of my toes in my new plimsolls, it only takes me a second to spot him lying on one side. There's white froth in his mouth and blood on his stomach. His eyes are open. I bless him with the sign of the Cross in the same way that I'm blessed when I get into a vest after a bath. It's then that I notice white socks soaking in the sink. When I get down off the box, my friend Sigurður offers me a piece of Wrigley's spearmint gum. Afterwards, I run into the field by the new building in my new plimsolls. There are puddles of red water, which smell of rust and must, and immediately colour my shoes. That night I soak my white shoe laces in chlorine.

The weather has cleared when we step into the yard and I notice Christmas lights hanging on the ridge of the barn. The family dog hops on me, but no one answers when I knock on the door. The light blue light of a television set glows in the living room of the bungalow so I knock on the window. A couple inside sit at both extremities of a sofa watching a swaggering police Alsatian in an Austrian cop series.

The farmer finally comes to the door with a smile that exposes his red gums.

"That earmark is not mine, it's my brother's, who lives on the next farm; let him tend to his own flock. My brother and I haven't spoken to each other for seven years. A dispute over borders. They've recently sent us another threatening letter, just because of the drainage ditches we dug. Now all of a sudden they think they've become the spokesmen for wader birds." Kinship is fatal.

THIRTY-FIVE

When I finally come to the end of the track leading to the neighbouring farm, for a moment it seems like we might be welcomed with open arms. The man walks slowly towards us from the yard, followed by his wife. Peering through the web of the cracked windscreen, I see that he has a yellow towel draped over his shoulder and a kitchen stool in his hand. He gives me no sign of acknowledgement, however, having probably just seen me come from a meeting with his wretched brother, which obviously does not bode well. They're more or less my age and could be cousins—same physique and hairstyle, a similar gait, both leaning heavily on their left feet. The man sits on the stool and, now that I'm out of the car, I see that the woman is holding a black electric razor in her hand. She starts shaving the back of her husband's neck under the porch in front of the front door.

"It's just to avoid any of the hair going on the carpet or sofa inside," she explains. "It's bad enough with crisps and the dogs."

The dog is going berserk and circles the car, barking up towards the window behind which the dead sheep lies, and makes several attempts to knock me over and scratch the paint-work off the car—not that it matters at this point—and finally jumps onto the bonnet, where he stands slavering on my neck.

"You've run over my favourite sheep," says the woman. "We had to call a midwife when she came into the world and then a vet. She had a caesarean birth." They examine the glazed-eyed animal after its shaky journey down two back roads to the farms of the two brothers, who live in this place where kinship is fatal and people haven't spoken to each other for seven years, although little cousins sometimes secretly play together through the gaps under the barbed-wire fences.

"Do you want to pay by credit card or cash?"

It transpires that the animal was four years old, was called Lind, had a truncated right ear and split-tipped left ear, always gave birth to two lambs, full weight: 40.7 kilos, twice the winner of a silver medal at livestock shows. She turns out to be more expensive than she would have cost me in a store, all carved up, spiced and marinated in cognac and vacuum-packed.

"Milk," says the boy, who has climbed out of the car and is standing right against me. I summon up the courage to ask if the boy can have a glass of milk. It's impossible to buy fresh milk in the petrol stations along the Ring Road.

"It's my husband's birthday in a week's time, a big birthday, so we were planning on slaughtering one anyway, I'll try to make some stew out of it," says the wife wearily, "we're expecting sixty guests."

"Not another of those spicy city recipes with beans," says the husband.

"We should be used to it," says the woman, "those animals are always getting run over, last time it was a pedigree horse that the priest reversed into. The irony was that he'd come to the wrong farm, no one had committed suicide here."

"Not yet," interjects the husband.

"We ate leftovers every single day for three weeks."

She leans over to whisper something into my ear:

"Add cayenne pepper and no one can tell where the meat comes from, whether it was an accident or clandestine slaughtering at the farm, any trace of their breed or origin vanishes in a second," says the wife. Then, striking a lighter and more sisterly tone, she chummily adds that they sell quite a few run-over animals to the Sand Hotel.

I wonder whether I should pass her the Irish goose recipe, which only requires it to be cooked with the stuffing for all signs of the crime to be erased.

"Go take a look at his paintings," says the woman suddenly, before lowering her voice to add: "if you buy a picture from him, I'll give you a good discount on the sheep. No one knows where his talent comes from, he's only just started, let's hope it's passed on to the children."

I follow the farmer up to an attic where he's created a studio for himself in the bedroom of his departed parents-in-law.

"It just started out of the blue, one day after dinner," he says, "it was as if I was being guided from the other side."

All the animals are in profile, like Roman emperors on those coins of yore. Most of the backgrounds are amber skies and sunsets. The prices on the paintings are quite low.

"*Hawaiian tropical sunset* is the heading an art historian used in a small article in the local paper," he says. "He was travelling around the country and devoted a quarter of a column to this quarter of the country."

The farmer hands me the cutting. The boy calmly looks at the paintings and the man alternately.

"Do you want a portrait of your sheep or just any one?"

I pay 3,500 krónur for the picture and he throws in an extra two kilos of potatoes, freshly picked in November. Auður will appreciate the pure tones of this picture.

"If the weather continues like this, we'll be able to grow crops all year round. Unless I start to paint all year round instead."

Blind kittens tumble over each other in the hallway by the shoes as I settle the payment for the sheep and the portrait of the sheep. The girl of the house invites the boy to play with the kittens; they're going to be drowned soon. The boy crouches over them by the pile of shoes and I fear they might be giving us another extra gift.

Once the transaction has been completed, the atmosphere lightens and the conversation turns to the weather. They mainly talk to each other.

"Yes, that's a lot of rain," says the woman.

"Yeah, very mild," says the husband.

"Nothing's the way it should be in the sky any more," says the woman, "it's all gone odd."

"It's all a sign that the poles will be reversing soon."

"We've almost reached the winter solstice and potatoes are still sprouting in the fields and we haven't picked all the summer carrots yet."

"Yeah."

"I don't ever remember there being weather like this at the end of November. We had the highest temperature in Europe here yesterday, even warmer than Rome."

"Yeah, imagine, just under the Arctic Circle. The potato plants are still sprouting and a lamb was born here two days ago."

"That journalist Ómar Ragnarsson flew over here in his plane today and is going to be doing a report on it in the news."

"Yeah, weird."

"Yeah, you can only be grateful for every day."

"Yeah."

"It must be coming to an end now."

"Yeah."

"Yeah, probably with an eruption."

"Or a flood," I finally interject to join in the couple's conversation.

"What do you mean?"

"Well, the rivers seem to have swollen up quite a bit, the water is up to the roadway of the bridges, the roads are wet, the glaciers have turned grey with the rain, not to mention the overflowing lagoons."

They look at me with suspicion.

As a farewell gesture, I apologetically pat the animal lying in the yard. The man tells me about a garage nearby where it will take them half a day to order a new windscreen.

"They're always ordering new ones for the machines they're using up on the dam."

As soon as I'm back in the car and have closed the gate behind us, a small little ball of striped hair appears from under the collar of the boy's hoodie. He looks at me through his glasses with moist, pleading eyes. In fact, four pleading eyes are now staring at me from the back seat. I give him an encouraging, understanding, approving smile, turn on the windscreen wipers and heater, and swerve back onto the highway. I'm back on track.

The best thing about this island's road grid is the Ring Road; there's nothing there to distract you, the back roads are only used to fetch milk and return any sheep one might have run over to the nearest farm. You can stop almost anywhere and pick up the thread again, without having to look at a map. It makes life so much easier not to have to dread new choices at every crossroad.

I turn off the weather forecast and slip in a CD. Pérez Prado and his band playing a forbidden tango, *Taboo*.

My vision of the world may be restricted by a cracked pane

of glass, but I feel I'm gradually gaining a better grip on things, and it would actually take very little for me to consider myself a satisfied woman.

THIRTY-SIX

We drive over three bridges, one after another, and the water level has risen further.

While the car is being fixed, we use the time to write the postcard and eat prawn salad sandwiches. The boy plucks four prawns out of his. It takes an hour and a half of my life to write the card for him. He dictates everything he wants it to contain for me. First, I jot down the words in my notepad, and then he takes a look at them and either nods or shakes his head. There's no doubt this boy can read.

Dear Mum,

We're on a journey in Iceland. The road isn't straight. There's a rear-view mirror in the car. I am well. It is raining. The sheep died and so did the fish. I have a kitten. The others drowned. I am well, but I will still come back to you. We send our regards (the last sentence is from me). All my love. Your darling son, Tumi.

That evening I call Auður.

"Guess who I met at my antenatal inspection this morning?"

"Who?"

"He looked up from a Norwegian gossip mag, he was peering at two-year-old photos of the royal family. The only man in the waiting room, because it was the middle of a weekday."

"How are you doing?"

"But I only saw the back of her, she was going in to be examined in a fairly anonymous-looking coat, so I wouldn't recognize her if I saw her on the street again."

"That's because you only saw the back of her. How are you?"

"She was wearing glasses."

"On the back of her head?"

"I caught a glimpse of her in profile."

"How are you?"

"I was expecting some brainless bimbo, but actually she's not unlike you, it seemed to me. Except you're more exciting, of course," she hastens to add.

"Because I'm your friend and you only saw her briefly in profile."

"Don't take this personally, but I thought he looked pretty good, new haircut and rested. Actually, he seems to be in great form."

"What are the doctors saying? Have they set a date for the birth yet?"

"What, mine?"

"Yeah, your twins."

"The 24th of December, provided there are no cock-ups, they're sisters."

"Is everything else OK otherwise? In the ward?"

"You can imagine, I've never led such a monotonous life. I'm trying not to focus on sex and death too much, my mind is mostly on food these days and I'm reading recipe books between meals. And it's always the same let-down when the food tray arrives, soggy biscuits and thick, lukewarm, tasteless cocoa soup."

Then I ask her if the boy can read. Not as far as she knows, she hasn't even had the time to teach him letters yet. She's got enough on her plate with his speech therapy, sign language classes, occupational therapy, physiotherapy, apart from the fact that he has only just turned four.

"Well, he can certainly write words," I say, "all kinds of complex words that he writes on the misty windows: MAMMY, FLY, OH, MIRROR, DADDY, WET, LAGOON."

"How do you like being with a child?"

"Tumi is a very special child, a wonderful kid. I've started to learn sign language, to read more about it, he's also teaching me, pointing at things and showing me their symbol."

"Is he changing you?"

"I guess he must be."

I can hear from her voice that she is fighting back some tears.

"Becoming a mother is the most important thing you can do in life. It's a wonderful experience to have a child. Then all of a sudden you have to decide whether you're just going to serve coffee or offer food at their confirmation parties and whether you should contact their fathers, or even go to a photographer's studio together. By law, fathers are obliged to pay for half the costs of confirmations and funerals."

"Well, first… they have to be born."

"I might die giving birth, all three of us might, it's such a big responsibility."

"Don't give me that, nothing will happen to you this time."

"But if anything does happen to me… to us, I want you to take care of Tumi. You're the best person I know. I've put it down in writing."

"Nothing will happen to you, you're so sensitive in your current state, they'll look after you."

"Precisely, it's the exceeding confidence in this ward that scares me, they all love their jobs and record episodes of *ER* for each other when they're too busy working."

"You're so vulnerable in your condition, if you like I could have a word with the obstetrician."

"I'm such a dreadful friend, blabbing away about myself and asking nothing about you. Have you met any exciting men on your travels?"

"No, it's mainly girls who operate the petrol pumps. Besides, I'm quite content to be alone with Tumi. We're up to 300-piece jigsaws now."

"I told you he'd change you."

As I linger a moment at the postbox and search for my car keys in my pocket, a man in an anorak with a fur-trimmed hood and a violin case in his hand turns towards me and speaks to me in Estonian in an amiable voice:

"Beautiful woman."

THIRTY-SEVEN

There can be no doubt that some major construction is taking place in the vicinity. Gargantuan machines, the size of three-storey houses, crawl along a strip of gravel road, blocking off both ends and creating an obstruction on the highway. I trudge behind them and it is not until I come across a side road leading to a farm that I have a chance to overtake them.

The beams of my headlights unexpectedly illuminate two men in blue overalls standing at the foot of a sharp landslide with their backs turned to the road. They stand there motionless, like identical twins, with a few metres between them and no vehicle in sight or nearby farms. They're looking up at the landslide; two sheep are perched on the summit and standing there perfectly still, looking down at the men. They simultaneously slip the rifles off their shoulders and take aim. I hear two almost concurrent shots and two balls of bloody wool come tumbling down the perpendicular mass of bulky rock. As I drive past the men, they turn to look at me. The white of their eyes looks yellow to me. I turn on the radio.

Water levels are steeply rising around the country after the uninterrupted rainfall of the past two weeks, says the reader of the lunchtime news. An increasing number of roads are becoming unfit for driving and muddy rivers are engulfing the pillars of bridges, which will soon have to close. A hundred-metre stretch of the Ring Road has already been cut off. Farms, horses and hay bales are surrounded by water, and fields have been inundated, locking people off on their farms, and there have been power cuts in many areas. In the highlands, the build-up of water pressure against the dam has exceeded expectations and rivers are beginning to overflow. The speaker botches his last sentence and repeats the detail about the overflowing rivers. He forecasts southern winds and persistent rainfall.

In fact I only have to glance through my windscreen to see that the country is half immersed in water; everything is quite literally awash in the sandy desert. The whole purpose of this pleasant journey around the island was to try to sort out my life, but now the thread has been abruptly severed. On a two-dimensional map, the world looks like a clearly delineated place, a fully defined and secure area in which rivers are just harmless blue strokes of the pen. Even though I may not know who I am, I can make out where I am and where I'm heading on this unfolded map.

Some of the countries further south are now experiencing temperatures of minus thirty degrees, the anchor continues unabated, while just 200 kilometres from the Arctic Circle thermometers are hitting plus eleven degrees. Such is the unpredictability of nature, which will always take man by surprise.

Since I'm travelling under my own steam and, what's more, with an unrelated child, I don't have the courage to tackle the dark brown mass of water on the other side of the sand in my car and therefore have to find somewhere for us to spend the night in the black desert in the middle of this dark winter day.

I scan the map that lies open on the passenger seat beside me, first to see how long this sandy desert extends for and roughly count the number of blue lines, and then to look for the red points that represent made beds and breakfast buffets with orange wedges, muesli and teabags. It's mainly on the narrow green strip along the coast that we have some hope of finding accommodation.

Ten minutes before reaching it, we can already start to hear the mounting rumble of the glacial torrent—dark grey, full of sand, stones and debris. We stop the car by the bridge to look into the water.

Tumi walks beside me, waving his arms about like a fearless man. Impossible to look at anything but the fury of the grey maelstrom, no firm point on which to fix our gaze. Drenched, we freeze a moment on the edge of the bridge, watching the enormous mass of muddy brown water run by.

By the time we get back to the car, it's as if an entire hour's worth of river had passed. I turn on the heater full blast and the boy writes two words on the foggy windows. Like an ancient Greek metaphysician: *Water runs.*

I take the warning sign, which the water-measuring experts have put up in the sand, seriously and don't venture out on any unnecessarily risky explorations. The question, though, is whether we should cross the next bridge and then be trapped on that side or carry on along this side of the river and then be forced to turn around. The first option seems slightly better; at some point one has to stop brooding over the past. Besides, we need to stop for the night soon. A luxury hotel has recently been opened nearby, complete with solarium, jacuzzi and bar. The area that seemed utterly deserted earlier is now suddenly busy with traffic. "Allow yourself to be yourself," the hotel's slogan reads.

As I'm about to cross the last river in the sand desert, I suddenly come up against a white car in the middle of a single-lane bridge and slam on the brakes, as does the man in the car opposite me. We both step out.

"I thought you were going to stop," he says. "I didn't realize you were driving over until it was too late."

"I somehow thought you were stopping as well," I say, still blinded by his headlights. The engines of both cars are running.

"I'll reverse then," he says, "I was actually thinking of turning back to spend the night in the hotel anyway."

"I can reverse too."

"Are you driving east?"

"Yeah, I'm having a summer bungalow moved there."

"Over Christmas?"

"Yes, over Christmas, are you going west then?"

"Yes, but I'll be back soon, maybe we'll meet again then."

His glasses are all misty, which makes it difficult for me to make out the eyes concealed behind them. I rub the sleeve of his jacket, which is an odd response to a complete stranger. He's dark and has such short hair that all his childhood scars are visible, both on his scalp and designer stubble.

"Are you a hunter?" I hear myself asking him.

"No, I'm no hunter. I came across some ptarmigan chicks on the road this summer and my car capsized when I slammed on the brakes. I've got a sick falcon in the car that I need to take to town. He needs some expert care, in the worst-case scenario he'll end up being stuffed. You've got to keep quiet about rare birds that stop off here for just a few hours before heading on to America, or someone will try to stuff them. They want to have everything stuffed in the south, causes them the least hassle."

When I'm back in the car, I realize I haven't given the child anything to eat for much of our drive across the sand desert, so I stick a straw into a carton of milk and hand it to him. He stares at the floor as he clutches the carton with both hands, sucking its contents dry. I bite the peel of a banana, feeling its bitter taste in my mouth, and hand it to him, without taking my eyes off the road, without slowing down, without breaking our continuity.

THIRTY-EIGHT

Hotel Sand stands in the middle of the desert, a brand-new blockhouse building with minibars, a satellite dish and loosely woven brown curtains in the rooms that don't fully cover the windows. We're surrounded by water, although the road men have started fixing the bridges on the eastern side of the desert.

"It's wonderful to pass through here," a foreigner confides to me in the lobby, "but I wouldn't like to be stuck here. It's different for you people who are used to sand deserts and darkness," he adds, "because you were born and brought up in this. Of course, it would be different if the sand weren't black but golden, and the temperature was about ten degrees higher, to be able to adapt I mean."

We book ourselves into the hotel, having been preceded by the Estonian male choir, which we seem to bump into everywhere it goes on its tour around the country. They've already stayed here one night and have another two to go. This evening they will be giving a concert, followed by a surprise number, which is already attracting guests from the dam construction site. The hotel was built in record time, I'm told, in true Wild West style, and apparently is an exact replica of a hotel in west Texas, the only difference being that the original model is 300 rooms bigger.

"We expect to be enlarging the hotel over the coming years," says the hotel manager in the lobby, "the growth potential is limitless."

The restaurant on the ground floor has small carved wooden doors that swing in both directions, just like in old Westerns or those changing cubicles in fashion boutiques. At the top of the dining hall there is a varnished wooden stage, equipped with microphones, and a dance floor in front of it with mirrors.

We throw ourselves on the bed with the kitten between us and watch the evening TV news. Maps appear with circles around the areas where rivers have overflowed and reservoirs seem to be on the brink of bursting. The presenter briefly mentions the

Estonian male choir and its accompanying troupe of young "artistic dancers" with a slightly smug air, before passing the ball to the sports reporters.

We zap through the foreign channels. Tumi is holding the remote and is therefore the master.

A naked snow-white woman crouches down on a golden beach to lean her head against a giant bottle of perfume, gently caressing its neck with the tip of her fingers and then rising towards the lid, stroking that as well, without, however, unscrewing it, before finally dropping her head and closing her eyes. The bottle is the size of a man, but the woman is small, fine and fragile. This bottle seems to be the only thing she has in the world to lean on.

We sit, stroking the cat and watching the woman in the commercial, mesmerized. It's on a French channel. *A woman is an island*, a velvety male voice says in the distance. This is followed by a moment's silence.

"Beautiful lady," says the boy, clearly and distinctly.

"Yes, beautiful lady," I say, laughing.

"Beautiful lady," he repeats before placing the palm of his hand on my belly.

"We're only allowed to serve alcohol with the food, if you buy more than chips," says a teenage waitress in the dining room.

Quivering bottles of soda and beer are being carried into the room in crates and technicians are testing the microphones. There is a sense of anticipation in the air, but for now everything remains relatively quiet and the hotel manager gives himself time to chat to us in the hall.

"Things will be livening up later on; we're expecting a group of foreigners from the dam construction this evening."

Adopting a mysterious air, he then lowers his voice as he leans over the counter between two palm plants:

"We're in an odd situation here. The cancellations due to the construction work on the dam have actually been far less than the number of bookings from the contractors above. We only get the odd ecological tourist who comes here to experience the desert. What's more they like to keep to themselves, hardly buy a single souvenir and bring very little currency into the country."

He has straightened up again now and raises his voice: "One has to look at the big picture."

We both slip into silence, the hotel manager and I. I'm waiting for the restaurant to open. The boy wants boiled fish with potatoes and butter, just like at his grandad's, if I've understood correctly. The kitten also wants fish. The hotel manager leans over the counter again.

"And then, of course, there's the commercials. We get quite a few film crews around here shooting their ads. Mainly for mobile phones. They're starting to bring in some currency. A foreigner recently said to me that he felt like he was living inside a mobile phone commercial here, nothing but sand and rocks, total freedom. Of course, some people are quite keen to track down these places with nothing around them. There isn't a single blade of grass growing here at the moment, although we're planning on planting a small oasis of pine trees in the sheltered area behind the building. We've been in touch with the Forestry Service and they've given us the green light. Unless we go for some mountain ash instead."

The boy's lips silently move, as he reads a sign on the wall in six languages. Once more the manager lowers his voice and turns on that mysterious air:

"And then, of course, there's a fair bit of local traffic from people in the area if there's something going on, people like to come here for a change of atmosphere and to give themselves a treat, gawk at the foreigners and have a drink."

There's a TV in the dining room so we watch a programme on some foreign channel while we're waiting for our food to arrive. A man from a small Alpine village in Austria, who keeps goldfish the size of trout in his garden, is being interviewed. He's taught them to play football, he claims, and to stick their heads out of the water to kiss him. His wife complains about how her husband spends all his free time kissing and fondling the fish and confesses that she is jealous. She invites the reporters in for dinner and chats to them, as she fries some brown trout. She is wearing a stained apron and seems to be quite chuffed by all the attention she is receiving from the cameras.

"We're out of fish" says the waitress, "it's mainly Italian dishes we have. Pizzas are the most popular. That includes soup of the day, mushroom."

I order milk for the boy and water for me.

"Is skimmed milk OK?" the girl asks. "People never order milk with their food here."

Tumi can only handle two morsels before the cheese seems to get stuck in his throat and he can't breathe and coughs into his glass of milk. Finally, he spits out the food into a green napkin I hold up to his mouth.

When I come back to the table, after washing his face, our plates have been taken away and clean sets of cutlery have been wrapped in green napkins on the table. The girl tells me that the kitchen staff agree that the Margarita and calzone weren't quite up to scratch and they would like to offer us hamburgers and chips on the house instead.

"All hotel guests are entitled to one free drink and a discount on two further drinks at the concert tonight."

Once the boy and cat have fallen asleep under the same duvet, I take a shower and finish reading *Gli Indifferenti* by Moravia. Feeling a slight chill after all my travels, I slip on a thick white sweater and return to sit in the dining hall. The place is steadily filling up with guests, who group into tables, according to their level of acquaintanceship and family ties. Many of them bear a striking resemblance to each other, with their red faces and freckles.

Two foreigners in anoraks by the entrance cast their dark eyes on me over their pints of beer. One of them has a rolled-up cigarette poised between his fingers. Scanning the room with my eyes, I notice a teenager, sitting slightly apart, about seventeen years old I would guess, with a bottle of coke and a glass full of ice cubes in front of him. He sips on the bottle, but doesn't touch the glass. There's something oddly familiar about him. He has a sensitive air and pale complexion, and I imagine he has started to harmonize the proportions of the various parts of his body and that he is no longer as lethargic as he was. He has dark, undulating hair, which he has clearly tried to wet and comb down.

I sidle up to his table and ask him if I can take a seat. When he looks up I see that he has beautiful green eyes and that he probably suffered from bad skin that has now started to heal. I order the same thing he's having and, before I know it, have leant over slightly towards him to ask him when his birthday is. His gaze shiftily darts in all directions, like the deserter of an enemy army who is on the point of disclosing information that could put him in peril of his life.

"At the end of May," he says, but without any hostility, pulling the hood off his head. A dark lock of hair dangles over his forehead.

"Are you from here?" I ask him bluntly, sipping on my soda. The youngster whitens and glances nervously over his shoulder, as if he were expecting someone.

"I see that you two have already introduced yourselves," says a man taking a seat at the table beside the youngster.

He slips a hand around the boy's shoulder, as if to tell him he's got nothing to fear, and smiles at me. It's the man from the bridge.

"Hi, and thanks for your help earlier."

"Same to you."

"We came to listen to the singing, but he'll have to wait a few years before we can watch the act that follows the choir," he says.

After chatting with them for a while, I tell him I have to go and check on Tumi. As I get up, he asks if I could do him a favour. He has to take the boy home before the show begins and he wants to know if I can mind the sick falcon for him while he's away, it's in a box.

"He's already been fed, so you won't have any worries. It'll just be for a few hours or until tomorrow morning at the latest. There's one place I have to stop off at on the way, but I'm pretty sure I'll be back at the hotel tonight."

Far be it from my mind to weigh the prospect of the company of a feathered predator against that of a naked man, I can clearly see that I will be given no choice about which of the two I would like to sleep or wake up with.

He follows me up to room ten, walking behind me up the stairs with the box in his arms, and places it on the bedside table. The bird gives us a hostile glare through the two little holes in the box. The kitten immediately arches its back and hisses at the feathered guest, fluffing its hair up in all directions. Before we know it, he's leapt out into the corridor and vanished around the corner on two paws, as if he had been swallowed up by the earth. The man from the bridge promises to help me find the kitten when he gets back, and tells me he is extremely grateful for the favour.

I notice how he rapidly glances around the room as he's leaving, and picks up the duvet, which the boy has kicked off onto the floor, and spreads it back over him again, showing the same care to all creatures great and small, just like those ptarmigan chicks.

"I'm a vet," he says. "I have to pop over to a farm to perform a caesarean on a calving cow."

I pull out a book, the posthumous publication of an early work by a French author, and read a story about a father and son who perished as the father was trying to save his ten-year-old son from drowning. The boy was then buried in his father's arms in the churchyard on the island, which they had planned to visit before returning on the ferry that evening. I'm having problems concentrating on my reading under the menacing stare of our overnight guest; not even the death of the hero manages to hold my attention. I decide not to sleep, but to wait for the return of the falcon's owner. The choir resounds from the floor below. They are being applauded now and will no doubt give an encore. I seem to have dozed off for a moment, because when I come to, I remember fragments of a dream: I'm lying on the grass under an apple tree and, as I'm looking up at these succulent red apples, I hear myself saying: "Opportunities will soon fall on you."

THIRTY-NINE

By the time I return to the hall, the lights have been dimmed and a rotating multi-coloured mirror ball has been lowered into the middle of the dance floor. An exotic bird is about to launch herself around the central pillar. She has travelled from far across the desert, considerably further than the choir even, judging by the colour of her caramel toes and violet nail varnish. Her eyelids droop heavily as she holds one leg suspended in mid-air, displaying a foot in a laced shoe with a thick sole and high heel. A heavy burden seems to weigh on her as she slowly allows herself to sink to the floor, until her black fringe touches the newly laid oak parquet. Despite the heavily dimmed lights, the scars are clearly visible under her breasts. The lights revolve, blinking green, red and violet. Huddled together up against the stage, the men form a protective wall around the exotic bird who has come from afar. Several of them are talking into their mobile phones in various languages, probably to the wives they haven't seen for such a long time. But the star of the male choir's secret surprise number is clearly having problems hoisting herself off the floor again, and eventually solves the problem by squatting and parting her knees to the audience.

After this, many guests join in the karaoke. The hotel manager and a group of foreigners burst into a rendition of *O sole mio*, and are followed by three men singing the song about the man who sailed home again across the sea, *I Am Sailing*. The last singer is a man with a long torso and greenish-blue tie whose bulging dry lips almost kiss the microphone as he stretches his long neck, while the rest of his body remains on the stage. He moistens his lips and tilts the microphone stand forward, as if it were a woman in a tango. The tune hiccups around the hall until the voice is suddenly isolated on stage with no accompaniment and the man eventually realizes that the playback has broken down. He stands by the mike, silently mouthing the words with his lips, as some men rush across the hall. Then the room erupts into whistles and applause, and the singer awkwardly adjusts his tie.

The heat and humidity are rising, the men have slipped their jackets onto the backs of their chairs, people are starting to touch, collide, rub against each other and step on each other's toes—the pairing off for the night has begun.

The owner of the falcon suddenly reappears again and sits down beside me in the corner.

"Hi again," he says, "did I miss much?"

"Loads, how did the caesarean go?"

"Well, it was a white calf with red spots, just like its mother."

"Was that your son?"

"No, he's the son of some friends; he was helping me out today so I invited him here for a meal at the Pizzeria Space."

He has booked a night for himself and the bird in room thirteen, which is just opposite ours in the corridor. When we get upstairs, the door is open and the boy has vanished from his bed. The box is still on the table. We run up and down the full length of the corridor, up and down the stairs, and rush to warn the staff at the reception desk that a child has disappeared from his bed. I'm so irresponsible and careless. There's no one at the reception desk. I think I hear a gunshot outside the hotel. A drunken guest reports seeing a dwarf in elephant pyjamas somewhere backstage. And that's where we find him, wide awake, holding the kitten in his arms, beside the striptease artist, who has almost completely changed back into her civilian clothing again.

The man from the bridge carries the boy upstairs, as I hold the kitten. The bird needs to be moved into the other room, but as soon as we approach room ten we notice something odd: the door is ajar, the window wide open and the fluttering curtains are more perforated than I remember. The box is still on the table but there's no sign of life inside. The bird is dead inside the cage—heart attack, says the expert, his plumage is still intact at any rate. We all move into room thirteen and leave the box in number ten until morning.

The girl at the reception desk can offer no explanation for how the lead pellets got through the open window. The male choir is sitting at the breakfast table with sombre faces.

"Well there might have been some shooting last night," she finally concedes with some reluctance, "the guests from the dam might have been trying to shoot some snow buntings to throw on the grill, the way they do back in their home countries."

FORTY

I settle the whole business over the phone and get the car dealer to take the old car back and send the box of chocolates that is included in the offer to my friend in maternity ward 22b.

We wait for the brand-new car to arrive across the desert before the evening, before setting off with some hot cocoa in the flask. I get a thirty-five per cent discount off the hotel bill because of the pellet holes in the curtains, an extra fifteen per cent because of the noise caused by the ball during the night and another fifteen per cent because there were no staff available to enable me to change room, thus forcing me to move into the vet's room for the night.

"Not that it would have changed much," says the girl at the reception desk, "we were fully booked." She then offers to wash and dry one load of clothes while we are waiting. The hotel manager hasn't resurfaced yet, even though we're well into the afternoon.

The boy shows considerable interest in the jeep when it arrives and gloats on it with the other men, kicking its wheels, as I transfer our things from one car to the other. He has slipped both hands into the pockets of his overalls. The hotel staff are very impressed by this exchange of vehicles out in the middle of nowhere. We don't have much further to travel now; tonight we'll be sleeping in the newly planted bungalow on the edge of a ravine.

"Thanks for last night," a voice close to my ear says, "it was nice to meet you, are you leaving then?"

They all say the same thing, "Thank you for your stay."

"Sorry about the bird," I say.

"And the pellet shots," he adds.

"Yeah."

"The rest wasn't so bad."

"No, the rest wasn't so bad."

We formally say goodbye to each other by the car. The hotel staff form a semicircle at the bottom of the steps, like the servants of a manor bidding farewell to a distinguished guest. The boy stands beside me and stares up at us, looking from face to face. He seems anxious:

"Can animals be handicapped?"

Being his personal sworn interpreter, I translate the expert's answers for my protégé:

"More often than not, they die shortly after birth. If not, they're normally put down fairly soon. Some of them are stuffed and end up in a natural history museum. A lot of people are fascinated by the sight of two-headed Siamese lambs and five-legged pigs."

I loosely interpret for him.

"What about deaf horses, are they stuffed too?"

"No, I don't ever remember coming across that in my work. But some friends of mine have two handicapped dogs that they are very fond of, a mother who is blind and a female puppy who's a dwarf. Their son is that boy who was with me yesterday."

"Is he an adopted son?" I think I might have then asked him, but I probably didn't, because I hear the vet asking me when we can meet again.

"I'm not sure that would be very sensible," I answer. "I was thinking of spending a month on my own. Alone with Tumi," I add.

"Well, if you happen to change your mind, I'd be delighted, my wife spends a lot of time away because of her work."

Before saying goodbye he leans over my shoulder, as if he were peering at the sand desert ahead of us, and murmurs into my ear:

"I know what you're looking for, but I wouldn't stir anything up, if I were you. The past should be left in the past. But I can tell you that he has a gift for languages and is scared of heights. He hopes to study abroad one day."

FORTY-ONE

The boy is asleep in the back seat under two down sleeping bags. Unusually, the kitten is awake and restless; maybe it's carsick or the tuna fish sandwich, which had passed its expiry date, from the hotel didn't go down too well in its stomach. As for me, I'm quite content with my lot, my glistening new car, the darkness and the heater that is working full blast.

I slip a disc into the brand-new CD player: a pantomime ballet by Béla Bartók, *The Miraculous Mandarin*. I shove the receipt I've folded into eight into the pocket of my flowery trousers.

Apart from the flowery trousers, I mostly dressed as a boy.

"Yes, you were one of the boys," says Granny. "You cut your hair like them, dressed like them and wore the same chequered brown sweater over your shirt all summer." I can't remember whether it was washed in the autumn when I got back to town or thrown away.

In stores I was addressed as a male. There was a constant stream of guests at my gran and grandad's place. And plenty of room, no matter how much of a squeeze it was. They even lent their own conjugal bed, if the need arose. People weren't supposed to stay in hotels; that was for foreigners. In August, all the kids from the area would gather, all the children that had been sent to the neighbouring farms in the name of good health and getting in touch with our rural roots, and we would spend the last week of our stay in the east in my granny's blue house down by the shore. That is where I would pass my time with my cousins, who weren't necessarily really my cousins, but also the grandchildren of some of Granny's old friends. No one actually knew exactly how we were supposed to be related to each other. Nevertheless, I called them cousins and they called me cousin too, although most of them were clearly unrelated to me. As the number of people increased in the house, we squeezed in tighter together and moved between bedrooms, as required, or up into the attic, with our synthetic quilts or blankets folded under our arms. Children under the age of fifteen slept without a down quilt. There were often fights for space that stretched long into the night. The main goal was to tightly wrap one's self in the synthetic duvet without the slightest draught.

I'd promised to get up first in the morning and heat up the cocoa and butter the scones. This meant that I had to stand up in the middle of the mattress and grope my way forward, balancing my arms like a tightrope artist, to avoid stumbling on the crowded mattress and get out of there without stepping on any calves, knees or, worse still, entire bodies.

As soon as I stand up with my hands in the air, I realize that the waistband on my pyjama bottom has snapped and the waist cord has slipped back into the furbelow during the night. I'm wearing nothing underneath because Granny is washing all my clothes. I clutch the waistband in the hope of saving myself any embarrassment and try to avoid waking up my cousins, but then realize that they are both awake and lying stiffly, on either side of the bed, watching my every move with new adult eyes.

I slow down, barely going over forty tonight. The mountain pass road twists and turns. Suddenly there is yet another pile of rubble ahead of us, a landslip that has crumbled from the side of the mountain, which stretches into the sea below. The car skids and adrenaline shoots through my body. There is no mistake about it; a mudslide has fallen onto the road in front of us, forming a pile of stones and sludge. Not a soul in sight and no way of turning back, a sleeping child in the back and a wakeful kitten in the front. There's a shovel in the boot, I noticed it when I was packing the car. As soon as I clear away some of those rocks and push all that mud to one side, I should be able to get past. If the kitten and I were to slip, at least I would have someone to hold onto for eternity; but the thought of the fate of my passenger in the back seat is just too overwhelming, the responsibility is paralysing.

I can't really boast of any clairvoyant powers, but suddenly a man springs out of the darkness and fog—the third man on my road to the east—seemingly materializing out of nowhere. Standing before me, he hurls himself into the beams of my headlights, like the sheep, except that this time the car isn't moving. He is so real, in fact, that it seems perfectly natural when he grabs the shovel from me and spares me the trouble of having to clear the mud away.

That's how far a woman's imagination can take her. His voice is clearly too deep for a man of this world.

"Are you travelling east?" it asks. It's painfully obvious that I'm heading east, since the road runs from west to east, like a coffin on the floor of a church.

"Could you take me some of the way?" he asks, "I'm stranded here."

He pulls out a silver flask and offers it to me first, as a token gesture, before taking a sip. As I drive, he tells me tales about country folk, most of them containing some supernatural element, stories of departed souls, guardian spirits, premonitions, shipwrecks. In between stories he praises my driving and tells me that, when he was a boy, he intended to grow up to be something other than what he is today.

"Are you a fisherman?" I ask.

"I don't practise my casting in the winter or make my own flies, if that's what you mean. Blood and entrails aren't really my thing, although I can gut a fish and stuff a bird. They'd probably put me in telecommunications if we were at war, or directing operations from some safe shelter away from headquarters. No, I was just helping a friend of mine who's cultivating a patch of land up there by the dam. We were planting dwarf apple trees under the cover of night."

As he's sitting there beside me, for a brief moment I feel a peculiar familiarity between us, as if he were closely connected to me, and my mind was trying to recall what my body clearly remembered. Once we've passed the mudslide, I know what he's going to say:

"Come with me, I want to show you something," he says in a very persuasive voice.

I stop the car. The boy is asleep in the back seat and will sleep until dawn. The headlights illuminate a stretch of path through the lava field. The glistening blue pumice squelches under the soles of his hiking boots as he walks. A woman in high heels would have a hard job keeping up with him.

I follow him blindly through the lava field, as naturally as one would follow a clerk to the screw and bolts section of a hardware store, without, however, ever taking my eyes off the car on the side of the road.

He is wearing a red shirt under his coat. The weather has cleared, with puffs of vapour hovering over cavities here and there, and tips of lava rock piercing through the moss. The moon follows us like a balloon, bouncing from the rim of one crater to the next, rebounding against our heels, rolling over the undulating igneous rock and swelling with every change of direction, like the pupil of an eye, with the golden glow of its sclera reflecting on our necks.

Suddenly, the moon vanishes behind a cloud and the world plummets into darkness again.

"I can't be long, seven minutes at the most; I can't stay away from the boy for too long."

"We're almost there." He scans the rocks to find a spot where he can relieve himself, since he has been drinking on the way.

We forge on, step by step, with about fifty metres behind us now. I would never have believed that darkness could be this black. It's as if I were walking across that creaking wooden beam back in my old gym, and were trying to hold my balance at its centre with both arms, the other girls watching me in silence. This is how far a woman's feelings can lead her.

I can no longer see anything, nothing but the hot vapour of my own breath in front of me. I grope forward, but my hands grasp nothing but a vacuum, the pitch darkness ahead of me is a thick wall that can't be followed because it delineates nothing, protects nothing, there is no way of distinguishing the outline of the world or its edges, the rugged lava field gives off no scent. Nevertheless I sense there is something extraordinary just a few arm lengths away from us, but what?

"What do you want to show me?"

"This," he says.

"This what?"

"The darkness."

"The darkness?"

"Yes, you're a city girl aren't you?"

I sense a colossal human construction in the middle of the darkness, and try to conjure up an image in mind. What kind of picture is it, though? A gothic cathedral that suddenly rises to the heavens in some old red-light district abroad, suddenly standing there, sky-high, at the end of a narrow paved road with dark, smelly corners. I'm standing on the edge of the imaginary, on the edge of the fear of darkness. The only thing one can do is grope for another human being. Suddenly I feel it is perfectly natural for him to slip his arm around me and for me to lay my head on his shoulder.

He has started to undress me in the drizzle, with swiftness and skill, ankles and wrists, zippers and tight necklines are no challenge to him. He spends the most time wrestling with my panties, which become entangled in his hands. It's a little cold, but he throws a coat under me and rolls me over back and forth. A lava bed may seem like an odd mattress, but in his own way this man has created a secure shelter for me, with the heavens above us and the earth below, and the two of us sandwiched in between—could one ask for more security?

Afterwards we linger a moment, sitting in the middle of the lava field. He rests his head on my shoulder and I kiss him, as if he were a child about to doze off. When he stands up he hands me a little stone containing the bright shape of a horseshoe in its centre.

"Next time, it'll be a silver belt or crock of gold." He smiles at me.

"I can take care of myself from here on," he says to me, once we've retraced our steps. "But I'll come looking for you later," he adds, "you're the best thing that's happened to me today by far."

FORTY-TWO

Many consequential events can occur in a woman's life in the space of less than twenty-four hours. Most mistakes are made in a fraction of a moment and can be measured in seconds: taking a wrong turn, stepping on the accelerator instead of the brake, saying a yes instead of a no or a maybe. Mistakes are rarely the outcome of a logical sequence of decisions. A woman can be on the brink of total surrender to love, for instance, without even pondering on it for so much as a minute.

The black desert is no longer ahead but behind us, and the summer bungalow isn't far off now, just one more little fjord and a heath. As I'm driving through yet another low-hanging cloud, all the way down to the lava rocks, it suddenly dawns on me that I am midway between the beginning and the end. I can't quite decide whether to measure the distance in years or kilometres. There certainly seems to be enough space ahead of me and plenty of time, and ample time behind me too. By not following the movement of the hands on my divorce watch, and by circling the island anti-clockwise, I have not only gained a head start over time, but also managed to constantly surprise and even, ultimately, catch up with myself.

If one were to summarize my experiences so far on this journey, one could say that I have caused the death of four animals (five if the city goose is to be included) and that I have successfully crossed forty single-lane bridges, tackled some difficult slopes and become intimately acquainted with three men over a stretch of little more than 300 kilometres, most of which was non-tarmacked and literally wedged between the mountains and the coastline. Even though the first 100 kilometres were fairly uneventful in this regard and I expect no major surprises in the last 100-kilometre stretch, it was nevertheless almost equal in intensity to the past ten years of my life combined. The fact that I couldn't tell you how many churches we passed on our journey may be indicative of my moral standing. I would have bought the souvenir glued to my dashboard no matter what it was, even a carved wooden model of a police station or a bank.

Analysing my existence from a purely statistical point of view, this works out as one man for every 160-kilometre stretch, which should be considered a fairly high level of activity in a country in which each inhabitant shares one square kilometre with his fellow man. According to my estimates, calculated on the basis of the length of the national Ring Road, which is 1,420 kilometres long, that should amount to 17.7 men before the journey is over. In terms of square kilometres, this corresponds to vast expanses of lava fields per person, extensive stretches of desert, reservoir basins, eroded land and withering lupin fields, as well as countless bridges, squawking seabirds and hamburger joints as one approaches the coast.

And then, I also ponder on the following: if I were expecting a child, there would be three possible fathers, or 17.7, considering the journey as a whole. This is slightly above the national average, on the basis of the total number of lovers a woman can expect to have in the course of her life. At the end of the day, one can always console oneself with the genetic fact that there can only ever be one father per child. I am fully aware of the fact that in many countries of the world I would have been executed many times over for less.

However, when I look into the rear-view mirror, I see a young woman with short dark hair, green eyes, pale skin and a loose lock dangling over her forehead—there's nothing sluttish about her, no make-up streaming down her cheek; an outsider might even describe her as innocent, pure and chaste. I see her looking at the world with sharp eyes, through the lock of hair, which she then confidently brushes away from her face, as if she imagined she was finally on top of things, as if she believed she was on the right path, as if she had a premonition of what she wanted, as if she somehow knew who she was. She turns on her indicator and sways into the car park of a petrol station. After swiftly rummaging through the fridges of the store, she dumps cartons of blueberry buttermilk yogurt and a smoked meat and Italian bean salad sandwich on the counter by the till. The boy is still sleeping.

FORTY-THREE

The mountain road is normally impassable at this time of year because of the snow, but nothing is as it should be any more.

As soon as I reach the outskirts of the town, I see that the summer bungalow has been delivered to its destination. Even though I haven't set foot here for seventeen years, it all looks familiar to me. The town is a tidy cluster of houses, with no actual centre or square, but a series of four or five parallel roads, one on top of the other, stretching out to the coastline, a bit like the grooves left by a gardening fork across the freshly turned soil of a virgin potato patch. In the furthest groove, closest to the shore, one can make out the colourful rooftops of the oldest corrugated iron houses, as well as the mini-market, co-op and savings bank, behind which are two streets of bungalows, and beyond which again are patches of brown gravel, with a little bit of heather in the summer, and the ravine, as well as the reservoir on top of the mountain road. Most of the inhabitants have tried to build sheltering garden walls to shield themselves from the blasts of the sea on their windows. Nothing grows in the vicinity of the open ocean, no shrubs or flowers, not outdoors at any rate. Indoors, on the other hand, the window views of the menacing blackness of the sea have been obscured by forests of window-sill plants. At this time of the year, every window also carries a shining Christmas star and seven-armed candlestick.

I can see the house from the chalet. It was built in the forties, maybe earlier. It all comes back to me. A group of people has gathered inside. It's as if everything were filtered through a veil of white silk or film, giving it a soft and blurred appearance, like the fading pages of an old psalm book or an over-exposed photograph. I think I'm in a white knitted woollen sweater. My cousins are also dressed in white, strange as it may sound, white tuxedos, so removed from reality, so close to the memory. Granny is enveloped in light, Granny is actually the sun. There is a large crowd at the funeral reception and everyone is in white, different shades of white, some fabrics are thinner and finer than others, others thicker: wool, cotton, silk, cloth, linen, tweed, polyester, polyviscose, crepe, chiffon, organza, veil, khakis—everything white.

I can only see blurred, slowly moving outlines. Granny is the most out of focus of them all. I watch her fade.

They've placed the mobile chalet on the outskirts of the village, just as I'd requested, on a plot of barren land on the edge of the ravine. It stands there aloofly in the dark, segregated from all town planning. Some people may not see it as the ideal setting for a sunny summer holiday, up there on the rocks, and even I wouldn't walk up there in high heels or in my bare feet after a Christmas ball; but still, it's better than living down there on the shore, where there was a constant flow of visitors and the constant risk of a knock on the door, at any time of day or night, from one of those strangers who had vanished at sea and left a puddle of water in the hall. The chalet stands solitarily on the western edge of the village, and the church stands equally solitarily to the east, on the other side of the valley, with a *Securitas* sign on its door.

The village seems deserted at this hour of night. Apart from the screeching of seabirds, everything is steeped in a deadly silence, like the siesta hour of a Mediterranean village. There is no sound of footsteps behind me and yet I know I'm not alone. Here and there, inquisitive eyes peep at me through seven-armed candelabra in the salt-beaten windows. One shouldn't be fooled by appearances. Even though the streets may be deserted, most of the life of this village takes place behind these walls, where people come to the door just as they are, dressed in soft, baggy garments.

It's the 25th of November and, as we approach the village from over the mountain road, out of the darkness and rain, it shines like a celestial jewel adorned with precious stones in the middle of the sandy desert. It wouldn't surprise me if this village were visible from outer space. Every window is decked with multi-coloured Christmas lights, as are the railings of the balconies, porches and steps, even the anchors in the gardens. The boy wakes up when I kill the engine.

"We brighten these dark winter days," says the man in the mini-market, who sells me milk, bread, cheese and candles, just before closing for the night. Most people add a new set of lights every year, so you can normally tell how long people have been married by the number of sets they have. Just like you can determine the age of a reindeer according to the number of its horns. I ask him if he has any Christmas lights that run on batteries.

"Afraid not, but you can get them at the co-op tomorrow."

He then asks me if I'm the owner of the summer chalet.

"And you intend to spend your Christmas there alone with a child and no electricity, is that right? We heard rumours that you'd done a runner on some bankrupt company and left your husband to pick up the pieces, that kind of thing. It'll be a little bit dark and spooky up there on the ravine. We were expecting you three days ago."

I tell him we took our time to do some sightseeing around the country. "We're on holiday," I say, and then add:

"My grandmother and grandfather used to live here."

Their names don't ring a bell with him.

"There was no need to bring a house with you," says the man, "there are plenty of houses for sale in this village. I could have found at least four for you, you could have had a bungalow with a newly tiled bathroom."

"I wanted to be slightly on the outskirts. I'm not going to settle here."

The boy points at a handwritten notice, advertising the sale of wooden toys at the old people's home, which includes an amateurish drawing of a blue van with rubber wheels. I ask the man where I can find them.

"This might not look like the most eventful of towns to an

outsider," says the man, leaning on the counter with both elbows, "but that doesn't mean that nothing ever happens. Couples split up, have their affairs and make a mess of their lives just as much here as anywhere else, no matter how stunning the nature may be. And occasionally, there are family tragedies that can never be fully explained. Those two brothers who lived on their own, for example. The one who survived was released on parole because the circumstances of the case were unclear, according to the police report. They said it was a case of accidental manslaughter, but the neighbours, who saw the scene of the crime, said it wasn't a pretty sight and that they'd heard at least seven shots being fired. Those wooden toys are made by the brother who survived, at the old people's home, or the Geriatric Health Centre, as they call it. That's where he lives. You can buy one of those vans from him there."

The man escorts me to the door as I slip on my hood and step out into the rain. I see through the rear-view mirror that he is standing in the yard by the petrol pumps, watching the jeep on its ascent towards the chalet. I think he's talking into a mobile phone.

I carry the boy in my arms into the chalet. Before going to bed, we clamber down the ravine to brush our teeth in the stream. We stand there in the ice-cold water with our mouths full of foam and then spit it out and watch the white trail as it floats away.

FORTY-FOUR

So much needs to be bought. We need two duvets and bedclothes. The boy chooses the duvet covers, a jungle with wild animals for himself and a pink flowery one for me, so that fields of nocturnal violets will expand in my arms in the mornings and spread across my tummy and breasts, as I stroke the quilt and ponder on how we should start the day, by going for a swim or paying a visit to the school library.

We also buy some new rain gear, thick sweaters and two pairs of leggings for the boy, a Barbie and Ken set with a caravan, cat food and rubber toys for the kitten, a football, colouring book and colours, a jigsaw, crossword magazine, several women's magazines, some towels and swimming trunks and a set of red Christmas lights that work on batteries to put on the deck. I get Tumi to try on a pair of blue hiking boots with laces and he is allowed to walk around the store in them. I also buy him a new pair of boots, which are only available in size 26, so they should last him a good while.

I gently throw him the ball in the toy section, aiming for his arms. He creates a hollow for the ball to fall into by pressing his elbows against his stomach and holding out his hands, as I try to gauge the distance and amount of force required for him to catch it before tossing the ball, which draws a small arch in the air, like a film in slow motion. But he misses the ball, which rolls into the underwear and socks department. I'll do it better next time and crouch down on my knees. I can manage playing with a child now, but he can't manage playing with an adult.

I ask them if they have any bicycles with training wheels and am informed that there might be a red one in the warehouse left over from the summer.

"Because it's winter here now," the man at the warehouse explains to me, as if I were mentally challenged. I use the opportunity to order three gas heaters for the chalet.

Tumi is mesmerized by the sight of a small Santa Claus costume in the clothes corner and asks me questions I don't quite know how to answer. It seems to be more or less the right size so we throw it into the basket.

"You can be Santa Claus's assistant," I say, although I'm not sure he understands me.

The Christmas books are in and I chuck them into the basket, practically buying all of them, with the exception of autobiographies, self-help books and a study on the genealogy of Icelandic horses. I place a novel that is set in the rain on top of the pile. It has a nice cover, but I'm not familiar with the author, nor, needless to say, is the shop manager, because only two copies of it have been ordered and it lay at the back of two towers of expected best-sellers. I also buy a book about the volcanic eruption of Mount Laki in the eighteenth century, some crime pulp fiction in English and a load of easy-to-read children's books for the boy, as well as some copybooks for him to write his foggy window words in.

With the help of the store manager, I find a book on the rearing of boys. I merely need to skim through the book and browse through the headings, captions and blurb on the jacket to realize that what the boy needs, above all else, is a strong male role model. I might be able to teach him how to catch a ball and cycle, and to fry pancakes, tie his shoelaces and read, if he hasn't taught himself already, and even to count up to five in Hungarian, but I can't teach him the value of words, how to be strong in spite of oneself or how to fight an enemy army.

We've almost filled two trolleys by now; he pushes one, I the other. He shows a lot of responsibility towards the home and is very attentive, pointing at the things we need here and there and fetching raisins, rice, spaghetti, yogurt, eggs, marinated herring, cottage cheese, caviar, stone-baked flat bread, smoked meat, olives, brawn, eggs, smoked salmon and cod liver oil—he's got quite a broad palate for a four-year-old. He also finds jars of vitamin tablets and helps me to find vegetables to make meat soup. There are four types: red cabbage, carrots, turnips and potatoes. The turnips are 1,000 per cent more expensive here than in Krakow. Then he returns with some perfume to give me and puts it in the trolley. I allow him to and take my place in the queue in front of the meat counter.

People prolong their shopping to observe us, not least the boy, the pair of us. Tumi looks at me apprehensively, signalling with his eyes that I'm not allowed to stare back at them, not to make an issue of it. Three people ask me if I'm the woman with the mobile summer chalet. Most of them are quite friendly and nudge their children to encourage them to offer Tumi some sweets. Digging into the green cellophane bags they're clutching in their hands, they hesitantly choose something that might have accidentally fallen into the mix, either too strong or too bitter, before formally handing it over to him with their sticky fingers.

Just as I'm about to reach the top of the queue, something rolls on the floor and the shoppers shift their gazes off the new arrivals to form a semicircle and look down at something glistening on the floor. It's a brown button.

The shop assistant is trying to hand a woman a parcel of weighed meat over the counter, but she's been distracted. Who lost that button?

Concerned and solicitous looks flash across people's faces and inquisitive glances are exchanged, before all eyes settle on me. Virtually no one is dressed in clothes that have buttons;

everyone is wearing comfortable and loose-fitting garments with elastic around the waist and ankles. Many of these villagers are related, but it is somehow deemed unseemly to behave in an overly familiar manner in the local co-op. It takes considerable practice to be able to pretend to be strangers to each other for five minutes, to keep one's kin at bay for a moment, and feign not to have the faintest idea that the person standing in front of them in the queue took a solitary walk down to the pier last night and, at exactly ten-thirty on that same evening, kicked an empty beer can into the ocean. At any rate, they feel no need to run up and throw their arms around their childhood friends and cousins every time they bump into them.

The man serving at the meat counter appoints himself as group spokesman and asks if I'm the woman with the summer chalet.

"He's a straight talker," a woman whispers to me, acts in the local amateur dramatics society apparently and practically knows Jóhann Sigurjónsson's entire repertoire inside out. But his most memorable performance was in the role of Lennie in *Of Mice and Men*. His female customers have hardly been the same since and obviously entertain fantasies of him stroking their smooth hair and touching them all over.

He asks me if it's true that I'm going to be staying in the chalet with the child in these awful conditions over Christmas, without even having any electricity? He wants to know what kind of company it was that went bust, was it an import-export business?

I'm about to point out to him that all the top chefs in the world cook their Christmas meals over gas when, for a brief moment, I seem to catch a glimpse of the man I met up on the landslide. As we're talking, people seem to lose track of their errands and begin to eavesdrop, with more voices gradually chipping into the conversation. I'm told that people normally go elsewhere to make big purchases of this kind. It's not done to buy duvets, clothes and children's bikes in the local co-op.

"Tomorrow," says a woman, "several mothers and a father will be meeting in the community centre to bake cookies with the children, everyone brings their own ginger nut dough. Your son is welcome."

"In any case, you'll be stuck here until the water level of the river starts to drop," the actor says finally, handing me the meat for the soup.

Our shopping list is long, as is our cash supply.

Finally, I pull the cloves, yeast, syrup and ginger out of the trolley onto the conveyor belt at the checkout. I mustn't neglect my maternal duties.

"That way I can make ginger nut dough tonight," I say to the adolescent on the counter. I reckon he's about seventeen. He's got a lot of gel in his hair, long sideburns and a meticulously combed parting—a hairstyle that seems to be shared by a lot of the youngsters in the village.

"The women around here try to entertain themselves at night as best they can."

He doesn't lack nerve for such a young man.

I count some thousand-krónur notes at the till and then dash out to the glove compartment of the jeep to get some more. It is only then that I remember I left the boy's old boots in the shoe section and rush back in to get them. By the time I get back, Tumi has vanished.

"He went out to his dad," the youth at the till informs me.

I see the familiar figure of a man standing outside in the car park, holding a big bag. It's my friend from the landslide. The rainbow-coloured reflections of the Christmas lights shimmer in the puddles. Tumi is standing right up close to him, holding onto his exclusive outdoors jacket, and once more I hear him say Daddy in a resonant voice. The man doesn't budge, but stands there as naturally as if he'd been waiting for his son and wife, who rushes out after her child. I see him stroking the boy's head and then back-stepping slightly to crouch down and speak to him in sign language. The boy is taken aback; he is more used to talking to people who don't know sign language, but suddenly has something to say with his hands, face and whole body. Who would have thought that so many images could have fitted into such a small, pale body?

"Hi, how are you, did you think I was an elf?"

"The thought had crossed my mind."

"I wouldn't mind experiencing more of those tales with you."

At that same moment, the clerk emerges from the store room with the bicycle, carrying it over to the car. He has finished screwing the training wheels to it. My friend and I stand in silence, side by side, and watch the boy clamber onto the seat of the bike and cycle between the puddles in the midday twilight, like proud and slightly apprehensive parents releasing their offspring into the world for the very first time.

When I've loaded everything into the jeep and am about to drive off, he says:

"I can teach you sign language if you like, give you some private tuition, I have a deaf sister. The boy can play with my dog in the meantime, she's very gentle, tolerant and child-friendly.

She's about to have puppies soon so she's a bit sensitive and not in the mood for too much horseplay right now."

With the hint of a smile, he opens his bag slightly to allow me to peep inside. There can be no possible doubt: red, white, black, a coat, beard, belt, furry lining—yet another Santa costume.

"I was just collecting it from the dry-cleaner's, the season is about to begin. This is the second time I've been appointed as a Santa Claus, obviously because I'm not a local. Children get suspicious when they meet their fathers in disguise and die of shame when they see them making fools of themselves in public. Families have plenty of other problems to be dealing with," he says with his alluring smile. "Besides, makes a nice break from my routine, getting to be someone else. This'll be my last Christmas here; then I will have had the change I needed in my life." He combs his hand through his thick, unruly hair and looks up towards the mountain road, as if he were trying to find his escape route.

As we say goodbye, he tells me he'll come and visit us one night, when the boy is in bed in his pyjamas and about to drift into his dreams.

"Then I'll knock on your window and sing a song or tell you a story. Unlike many of my fellow Santas, I have the advantage of being able to play the accordion. If nothing else I can slip a little gift into his shoe."

FORTY-FIVE

There are two bedrooms in the chalet and we sleep in one of them with two gas heaters. Tumi is responsible, and we help each other to clear up and make things cosy in the newly planted chalet that smells of Norwegian wood. Water runs out of the tap when it is turned. Through the window, there is a view of the Ring Road.

We play outside in the ten-degree heatwave, sheltered from the rain by the edge of the roof, which stretches over the deck.

He adroitly cycles in clean ellipses and by now has mastered the skill of taking sharp turns on the training wheels. He rings his bell every time he passes the deckchair I'm lying in, studying the conjugation of sign language verbs. He can hear the bell too. I wave at him and sip on some hot tea.

It's important to address the verb to the right person, the book tells me; that seems pretty logical to me.

Tumi nods his head to indicate that he's understood me, that I'm making progress, he's a good teacher. He just doesn't have the time to talk to me at the moment, we can't always be yakking together, because he needs to use his hands for something else. He has started to draw.

I suggest we go off on a reconnaissance mission and fill the flask with cocoa. We take an extra cup with us.

The murderer who slaughtered his brother is now ageing in the Geriatric Health Centre. He chisels pieces of wood and makes children's toys to keep himself busy and kill time until he goes to meet his brother. We are escorted down a corridor to his bedroom, which faces the mountain road. An odd odour hovers in the air, a mixture of strong detergents and weary personal objects that have been removed from their original setting: a chest of drawers, chair, kitchen clock and old family photos in silver frames. A large portrait of his departed brother hangs over his bed. He receives us in chequered slippers.

The table in the bedroom is crowded with little carved figures, skinny, elongated beings with no ears. Their eyes are the heads of nails that have been hammered into them and sometimes pierce their necks. Garments have been painted onto their carved bodies in red, blue and green. On the bedside table, two porcelain hands intertwine to form a ceramic flame. I was later to discover more lamps of this kind around the village. I unscrew the lid of the flask and pour cocoa into the two men's cups. They sit side by side close to the bed. There's eighty years between them.

"I remember your granny very well, she was so gentle and shy, your granny was, when she was a young girl. We used to pop in there sometimes, me and my brother, to drink some coffee with a sugar cube and jam cake."

He cautiously sips the cocoa from his cup, sinking into a long silence.

"She was a warm lady with a serene mind, your granny was, never judged anyone. That was an accident with my brother Dagfinnur. And the woman who took the child was good too. Your granny was a bit upset by the whole business. That it all should have happened while the girl was staying with her."

He takes another sip from the cup and shuts up; he's got nothing more to add.

I tell him I've come to take a look at the toys. He doesn't have that many at the moment, but he pulls out a lorry with a red cabin and rubber wheels—beside his chamber pot.

"These aren't obligatory," he says, "but I can't be bothered getting up five times every night. Some of my mates have sinks in their rooms that they can piss into, not me."

No such thing as privacy in here, everything is public

knowledge. He ties some string to the truck with his trembling hands so that the boy can tow it down the lino floor in the corridor.

FORTY-SIX

An almost imperceptible high-pitched sound awakens me in the pitch darkness of the night. I sit up to locate its source. No doubt about it, the boy is humming in his sleep in a different voice to the one he uses during the day. His duvet is on the floor. As soon as I pull it back over him, the sound seems to be cut off. He sits up, awake.

"I'm blind."

He gropes through the air, searching for his thick-lensed glasses, and I turn on the light so that he can see me talking to him.

"It's night time," I tell him, "it's dark. I can't see anything either. There are no pictures at night. Shall I tell you a story? Shall we invent a story together?" I try to create a story for him, speaking slowly and clearly, using the sign language I have learnt.

"No," he says, "not like that."

Every time I try to pick up the narrative thread again, he protests. He wants the story to be different. Finally he buries his head under the pillow, he doesn't want a story. He just wants me to go away. I lift the pillow.

"Don't you want to know how it ends?"

"No."

"What about tomorrow?"

"Maybe," he says unenthusiastically.

"Do you want to sleep in my bed? Do you want to climb in with me?" This is the permission he was waiting for. He swiftly bolts up again and drops his feet to the floor.

He takes his pillow with him and plonks it right beside mine. Then he fetches three fluffy animals, which he carefully lines up on the bed, side by side, with the smallest one wedged between the other two. I grab his duvet.

"Tomorrow we'll go down the ravine with the truck and the shovel and we'll build a dam in the stream," I say, moving over in the bed to give him and his animals more space.

"Then we'll make pancakes and go for a swim."

When I wake up in the morning, the boy has disappeared and is nowhere to be seen. His duvet is still warm. I search for him everywhere and then rush outside calling out his name, but naturally he can't hear me. I run around everywhere in my boots and the white woollen sweater I've thrown over my silk nightdress, and then clamber down the ravine. Finally I see him silhouetted against the faint twilight, in his bare feet and Superman pyjamas, standing on a rock by the stream. He doesn't budge, even after I've walked right up to him.

When I phone Auður, she confesses to me that Tumi's quest for his father started one day when she collected him from kindergarten. That was when he'd asked who his father was and why he didn't come to collect him.

"'It's a long story, I'll tell you it when you're five,' I told him. That's next autumn, so at least I have a year's respite. Then, a few days later, as I was standing in a bookshop in town, the boy threw himself at a man who was a few places ahead of us in the line, wrapping his arms around one of his legs and endlessly repeating Dad Dad Dad. It was pretty embarrassing, not least because it was that sports presenter on TV, the one who always gets on my nerves. After that, he played the same trick on several other men, all very different from each other. It's totally unpredictable, like his sleepwalking."

We say no more on the matter and she asks me to help her find a word, an adjective to qualify something that falls on mankind, although not necessarily something of a meteorological nature, like rain, but a word associated with the apocalypse of the human soul and heart, but not in any direct way, more indirectly, like rain in the soul and nature oozing tears, she explains to me. Something like the smell of a birch tree in the rain, just one word. The obstetrician claims that no word could encompass that much, no single word could ever be that big.

"Could you think about it and give me a call tomorrow and maybe look up the ancient Greeks for me, if you get a chance, when Tumi falls asleep tonight?" The connection is rather poor and Auður's voice sounds like she's 5,000 miles away, although I can hear that she's on a high, happy with her life and the weather.

"I've ripped off my clothes here," she goes on, "and I'm about to go out into the rain in nothing but my socks to roll myself in the grass, just for the sake of breaking up the monotonous view patients have of the lawn. Too bad if the people in this ward have never seen a happy future single mother of three before. I recommend you do the same," she adds. "They're all at a meeting right now, trying to work out whether I should stay in the maternity ward or be transferred to the psychiatric one, just because I'm happy. If I die tonight I'll die happy. Then there's always a chance I'll die giving birth to my twins."

The voice has almost faded down the line. She has started to cry:

"I'm so scared of him sleepwalking, of him wandering into the water. I want to ask you not to sleep anywhere too close to the sea. Don't go anywhere near water or snow with him."

Then, switching topics, she adds: "Did you know that in the Bible there are 153 references to the past, but only fifteen to the future?"

FORTY-SEVEN

Darkness looms over the pool and butter-coloured vapours dissolve into the sombre misty November sky above, as faces vanish and materialize, the diving board only half visible in the haze.

The best way to establish any real intimacy with the inhabitants of this village is in the hot tub, the best way to meet one's fellow man is in this natural primeval state, where each person is as vulnerable as the next. Huddled together in a tight jacuzzi with my knees pressed against my chest, I can feel the burning warmth of strangers' bodies in the sulphurous mist. This is pretty much the state God created me in thirty-three years ago, if one adds the swimsuit, sexual longings, life experience and obsessive memories.

People have just got off work and are tired. The summer colours have been drained from their bodies, and they've grown all pale and flabby again. Everyone reeks of the same blend of chlorine, this is about as equal as people can get. Most of them are with packs of small children who potter about in the baby pool, mostly unsupervised. The majority of the infants, who wear nappies on dry land, have clearly learnt how to float a good while ago. Next summer they plan to enlarge the pool and build a slide for the children and their fathers.

As Tumi is putting on his new swimming trunks under the shower, he says he wants to be like me. Be like me, I get that much.

"What do you mean like me?"

I think he says woman.

I slip two armbands onto him to make sure he always returns to the surface.

"I want you to stay put right here," I say, trying to improvise the appropriate sign language with my hands.

"Stay put, only play in the splashing pool."

He jumps up and down into the shallowest part of the pool, releasing all kinds of joyous shrieks, which he himself can't hear. He is utterly transformed without his glasses and hearing aids, and looks even smaller and skinnier. His facial features seem to lose the sharpness his spectacle frames give them and blur into each other. I remind myself to pop into a store on the way home to buy some protein powder to stir into his cocoa.

I've never seen him this lively. He spatters and splashes and makes the jet of the fountain arch over the other children, who huddle together at the other end, following his moves with mute gaping mouths, wondering whether they should get their own back by pushing him under the surface or emptying a receptacle of water over his head. At any rate, this seems to be the only kind of communication Tumi is interested in.

I'm taken aback by the number of tattoos in the tubs, both on the women and men. Virtually all the women have intricate motifs around their arms, and many of the men sport tattooed outlines of reindeer horns in the same area. There were also plenty of tattoos in the swimming pool on the other side of the sand desert, 150 kilometres from here, but the patterns are different over there, mainly of animals and roses.

"If we're heading for a reversal of the poles," says a man in the tub, "we'll have to refigure what's north and what's south again, compasses won't be reliable any more."

"I can bring you the recipe tomorrow, if you like," says another woman. "Instead of using ordinary crème fraîche, you can use bacon flavouring."

"You'll never have any fun in this life, if you're never willing to try something new," an elderly man interjects.

"But you don't necessarily always have fun, just because you're trying something new," chips in another woman.

"No, I'm not saying that one always has to be trying something new," says the man.

"But it's also true that you'll never see anything new if you never go anywhere," says the woman.

"Exactly, one has to go somewhere to see something new," says the man.

"Yes, to meet new kindred spirits," says the woman.

"Exactly."

As I shift towards the massaging jet of the jacuzzi, I accidentally brush against the hairs of a man's thighs. This earns me a stern look from one of the ladies; she's not happy. I'm on the point of telling her that I didn't do it on purpose.

There are clearly several specimens of the opposite sex in here. Not that I'm shopping for men. It's not as if I were eyeing them up, in search of potential candidates, as that woman's censorious glare seemed to imply. It's not as if I'm looking for anything special in this village. All I want is a break and a change. To take a long-overdue summer holiday in November.

The furthest I go is to loosely compare the men in my direct line of vision in the tub with my ex-husband, but only very roughly, glancing at their outlines. He's starting to fade. I really have to concentrate to summon him up in my mind.

There must have been problems interpreting the sign in the locker room that says in five languages that all patrons are required to shower nude before entering the pool, because five explosive experts from the dam construction site have just appeared at the edge of the pool, stark naked. The lifeguard chases them vigorously with his whistle as they climb the ladder in a single file to the diving board. This brings the conversation in the tub to an abrupt halt, as all eyes turn to the men's fronts and behinds.

"They need to have that sign in forty languages, since they've started work on that dam," says a woman wearily. She's no longer staring at me.

I close my eyes.

When I open them again, a new crowd has entered the tub.

Another man is sitting opposite me in the mist. I glance at him, unable to distinguish his face, and have to squint through my wet lock of hair for some time before I realize that it's him again—the man from the landslide. The elf looks back at me with a teasing air, as if he'd been waiting for me to discover him and manifest my surprise. He seems a bit tense, though, slightly awkward, even a bit shy perhaps. I smile at him and shift, as a fresh jet of hot water spurts out from a pipe on the wall.

He returns the smile, but then starts talking to a woman who has been waiting for the opportunity to say something important to him. I close my eyes again and stretch back in the water, allowing my head to rest on the edge of the tub. I'm beginning to be able to picture myself living in this dark place, even if the mountain road is impassable and nothing seems to happen here.

The woman who was talking to him has stepped out of the tub, leaving only six of us behind.

"I was hoping you two would visit me," he says finally. "I would have cooked something nice for us, I rarely feel like cooking just for myself."

He has a peculiar round tattoo on his shoulder which looks a bit like a labyrinth, but could also be a spider's web.

Apart from our conversation, a highlands silence has fallen on the tub, people have stopped exchanging recipes. He sidles up to me and we sit together, side by side. The others have shifted and withdrawn to the other side, as far as they can from us in this circular tub, and the four of them, two men and two women, sit there mutely, trying to remain as inconspicuous as they can, by veiling themselves in the mist and sinking into the water up to their chins. The steps are on our side of the tub and no one has the courage to draw attention to themselves by climbing out at such a delicate point in our conversation. He floods me with options:

"Anyway," he continues, "I'd be willing to see you again. We could find things to do."

Then, leaning forward, as if he were about to climb out of the tub, he stoops over me:

"My private tuition offer still stands," he says, gently brushing against my shoulder.

He stands up and water pours off his body. The others quickly follow his example and exit after him, like a mass walkout at a trade union assembly. The water level drops considerably and I'm left there, sitting alone.

I suddenly catch a glimpse of a woman in the corner of my eye who seems familiar to me as she rises from the depths of the pool, swimming towards me.

It was on the same evening I'd taken the flower out of my hair, but kept my curly locks. It was Holy Thursday and all the shops were closed. I combed out my curly locks as best I could and tied my ponytail in a yellow band. I was wearing a new jacket and everything was new and strange in my head and I wanted to get away. But instead I went for a swim with my best female friend. My hair was much heavier than normal and stuck together. It was like carrying a new living organ on my back that I couldn't free myself of. It must have been the varnish or stuff that had been mixed into it out of so many bottles.

I hear the sound of someone diving close by and the ripples of water travelling all the way over to me. Someone swims below the surface to the bottom at the deep end of the pool. I suddenly feel a wave breaking against my thighs and a hand grabbing my leg and pulling me down. Then my other leg is tugged and I sink and feel the need to cough.

I shoot up and try to cough, but my friend is still holding my leg and tugs it away from the edge again, laughing. I try to break free and kick her, but she obviously feels it's all part of the game and tightens her grip. I swallow more chlorinated water and feel it freely invading my lungs. My vision begins to blur; I'm losing the game, without ever having travelled abroad. My friend still doesn't get it when I suddenly free myself and manage to grab onto the edge of the pool. I cough and cough, tears streaming down my cheeks, and try to spit the blood-tinted slime into the side gutter, but miss, and see how it spews out of me and floats straight towards my smiling friend.

When we got home she insisted on reading my fortune so I pulled a few cards out of the deck and placed them on the table. She reckoned I would be about thirty-three years old, but made no mention of a man or children. I was thirteen back then so it seemed like a reasonably ripe age, since I didn't know that her granny had just spoken about the death of a thirty-three-year-old woman and my friend probably just wanted to sound like a credible fortune-teller.

FORTY-EIGHT

The boy doesn't want to play with other children or the ball I bought him. He prefers to stick close to me, and sit outside on the deck under the porch, watching me read or looking up the myths of ancient Greek gods. He also likes to lie on the floor by the fireplace, writing words and drawing pictures. One of them is of a little child holding the hands of two women, one of whom has a swollen tummy. After that he draws thirty pictures of Hercules in a row.

"So, you see, his macho-ness may not be buried as deep as you think," I say to the music teacher and mother of this deaf child.

"Are you afraid of the other children? Are you afraid of what's outside? I don't ask him these questions; they're not the sort of questions one asks a child."

Sometimes the child sits totally still for long periods, as if he were somewhere far away. Or he rocks to and fro like an old man.

But in between, he's like just any other kid, always agitated, like the sea. He reminds me of one of those deadpan actors from the days of silent movies or a professional mime artist from the south, whose facial expressions can switch hundreds of times in the space of a few moments. His hands create images that I can understand, although not all of them yet.

Someone knocks at the door at ten-forty one morning, a potential friend for him of about his age, holding a DVD for over-twelves in his hands. It's his father who has brought him here. Tumi's eyes light up with hope as he stands beside me, eager with anticipation.

"I saw you at the co-op and it occurred to me that they might get on," he says, pushing his boy in and trying to close the door, which is suddenly blocked by his son, who sticks his foot through the gap.

"Don't you have a DVD player? Or even a TV?"

The man quickly sizes up our home, which we've decorated with the model of the church, the portrait of the sheep, the foggy window words Tumi has copied onto paper, and thirty drawings of Hercules on the wall. Then the man walks one circle around the living room, knocking on the walls, as his son follows right behind him.

"Well then," says the father, "this obviously won't work out then."

He tugs on the sleeve of his son, who seems to be quite interested in the flames in the fireplace, and drags him back towards the entrance where he shilly-shallies at the door.

"I remember your grandmother very well," he says finally. "I used to stay in the blue house sometimes when I was a kid. I used to play a bit of guitar back then and compose. I still write a bit of lyrics." Then he suddenly shuts up, as if he'd suddenly remembered something more important:

"Are you here to protest against the dam and stuff?"

I hear him say goodbye as he quietly closes the door behind him. I can't quite make out whether that's a look of regret I see on Tumi's face, as we melt a whole tablet of chocolate into two cups of cocoa and spread butter and jam on some bread.

FORTY-NINE

The sun sets over the harbour in the mid-afternoon, as the boats unload their catch. There isn't much to see, travellers passing through here would say. But they'd be greatly mistaken, because they don't know what goes on behind closed doors.

I'm beginning to be able to picture myself living here with my boy and to be able to imagine that, in fact, I've been living here for the past thirty-three years and that, even though I may have gone away for brief spells every now and then, my life is rooted here. This creates a new feeling in me that grows in these surroundings.

Bare-footed in my plimsolls, I await my fisherman on the pier. I spot his blue sailor's sweater in the wheelhouse of the boat heading for the harbour. The yellow fish glisten, yes, that's right, the fish and sea water are soaked in oil. He stands at the bow, as the boat pulls into land, coming home, smudged in fishy scales and slime.

The men look at me in wonderment. The other women are at home preparing dinner and getting the children ready for bed. I don't have to prepare my child for bed, he's big enough now and rehearsing with his band, I think.

"You're lucky to have a man like him," says another sailor's wife to me, "when mine's not at sea, he spends most of his time down on the shore."

That's how I picture it all.

A man walks off the boat and crosses the gangway in two steps. He reeks of fish and his fingertips are salty when he slips them into my mouth, one after another, to make me lick them. A slightly odd ritual to an outsider's eye, but that's how it goes.

Afterwards we draw the curtains his mother made for the windows. The teenager is still practising on his bass guitar in the garage, I imagine, which is why we allow ourselves to draw the curtains.

"Are you going to eat bare-chested?" I ask the man of my life, once we're seated at the table with the freshly pan-fried catfish.

"Hang on, does it matter? It's just the two of us, you and me, right?" He's forgotten the teenager, just like I have.

"Yes, but I was brought up to expect people to come fully clothed and combed to the table and to talk together. Dad often told me, my mother and brother stories at the table and we'd also take it in turns to tell each other how our days went. One day Dad told us the story of an unemployed pianist, who often lay awake at night. On one of his sleepless nights he invented a special screw for the propeller of an airplane, or a bolt or something simple like that, that made him filthy rich. And not just him, but three generations of the Jack Wilson family."

"You don't have to tell me all the stories in the world just to get me to put a shirt on."

"And Mum used to doll herself up before he came home for dinner, put on lipstick. Then she'd put me in front of her so that

I'd run over to him. She always let my brother be. I sometimes felt it was a bit unnecessary to be pulled out of a game and to be appointed as my father's welcoming committee. It wasn't that my joy was faked, since my days were pretty uneventful anyway, and it was always better to get a visit from Dad in the evening and night than nothing at all."

"Would you like a little house reading maybe, to read from the Bible?"

First row. It's the conflict of opposites that keeps life going. I admit that I find it difficult to get the adolescent to help out at dinner time. Nevertheless, I clear the plates and keep the food warm, in case he re-emerges from the garage before we go to bed.

Afterwards, my husband empties the washing machine, stretching socks and shaking T-shirts before hanging them up on the line. We laugh a lot, though, on most evenings and sometimes into the night. Too bad if we sleep in an unmade bed at night. The boy hasn't come back by the time we turn in. Sometimes we also have a giggle in the morning, except when we say goodbye; he's always surprised to see how sorry I am to see him go.

We'll be seeing each other again this evening, at seven-thirty, he says, trying to lighten the separation. The boy isn't up yet. I'm not even sure he ever left the garage last night.

I lean back in the deckchair under the porch and put down my book. It's four o'clock and darkness is falling again. Tumi is in view pottering about on the side of the deck in his rain gear and balaclava with four baking moulds. I've got the fourth pair of dry stockings ready in my hands. He smells of cold, wet clay when he comes in, the scent of stripped soil. His mouth is smudged in brown, but he shakes his head when I ask him if he's been eating clay. He opens his mouth as evidence. There's also sand and soil on his molars, maybe he needs iron or magnesium; I must remember that when I do my shopping tomorrow.

I'm beginning to be able to imagine that I went away for seventeen years and have now come back to settle here, that this is where my home is, that I have a life here. I'm alone and move into my sailor's place on Monday.

Everything at his place is in shades of yellow and brown and his Sailor's Day badge from two years ago is still pinned to the beige curtains in the kitchen, which his mum sewed for him when he moved in. On the living-room floor there's a log of driftwood, which is used as a stand for a bottle and four glasses. Bit by bit, I discreetly begin to make changes, move things around, putting some into boxes, and use the opportunity when kids come around to collect things for a raffle to give them the Christmas gifts he received from his mum. The last article to go is the intertwined porcelain hands holding a flame. But I still don't have the courage to move the ship in the bottle yet.

For a long period, he makes no remarks about any of this, but then one day, after three months, as we're eating chicken in coconut milk with corn, beans and rice, because he'd rather not have fish, he says between mouthfuls:

"Feels a bit empty around here, have you changed anything?"

It has taken me four months to muster up the courage to mention the kitchen curtains, and I tread carefully.

"What's wrong with those curtains?" he asks. "Mum made those and it was enough hassle getting them up. She went all the way to Reykjavík to buy that material and had to extend her stay by two days. My brother Daddi had to drive her all over the place until she finally found the fabric in Mjód. Then she insisted on

sewing them here, so she moved in here with the sewing machine and took over the entire living room. Two of her friends helped her to put them up. What's wrong with the curtains?"

I stroke him like a cat, gently running my fingers over his tummy until he becomes totally docile. Afterwards he tells me that I can change the curtains if I want to, but that I needed to explain this to his mum, who already views me with plenty of suspicion because I'm skinny, boyish-looking and divorced and I make a living correcting papers.

"I feel there's no need to have curtains in the kitchen," I say. "Besides, there's nothing but the sea in front of us. I feel I lose sight of the horizon with those frilly drapes up there."

"So you want the place to look like a building site?" he says. He's gradually changing.

"What are you reading?" he asks. I tell him about the subject matter of the book as he looks back at me with an unfathomable air.

"I don't see any point in reading a book that you've read before me, because then I'd be experiencing it after you, but I'd be willing to try being a woman and to see what it's like to give birth to a child. I think it must be a totally unique experience to split into two," says my muscular, macho sailor as he slips into a blue salt-beaten sweater that his mother knitted for him and must never be washed. He's going off to sea.

FIFTY

The house stands below, virtually on the shore, almost unrecognizable. But it still has that same low ceiling, which a tall man could barely stand upright under. He is by the stove in a white, newly ironed shirt, holding a tray of freshly fished pink lobsters. Six boats are approaching land with their catch on the horizon, all of them with their lights on. They seem motionless, as if they were preparing a surprise attack, a raid on the village just after the evening news.

"It's the location I fell for," he says, nothing but the sea through the window. "It was empty when I moved here and I'd no idea it was connected to you in any way. Because I didn't know you back then," he says teasingly, "so I hadn't even started to think about you."

I walk from room to room in this both familiar and alien house, Tumi at my heels, and gently stroke the faded flowery wallpaper.

"I sandpapered and varnished the floor. Those are the original floorboards. The musty odour has gone now."

I try lying on the bed.

"The place was empty when I bought it, apart from the bath in the basement and some boxes up in the attic, old stuff I couldn't bring myself to throw away and that I haven't had the time to go through yet. You're welcome to take a look if you like."

I speedily skim through the contents of the copybooks in Granny's neat handwriting. It is the month of May, the rest of the date is illegible—humidity has eaten into some of the pages:

A gentle summer breeze after this morning's rain. A boy is born at 16:40. The couple came to collect him at 18:10. The wind is shifting to the west. Everything is fine.

"I hope you're hungry," he says when I come down, "this is at least three kilos."

The boy places three plates on the table and makes a fan and two rolled telescopes out of the napkins, which he sticks into the glasses, and then goes out to play with the pregnant dog in the garden.

"I got her as part of my divorce settlement," he says, "she'll be having the puppies in three weeks' time, on 24th December, they'll be my Christmas presents this year, along with some socks from my mum and whatever my daughters make at school. Last year I got a paper mobile sculpture from my daughter and a rug and muffler for the dog from my eldest. They miss the dog, we're one in their eyes, the bitch and I."

A photo of two adolescent girls sits on one of the bookshelves. The eldest looks slightly anxious and resembles him. The other is blonde with a parting in the middle and a pigtail, fine features and a smile akin to that of the woman in the skiing outfit in another picture, standing between her daughters with her arms around their shoulders.

"That was the last holiday before she gave up on me and vanished with a pal of mine. I'm so unbearable to live with," he says, coming right up to me so that I can smell his aftershave. I recognize it, Yves Rocher, *Nature pour homme*, the essence of manhood in a bottle.

"I mostly took care of the children while their mum was having her honeymoon, and now I try to go to Reykjavík to meet them at least every second weekend. We stay at my mum's for the moment and she washes and irons everything for us and neatly folds it all into cases, one for her granddaughters and one for her son. I didn't start wearing ironed underpants until after my divorce."

Or perhaps he doesn't actually say that; in fact it's fairly unlikely in this setting, right in the middle of cooking, that he would have said something like that and mentioned ironed underpants.

"I'm doing the house up myself; I tiled the kitchen during my summer holidays. I admit the chessboard floor is slightly audacious."

He stoops over the stove a moment on the carved stone tiles of the chequered black and white kitchen floor. He's on a black square and I'm on a white one, with half a chessboard between us. Once he's lowered the heat, he swivels around and moves forward one square, from a black one to a white one, so that we are now both standing on white squares, with just one black square between us, and we just have to stretch out our hands to be able to touch each other. But I need more time to think, so I make little moves at a time, first to the side, from white to black, and then back onto a white square again, as if I might even be thinking of leaving the kitchen altogether and vanishing. But I appreciate his appreciation of me. He launches a diagonal attack on me, like a true knight. His hand slides down my back at the same time as I start to feel something wet in the palm of my hand. It is the tongue of the drenched dog, followed by the boy at the other end of the leash.

"You're just on time," he says. "Food is ready."

FIFTY-ONE

As I'm posting my latest translation, I take the opportunity to give Mum a call. I realize it's not very sensible to have no phone, with Tumi in my care. What if he had an ear infection and I had to call a doctor? He wouldn't know how to cope if something happened to me. He might run up the moor on his own instead of finding his way down to the village. I'll buy a phone and immediately write down the emergency number for him on a piece of paper this evening and stick it on the wall beside Hercules.

"What kind of a man is he?"

"What man?"

"I wasn't born yesterday, you haven't phoned for two weeks, we were getting really worried."

"He's divorced, has two kids."

"Does he still talk about his ex-wife?"

"Hardly ever, he showed me a picture of her, though."

"He showed you a picture? He isn't over her yet."

"She was standing between their two daughters in the photo, he couldn't have cut her out."

"I've collected some clippings for you."

"Mum, I'm still in Iceland, they get all the papers here too, you know."

"You don't read them."

"They speak Icelandic here, if it weren't for the flooding I could be at your place for coffee this evening."

"I've given up coffee; I've made some changes in my life."

"Anyway, I've got plenty to read and do with Tumi. He's learning how to dance and embroider."

"Is that what you're teaching that fatherless boy? To dance and embroider? I've no recollection of ever seeing you embroider, neither as a child nor an adult."

"It's just simple cross-stitching. I let him try whatever he feels like. We bought a pattern with the picture of a horse; he wanted to embroider a blind horse."

"A blind horse?

"Yes, we altered the pattern slightly and closed the horse's eyes with the same colour as the crest, we've only changed it by four stitches altogether."

I don't tell her that he also swaps the colours, that he's made its tail bright red and used the green yarn that was supposed to be applied to the grass on the mane, and that he then wanders with the yarn between different parts of the horse's body, jumping from the unfinished head to the withers to do some stitching there and then skips to its flanks, which he chooses to stitch in sun-yellow.

"We're mainly learning ballroom dancing and free style."

"Don't you need some food?"

"They have shops here just like anywhere else on the island, we get plenty."

There is a long silence at the other end of the line. Tumi is getting restless in the play corner of the post office, having assembled the twelve remaining building cubes in every possible combination and being eager to move on to the promised visit to the bakery next door, where there are round tables and chairs and they serve hot bagels with cream cheese and cocoa.

"Anyway, Mum, I'll talk to you again soon. Tumi is waving at you as we speak, we're at the post office, I'm in a coin box."

There's a silence at the other end of the line. Finally, she speaks again:

"I heard from Thorsteinn yesterday, he was pretty down and didn't look too good. He's not a happy man."

"I thought you said you'd *heard* from him, not that you'd *seen* him."

"Well, he just popped by. We're worried about you, you just vanished."

"I've stopped thinking about Thorsteinn; right now I'm just thinking about me and Tumi."

"He's stuck in a predicament he has no say in. That woman seems to have him under her thumb."

FIFTY-TWO

The boy wants to learn how to knit to be able to make socks for his unborn sisters. I've found a woman who can teach him garter stitching. She lives in the house next door to my sign language teacher's, is eighty-six years old and every month delivers a hand-knit Icelandic woollen sweater with a reindeer pattern to the co-op. But I still feel I need to get Auður's approval before buying the yarn and number three knitting needles. She thinks it's the best plan she's heard in a long time.

"I think he's growing and getting taller," I tell her, "the clothes I bought for him last month are getting too small; I think he's stretched by about two centimetres."

"New clothes often shrink in the wash. And what about you," she asks, "have you met some fun people? Have you revived any old memories, done any long-line fishing on the pier?"

"I'm not sure I want to be taken care of," I say.

"What do you mean taken care of?"

"The men here are so considerate; they want to fuss over me."

The boy chooses a yellow ball of wool and a green one. So that the babies won't be confused with each other when they lie side by side on the bed, he explains to me in sign language.

The old woman receives us in a spotted dralon apron and hunched back. She's quite a lady, her neighbour tells me, a well of knowledge on premonitions and guiding spirits. We walk into a roasting living room; all the radiators have clearly been turned up to the hilt and the windows are closed. There are four woollen rugs on the floor. On the dining table there is a pile of thick-buttered *skonsur* pancakes with pâté and a plate of cookies. She's done her Christmas baking, and I recognize some of Granny's specialties: *spesíur* cookies, half-moons, vanilla rings, Jewish pastries and raisin buns. There are also marble cakes and twisted *kleinur* doughnuts, as well as bottles of soft malt and orange. Our contribution is a large box of chocolates with a picture of the Dettifoss waterfall on the lid. She takes it and says there was no need, before swiftly slipping it into a cupboard. I seem to catch a glimpse of other Dettifoss waterfalls beside the neatly folded bedclothes.

The boy knows how to behave and immediately sits at the laid table, after greeting the old lady, and spreads the napkin on his lap. The woman sits opposite him with the knitting needles and a ball of light green wool. They're both wearing hearing aids and glasses. It transpires that she's recently had a hip replacement, feels totally reborn, and has enrolled for a country line-dancing course. She asks me if we're cold and if we can feel the draught; she's had problems with her heating, apparently. By the time I leave them to go into the next house for my sign language class, Tumi is placing his third slice of cake on his plate and has downed half a bottle of malt, while the old lady has already knitted the first row of a light green sock.

The neighbour's quilt smells of mild washing powder; I think he's only been able to sleep there once since the bedclothes were last changed.

FIFTY-THREE

A balloon flies into the air, as a child releases the piercing shriek of a throttled pig. I think those are rabbit ears I see gliding over the highlands.

"The Winter Festival is held during Advent, and we organize all kinds of happenings and events around it that are designed to encourage those who have left to return," explains a woman as she wraps candyfloss around a stick for the boy.

A giant crane that has been set up to deepen and enlarge the harbour is going to be used for bungee-jumping. It's ten degrees and drizzly, which doesn't stop the girls from wearing open high-heeled shoes, heavy make-up and their best clothes. They move in invincible groups of six or seven, giggling wildly. The neon lights of the classroom have been covered with crepe paper and the blackboard has been adorned with a multi-coloured chalk drawing of Mary, Joseph, a cow and several sheep with short tails, but no sign of Jesus. Tumi wants to play an angel, like the girls, and to pluck a cardboard harp. Baked ginger cookie fingers lie waiting on paper plates on the table. The local dentist will be livening up the ball on his synthesizer this evening.

The guests of honour of the festival will have to travel here by sea or air. The ministers for industry and the environment were both supposed to be coming to visit the freezing-plant and examine the new candling table that is being used for spotting ringworm, and take a day trip up to the lagoon, where there are plans to store amphibious boats in the future. But the Minister for Industry has a nasty bout of flu and the Minister for the Environment never takes domestic flights—too much turbulence in the air, according to the local paper, too much claustrophobia. According to other sources, though, he's on holiday in the Canary Islands, and it is precisely these contradictory alibis that awakened the locals' suspicions. The leading parliamentary representative of the constituency has agreed to come in his place, however. After all, his grandmother originally came from this region, a detail that has won him some precious votes and a seat in parliament.

Legs wide apart, the MP has planted himself in front of the entrance to the tent where the Women's Association has set up camp with a huge pot of Swiss Miss cocoa. He claims to get no peace in his own home; his two adolescent children are kicking up such a fuss about the reservoir. He just hopes that they'll be so absorbed in their computer games when he comes home that they'll forget to come down for dinner.

The MP insists on being the first man to be lifted up in the air on the crane, but when the time comes he's too drunk, and the new challenge becomes finding a suitable place to put him down. He nevertheless continues to greet people as best he can, old colleagues, relatives on his mother's side of the family and fellow party members. In his place, it is the mayor's secretary who is hoisted into the air by the crane in a harness, the first inhabitant to launch himself into the void and to bounce in the air several times, the tip of his nose almost touching the surface of the water.

I find myself in the middle of a small but compact group at the harbour staring into the air. I quite like being in the middle of a crowd, in the heart of a scrum of strangers pressed against me in the rain, listening to the racket of a brass band, and yet I'm not a particularly gregarious person. Nevertheless, I can see the advantages of not straying from the centre: for one, you don't need an umbrella, but still don't get wet, thanks to the shelter provided by those of others. The best thing about being in the middle, though, is that one can become invisible. I slept in the middle of the big mattress on the floor sometimes, but that doesn't mean that I have to be a middle woman for the rest of my life. Although I normally prefer to be chosen than have to choose myself, I still know how to take a risk. In fact, I'm continuously getting better at it and might even be getting to like it.

I watch the mayor's secretary dive head first from the crane, plummeting to the multi-coloured circles of oil and fish mucus on the surface of the water, and then bounce back up and down again at the end of the elastic until he is pulled to safety on his wobbly legs. Meanwhile, the next man is hoisted up in the basket. Bungee-jumping is one of the things that terrifies me the most and the last thing I would want to try. It's about as un-me as you can get, in fact—first because of my fear of heights and, second, because of the jump itself, that head-first leap into the void, the idea of hanging in mid-air from the gallows, swinging to and fro, like a wreck. Mind you…

"This is your big chance to take on the insurmountable and challenge all those paradoxes inside you," says a deep voice beside me.

He's absolutely right. Maybe this is the moment to conquer my vertigo and put myself to the test, even if it means bursting the blood vessels of my eyeballs. I smile at the man beside me, ask him to hold onto the boy's hand and register my name on the list, putting down my mother's name as next of kin.

The seventy-metre ascent above sea level is petrifying. I'm scared shitless, I will confess.

The surface of the ocean is infinitely distant below me, and is being circled by seagulls the size of insects. A young man is busy strapping me into a harness behind my back and finally hooks an attachment to my ankles; I hear the sound of metallic clicks. I'm not feeling too good and have started to tremble in the rain. There's more life in the withered grass of the moors than there is in me right now. Those who knew me well will say that it was unlike me to come to such an end, having just embarked on this new life, and now about to leave it abruptly. And yet almost all of the best women and men of this world have taken this path well ahead of me—there's nothing particularly original or significant about dying.

Right now it's a bit difficult to evaluate how many people might be moved by my passing, I've been away for such a long time; maybe enough to fill eleven pews in the church once everyone has been counted. Then some deeply distraught stranger that no one in the family has ever seen before will appear dressed in black; the unexpected can always happen, even in death.

I have to admit that my ex-husband would show more originality at organizing my funeral reception than my mother would. He'd go for sushi, whereas she'd have a four-tiered sandwich cake cemented with mayonnaise, the whole thing crowned by a thickly spread layer, adorned with four thin slices of boiled egg with light reddish yolks sunk deep into the dressing.

From this critical viewpoint, I have a bird's eye vision of it all. Could any woman have asked for a more ideal setting and luxurious view for her departure?

No, I think not.

I pan the horizon, starting with the chalet with no curtains that is visible on the edge of the village, my mobile home complete with deck, grill, fire extinguisher and smoke alarm, and then move to the mouth of the river and the sandy embankments that will fill with violet flowers in the spring when I'm no longer here. Even from a height like this, I can distinguish the colour of the flowers, my eyes skim over the soggy, mossy lava fields which stretch and lose themselves in the mist, fusing with the hues of the dark ocean, and in the distance the tongue of the glacier, woolly grey and cracked and, beyond that again, the enormous reservoir. The only things linking me to my former life now are these attachments fastened to my ankles, the only thread that can lead me to the meeting with my new self, if all goes well.

The young man standing on the gallows pats me reassuringly on the shoulder. He is wearing a blue woollen bonnet and a polo neck under his leather jacket.

"Most people prefer not to think about what they're about to do and just step over the edge."

I ask him how old he is and then, to delay the moment even further, when his birthday is. Since I'm showing no sign of wanting to jump off, he offers me a cigarette.

"Would you like me to push you?" he says after I've taken my first drag, "some people don't have the guts to jump on their own."

People are clearly growing restless below. We stand together on the gallows, my executioner and I, and he's about to kick the stool from under the woman who is to be hanged.

"Would you like me to push you?" he repeats. "This is the opportunity of a lifetime to throw yourself into the air, don't be scared, you'll bounce right back up again. Don't you want to experience what it's like to hang in loose air? Are you scared of that freedom?"

I finally compress all my experiences into a single memory that goes something like this:

I was seven years old and tending to chickens in the country, where I soon realized that the richest chickweed grew on the mounds of manure by the shed. If I managed not to sink through the outer layer and, moving swiftly, not to break the crust, I could clip a nice big cluster of green herbs with the big rusty pair of scissors. Two days later, the hens would lay eggs with orangey-red yolks, and not yellow ones like those sold in the supermarket. That is where I learnt how to take risks, to push myself to the very edge. On the other hand, there was always the risk that I would crack through the crust and sink into the cow shit up to my neck. Since then, I've very often pierced through the crust and ended up in excrement up to my chin. And yet flowers can still grow out of manure. Chickweed produces beautiful flowers, has a sweet taste and is good in salads.

In fact I could barely be happier because I am beginning to know who I am, I am beginning to be someone else, beginning to be me. The last thing I see before I jump is the boy below, with his big ears and gaping mouth releasing a silent scream. That's the last thing I remember.

FIFTY-FOUR

"You're incredibly unlucky," the doctor tells me, "it's almost incomprehensible. You seem to have jumped to the side and somehow managed to do the impossible, to bang your hand against the edge of the *Guðfinna Kristjánsdóttir* capelin ship."

He looks like a doctor out of a novel, a handsome man who inspires confidence. He has small hands, though, hands are rarely mentioned in books that feature doctors.

"We've gone over all the security measures and couldn't find any faults there. Eleven people jumped off ahead of you, no side winds or anything like that, you don't have any suicidal tendencies, do you? Luckily, it was the contraction of the elastic that saved you and made you bounce back up when you landed; the radius of your right wrist is broken, you got off quite lightly, all things considered."

Then I suddenly remember:

"Where's the boy?"

"Your son's in the other room. He's doing a jigsaw."

They usher him into the room of the health centre and position him at the end of the bed, from where he looks at me with anxious eyes.

How irresponsible of me, my son was on the point of becoming an orphan.

Once we've embraced each other as much as circumstances will allow, the boy opens his mouth to the doctor and points at a tooth. It's loose.

"He's a bit young to be losing a tooth," says the doctor, "but it does happen." The boy closes his mouth. Then the doctor turns back to me.

"How are you feeling?"

"Fine."

"Don't you remember me?"

That's what they all say, it's hardly very original. This is the third time in about as many days that I'm being asked this unfathomable question.

"No, should I?"

"We were at secondary school together and left at the same time. I often looked at you, without ever hitting on you. You were a bit too boyish-looking for my taste—but I remember your special linguistic talents and how you spoke all these exotic languages, even ones that weren't being taught at the school."

I remember him now. He immediately had a girlfriend. They sat in the corner and held hands, in a world of their own, and didn't show up at parties. They're still together, in fact, because she now appears from behind him to wrap a blood pressure cuff around my arm. He does the introductions for both of them:

"Don't you remember Gugga? She went on to do nursing." She greets me with professional detachment, without being distracted from her task.

A woman enters and places a tray of food in front of me on the bed. She offers Tumi some too, but he shakes his head. I'm not hungry, but am used to doing what I'm told. I manage to eat almost half of the sausage and a bit of the white sauce with my good hand before I throw up.

It is then that I get a shot of pain through the left side of my chest: my heart skips a beat and I feel as if it had just been clutched by a hand. For a moment it stops to beat, while it waits to see if the hand will squeeze it. I'm finding it difficult to breathe.

I tell them my heart hurts.

"You need to work out what you want. It was a warning. Why did you jump?"

"What do you mean?"

"That horse meat sausage was a test of your free will," my

doctor says, looking at his nurse. I sense they belong to the same world, that there's a strong personal bond between them.

"Wasn't that veal meat sausage?"

"No, horse meat, but it all comes down to the same thing, it obviously didn't agree with you." Once more the doctor and nurse exchange meaningful glances.

"Isn't this just what all the patients get?"

"What do you enjoy doing?"

He talks to me as if I were a four-year-old, without taking his eyes off his wife. I answer like a fully grown woman:

"I enjoy being with my son and jogging," I say, looking at my fingers protruding from the virgin-white plaster. "And I also like to go skating," I add. I don't feel it is appropriate to add anything else.

"That'll be good for you when the weather picks up," he says.

When we step out of the health centre, I see that my sign language teacher is waiting for us in his heated car.

FIFTY-FIVE

He feels awful about having encouraged me to jump and looks seriously worried.

"I didn't expect you to do it. I didn't mean those words I said, it was just bullshit, I didn't realize you were so docile."

He has to go to Reykjavík for the weekend to see his kids and wants us to stay in his place while he's away, so that I can recover. He is afraid it will be cold and damp up there in the chalet. I'm still in too much of a daze to be able to formulate any objections. Otherwise I could have said something like:

"Thanks for the thought, but I already have plans and I'm fine."

"The fridge is full of food, for a change, I did some shopping. I'll leave the dog behind, all you have to do is feed her and let her run in the garden. Don't worry," he adds with a smile, "the puppies aren't due for another two weeks and I'll be back on Sunday evening. She's feeling a bit delicate too, so you'll be good company for each other."

"Thank you."

"The kitten is no problem either, not for the dog at least."

That is how we move down from the ravine to the shore, the boy, the kitten and I.

As he's leaving, he pats the dog from top to bottom; he's good to her. Next he pats the boy and then finally strokes me, adjusting my sling.

When you live in the home of an absent person, sleep in his bed, eat off his plates, skim through some of his books, occasionally opening one to read a small extract, you slowly develop an odd kind of understanding of him that isn't far from affection. Or wonderment at what kind of man could be behind these books about saints and Japanese bonsai gardens?

His shirts hang in a doorless wardrobe with even gaps between them, most of them white, except for one that looks particularly gaudy. He doesn't seem to own any ties. The fridge is crammed with food. He's even bought cans of food for the cat. Without trying to actually work out the owner's culinary tastes, I can't help noticing that there are four types of olive oil in the house, and an equal number of bottles of vinegar.

"I roasted some lamb for you in the oven," he said as he was leaving, "I hope that's OK. You just have to heat it up, you can handle that, it was especially conceived for a one-handed person and slowly roasted for four hours—you could almost eat it with a spoon."

The post-divorce bedclothes of men are always new. Very few men take bedclothes with them when they split up. They generally buy a set of two in the first round, and then another two a few weeks later, all the same type, rarely white, normally stripy blue, like the ones we're lying in. The plates and cups also match and are still unchipped; the whole lot has been bought in a single trip, a complete set without the interference of any woman.

The dog seems to be tolerating the kitten quite well and treats him gently, almost with a touch of motherly care. Then she keels over to one side, spreading out her tummy and teats. The kitten vanishes under the sofa. The dog doesn't want to eat, doesn't want to drink and doesn't want to play. The boy lies down beside her, patting her, and pulls a quilt over her. But she doesn't want to be patted either and staggers about on four legs, moping aimlessly around the house for a good while, investigating every nook and corner, before finally lying down behind the door of the dark bedroom that is furthest from us. The boy sits on the sofa and finishes knitting a new yellow row in the sock. I feel quite weak and might even be running a temperature. The dog also looks weak to me and feverish in her eyes; she obviously has a temperature too. By the time I get to her with some water for her to drink, the first puppy is born. She is licking him and the next one is beginning to emerge. There will be three in all, by the time she has finished, all covered in yellow spots, and throughout all of this she doesn't utter a single sound.

FIFTY-SIX

Low-pressure belts are lining up above the island, piling up, one on top of the other. It's been almost six weeks now, the drainpipes can take no more water and in many places basements have started to flood; water leaks into boots and down necklines, and children need dry socks and trousers several times a day. The weather clears for short intervals to allow people to run down to the video store to change DVDs and buy a snack, although many stay in, without noticing the brief dry spell that would have enabled them to see December's half-moon.

Dawn is slow to break; it's not before noon that a glimmer begins to form over the harbour, a streak of daylight through the muddy darkness. Huddled up in bed, we linger there solving crosswords. He's helping me to find a feminine noun beginning with b.

After that, he fixes the pyramid in the bowl of mandarins; he wants it to be tall and impressive and is constantly adjusting the fruit.

The tiger kitten scuttles several times diagonally across the floor. He no longer zigzags, has stopped galloping sideways and has recently developed the ability to walk along a straight imaginary line—on four legs. He eagerly observes the small birds on the deck outside; he is slowly but surely turning into a shrewd hunter. One morning there's a dead snow bunting lying on the floor; the kitten pleads innocent and makes itself scarce. The boy picks up the bird and holds it tight to his chest. I tell him we'll bury it later in the day. A short while later I find the bird under his bed, beside his treasure chest.

By the time we've finally climbed into our rain gear and are ready to go out on an exploratory mission just after noon, the end of this very short day is already approaching. Our first and final destination is the playground. I lead him with my good hand. He's wearing a new green cable sweater under his overalls.

Tumi weighs thirteen kilos and I weigh fifty-three, so in order to get some kind of balance I have to shift closer to the middle of the see-saw. He's not interested in trying to tackle the climbing frame. When he walks up or down steps he always moves forward with the same foot; three steps are like a steep cliff to him. Afterwards, we sit on the white plastic chairs by the shop and have an ice cream with chocolate sauce.

He has finished decorating my cast and drawn a bulldozer on it, but also fish and marine vegetation. We are not likely to be going to the swimming pool for at least a week. My friend offers to take him along with him. That would be the first time in six weeks that I would be separated from him for more than an hour.

"I'll keep a good eye on him," he says, "don't worry."

The boy seems pleased.

While the two boys are at the pool, I lie on the deck with a trashy novel and a scarf coiled around my neck. How many women in the world can allow themselves such a luxury at this precise moment in time? Could a newly liberated woman ask for any greater bliss than this?

"See what I've got for you?" says my father in the middle of a pile of books. We are visiting a second-hand bookshop.

"There you go, that's for you", he says, blowing the dust off a book in front of me. "There's so much music in the words, if you don't hear the music, you won't get the story," says the man whose

favourite composer is Bach. "There are a few pages missing from it so it ends in mid-sentence. You can decide how the story ends, invent your own ending, aren't you lucky?"

I read it many years ago and remember only being moderately happy about the ending. I expected something more decisive to happen between them. A woman doesn't brush fluff off the shoulder of a man's jacket at a dinner party unless there's something intimate going on between them, or does she? "Your ending will be better," he says, smiling, and then pats me on the cheek.

FIFTY-SEVEN

Across the chasm there is some kind of stone arch or bridge. It has been considerably eroded since I last crossed it, but I decide to give it a chance and lean forward, at first only gently pushing against the stone with one arm. Then a bridge automatically stretches across the abyss; it obviously has hinges. I tell myself that this is an ingenious invention. But as I'm pondering on whether I should leap over the chasm or not, I'm awoken by the phone. I leap out of bed, searching everywhere for my new mobile, our renewed link with the vanished world, and finally find it in the pocket of my raincoat. It's 04:07.

It's my ex-husband calling from the capital from some bar where he says he's been drinking beer for the past two and a half hours. He tells me he's been trying to track me down for three weeks to tell me he's had a daughter. He's emailed me a picture of her, but I obviously don't answer. He got my new number from his ex-mother-in-law.

"She's lovely, tiny and soft," he says.

"Congratulations."

"You didn't have to run away like that, just vanish. You've got a new address, a new phone number. What crime did you commit?"

"I'm not running away, I'm taking a break."

"Just because we're divorced doesn't mean we have to lose all contact, does it?"

He wants to know if he woke me up.

"I hear you injured yourself."

"Who told you that?"

"Your mum, when I finally reached her to get some news about you, she just got back from India."

"That's a bit of an exaggeration, the cast was removed yesterday."

"How are you anyway?"

"Just fine, thanks."

"I was thinking of visiting you, coming to say hello?"

"I thought you were tied down, with a woman and child."

"Tied and not tied."

"What do you want from me?"

"Do you know what the special thing about you is?"

"What?"

"You're always so sexy when you've got that sleepy tone of voice, when you've just woken up."

"I'm not sure it would be a good idea for you to come."

"Your mum told me the roads are impassable so I guess the flying instructor will just have to come on his plane."

"What does Nína Lind have to say about all this?"

"You can barely reach her or the child, she's got so many of her girlfriends around, the house is always packed right up to the front door. When they aren't at our place, she's at their places with the baby. When I walk into the living room of my own house, there's a sudden silence and awkwardness. Easy to guess who they're talking about and what the nature of the problem is."

FIFTY-EIGHT

We hear a banging engine sound long before the yellow contraption comes over the mountain and down a grey cloud. The boy sees the plane's swaying wings as it flies over the chalet. There can be no doubt as to who the pilot is.

I had borrowed my mother's car and when I came out of the restaurant with Auður, there was a white paper rocket under one of the windscreen wipers. Seventh heaven. Private flying lessons. Ten lessons special offer. Make your Icarus dreams come true. First lesson is free, eleven per cent discount on the following two. Negotiable payment options.

My fear of heights is legendary and I purely look on airplanes as a means of getting me away from the island. Nevertheless, I think the reference to Icarus is an interesting one, since it was precisely his dream that led to his demise. Despite the warnings I get from Auður, who sees no interest in this message, I decide to call the man who will later become my husband. It eventually transpired that the ad had been solely aimed at me and no one else and I've yet to step on his plane.

The silhouette drifts over the barren plain in the midday twilight and up the hill, heading straight for me. I see him standing outside on the deck in an orange anorak. What is he lingering there for? Is he going to come in or stay out? He strikes a match. I see the red glow of the tip of his cigar and then myself, reflected in the window, but don't budge. He seems to have spotted me, because he casts his cigar away and walks straight towards me.

The man looks both familiar and alien to me, as he stands there with his hands buried deep in his anorak pockets. My memory of him is somehow different. Older or younger? Did he maybe have a beard? That's the first thing that strikes me, his beardlessness, it sharpens his facial features. Wasn't he taller than that? He seems to be of average height, standing there by the doorway. Could be the shoes I guess. Not only are they unfamiliar to me, but they're worn out and part of some new sphere of experience. Even the colour of his eyes surprises me; I could have sworn the eyes of my ex-husband were brown, but now they seem to be grey. He hands me a cardboard box and pecks me on the cheek.

"Your mum sends her love; that needs to go into the fridge."

The box contains salmon, halibut, scallops and prawns, as well as fried fish balls. At the bottom of the box there's a wrapped parcel with a blue ribbon for the boy. Through the window I can see the freezing-plant this fish probably all comes from.

"Aren't you going to invite me in?"

The boy stands by my side in the doorway, holding my hand.

"There's a button missing."

Tumi points at a loose thread sticking out of the man's anorak. Thorsteinn is normally very meticulous about these things. I interpret.

"Biscuit," says my boy in his resonant, metallic voice, pointing and sniffing at a protrusion from the man's pocket.

"Can I have a biscuit?" I interpret, and by way of confirmation the boy stretches out his hand with a pleading look.

My ex looks embarrassed and the sparkle in his eyes instantly fades as his gaze moves away from my neck. He pulls half a glistening and crumpled packet of chocolate biscuits out of his anorak pocket. The boy smiles.

It is then that I realize, as if I'd found the missing piece to an old jigsaw, that he has the same taste as a cream biscuit, his skin, his entire being has the exact same taste as the vanilla cream inside those biscuits.

"Doesn't he play outside with his friends? Can't you get someone to mind him?"

He continues to empty his pockets as he talks, like a condemned man, guiltily placing all his belongings on the table, or a visitor standing in front of a prison warden, before going in to see an inmate. The boy clutches the packet of biscuits with both hands, trembling with excitement. Finally, my ex pulls out a picture of his daughter to show me. She is small and dark with a red face, like all babies. He pulls off some layers of clothing: his anorak, shoes, sweater and then even his socks—I wonder if he's going to go to bed.

Once he is seated, he tells me she's jealous of me and asks if I'm also jealous of her. I say no. He wants to know why not, am I not fond of him any more? I say to a certain extent, but that he's starting to turn into a stranger, that I no longer see him behind me, like a mirage in the corner of my eye in the mirror, when I brush my teeth, that he no longer pops up in my mind when I'm thinking or reading, that he has started to fade, vanish, that I find it hard to picture him any more, that I'm starting to confuse him with other men, that other men are starting to supplant him. I tell him that I am, nevertheless, still relatively fond of him, at least fonder of him than I am of the local priest whom I haven't met yet or the vet whom I have actually met. He takes out his nail clippers as I'm talking, and starts to clean his nails.

I allow him to digest the information and move away to heat up some cocoa. The boy follows and arranges the cookies on the plate for the guest.

"You've changed somehow," he says when I return, "I can't quite figure out what it is, your hair maybe, did you have it cut?"

"No, I'm growing it."

Then he tells me his relationship isn't working out the way it should:

"In the beginning she was open and willing to be guided."

"Maybe you can teach your daughter something instead."

"If things don't work out between Nína Lind and me, which seems likely, could we give us another go?"

"I thought you didn't love me any more."

"Love or not love, you haven't answered my question."

"No, we can't do that."

At some stage you have to decide to stop, not necessarily because it's totally over, but because one decides to put it aside. Then I also tell him that I've changed, that I've experienced so many things without him.

"In forty days?"

"No, over many years."

He looks disappointed.

"We can still meet, though, and go out for dinners together?"

"I don't think so."

"Can't we be friends then?"

"Isn't that unnecessary, since we don't have a child together?"

"Hang on, who was it that didn't want children?"

"Me, I suppose."

"God, you've changed."

He slams the door behind him, but comes back fifteen minutes later and stands there brooding in the doorway with his hands buried in his pockets. He can't fly back in the dark, he says, and he wants to know if he can stay the night. I tell him that he can, but that the space beside me is occupied.

"Couldn't we push the kid over a bit when he's asleep?"

"No, that's out of the question."

Tumi looks at me with a triumphant smile, as he puts on his elephant pyjamas.

FIFTY-NINE

When I re-emerge the following morning, I find him half out of his sleeping bag, with one arm dangling on the floor, a familiar but alien body. Saliva is dribbling out of the corner of his mouth onto his chin, the same chemical composition as the thousands of waves in the sea, I tell myself, and there's an entire ocean between us. When he turns over, I catch a good glimpse of the scar on his back. If I run out of topics at the breakfast table, I can always ask him how he got it; but when the moment actually comes, I find I'm not interested enough in the answer.

A butterfly flutters over him, drawing irregular circles in the air. Then, suddenly losing its force, it falls to one side and tries to stumble to its feet again on his slippery chin. My ex tries to wave the itch away with his hairy arm. I observe the butterfly's struggle and suddenly feel the irrepressible urge to save it while I still can. I try to scoop it off him with a sheet of paper, without waking the sleeper, but to no avail. Finally, I grab a jar on the table and press it, mouth down, against my ex's cheek, perhaps a bit brusquely.

He springs up. There's a red circle on his cheek.

"Did you just hit me?"

"I was saving a butterfly."

"The last time you hit me your excuse was two flies in October. This time it's a butterfly in December."

"It's vanished."

"You're not normal; you hit me every time we meet."

He glances swiftly at the clock and has to go out onto the deck to make a private call. Like some marsupial creature, he staggers outside with the sleeping bag still wrapped around him; there's better network coverage outside. I prepare breakfast, while he is recovering from the assault.

I can't remember how he likes his eggs. Softly boiled, medium-boiled or hard-boiled apart from the innermost core of the yolk? Fried? How did it ever occur to me to offer a man such a complex breakfast? The boy stands beside me so that he can time the boiling of the egg with the divorce watch, which he's wearing on his wrist with a new strap. My ex believes hen's eggs require seven minutes. The boy toddles around the guest, occasionally glancing at the watch.

"Hang on, isn't that the watch I gave you? Why is he wearing it?"

"Yes, he's got the watch now."

"Did you take off the golden bracelet with the inscription on it and replace it with a strap instead?"

"Was there an inscription on the bracelet?"

"Yes, there was an inscription on the bracelet. Are you going to tell me you didn't even read the inscription?"

Sometime later, I notice him peeping at my diary, rapidly skimming through it. I think he might be saying something in the living room, but the whistle of the kettle prevents me from hearing what. When I return he is sitting in white socks and underpants on the sofa bed and has rolled up the sleeping bag. I get the feeling he might have been crying.

"The good thing about you is that you never placed any demands on me."

Then I sit down beside him, pat him on the arm and, after a moment, say: "Yes, I can well understand you, but sometimes people have to make decisions, go home to Nína Lind now."

"I might be pathetic, but I'm not a bastard."

He has stood up and walks towards the living room window where he pauses a long moment, his back turned to me, peering into the morning darkness.

"It sure is incredibly dark here."

When he is about to leave, he can't find his scarf.

"If you ever find it, it's purple with yellow stripes and a brown fringe, Nína Lind knitted it."

Before leaving, he asks me if there's another man in the picture. I don't answer.

"You're a quick operator," he says. "I take my eyes off you for one second and you're already hitched up with someone."

"That's a bit of an overstatement."

"We could have such a good time together, travel and do lots of things."

Stepping out onto the deck, he abruptly swivels on his feet to pull me into a tight embrace. I can tell it's a quality imperme-able anorak that he's wearing, it insulates well.

"I just wanted to tell you that I just texted Nína Lind to ask her to marry me." He then moves away a few steps before turning one final time to ask:

"Have you any idea where the box with the Christmas decorations got to?"

"Wasn't it in the garage?"

"Wait a minute, did you leave all the stuff in the garage?"

"I forgot it, didn't you take it? The sleeping bags were there."

"Jesus Christ, did you give the new owners a year's supply of toilet paper, the bag of walrus teeth from Greenland and all the Christmas decorations, including the blinking singing reindeer?"

When I walk back into the house, I see that he has left a handwritten note for me on the table.

SIXTY

Tumi is knitting and I tell him I'm popping out to the shop to buy some prunes to make halibut soup, and that I'm not taking the car, just running down the hill. I say it to him in three different ways:

"I'm just running down to the shop, you just stay put in the meantime and carry on knitting."

He nods and sticks his needle into the stitch, with some yellow yarn double-wrapped around his middle finger.

This is the first time I leave him alone so I hurry. The prunes are carefully hidden away in the shop, so I have to ask the girl at the till to help me find them, but she needs to finish serving two other women first.

When I come running back up the hill I see him rushing towards me, soaking wet in his socks, with outstretched arms. I lift his feather-light body into the air. His face is twisted with worry, all wrinkled like an old man, and I can't see his eyes through the lenses of his glasses, which are all fogged up with tears. His heart pounds furiously like a little bird's. Auður's descriptions of him as a premature baby in the incubator spring to mind—almost transparent in colour, his skin so thin that one could see his underlying organs.

"I could have died", he says. "I thought you'd left me." He wraps his wet arms around my neck.

I show him the bag of prunes. "Come on," I say, "let's go make some silver tea. Then we'll make some soup the way your mummy does and, after that, we'll go to the cinema. Have you ever been to a cinema?" I don't tell him I've been invited out to a film and that I'd been thinking of getting a babysitter for him.

There's an Italian film festival in the village, three Italian movies are being screened on three consecutive Thursdays, at eight. That means we'll be back in the house at about ten, which is a bit late for a four-year-old child.

We take the car. The youth in the box office assures me that, even though the film isn't advertised as a kid's movie, there's nothing in it that would disturb a child. We join the queue by the door behind eight other spectators, with Tumi clutching the tickets in his outstretched hand. Everyone is staring at us.

My friend appears, kisses me on the cheek and shakes the boy's hand, greeting each other as equals, man to man. The viewers are watching us. I ask Tumi if it's OK if our friend sits with us. It's OK. We lead him into the cinema and he chooses the third row in the middle and wants to sit between us. It's a bit too close for comfort, but I'm not sure how well he sees the screen, with his eyesight. It's bad enough that he can't hear the words or the music properly. The other guests spread out in the back rows, leaving a gap of about half the cinema between us. We're segregated from them, just like our chalet. *La Vita è bella* begins.

The boy is no bother in the cinema and sits perfectly still throughout the film, watching events unfold on the screen. He's not interested in any of the pastilles because he's too busy watching the movie. I frequently glance at him and don't know how much he is taking in, or whether he wants me to interpret it for him, tell him the story. He does, however, seem to be reading the subtitles. Then I notice that he sometimes stares at me at length, that they both sometimes look at me, the two men, together. I smile at them.

During the break Tumi eats a pastille and gives one to me and one to my friend. Then he closes the box. It's a drag for him not to be able to lip-read the actors on screen and follow their mouth movements. He sees nodding heads, people squinting their eyes and laughing, but he can't grasp the words.

His eyes barely reach the top of the seats, so I lift him up and sit him on my lap after the interval. He's no taller than a three-year-old child; I can see the screen over his head. Our friend slips into the boy's seat.

"Was that for pretend?" Tumi asks when the lights come back on.

Should I tell him that it's all for pretend? That you can see the reflection of spotlights in those make-believe tears?

"No, the things that we experience and imagine are also real," I say, and he knows exactly what I mean.

"You don't need a man," he says from the back seat as I'm fastening his safety belt in the car, "you have me."

"Who says I'm looking for a man?"

"You look at him."

"Really?"

"And he looks at you."

I don't tell him I'm expecting a guest when he falls asleep.

SIXTY-ONE

Everyone gets a nocturnal visit at some stage. There are no curtains in the windows, no point in locking out the darkness when there's nothing but brown lyme grass and heather in front of them, and nothing behind us but the brown moors. Everything is still in the darkness outside. Five degrees, and for the first time in ages there is a ray of moonlight, which filters down diagonally from the top left-hand corner of the window, like a subtle reading lamp. Despite the day's rainfall, some clothes are still hanging on the sheltered line on the deck. Inside the scene is as follows: I've finished reading a story to Tumi, who is now sleeping with the kitten. I limit myself to the candlelight in the living room, coupled with the glow of the moon, that spotlight provided by the Almighty above. On the window sill there is a blue boot with a yellow rim, size 26, and our pet butterfly is up and about. How much longer can it live for? The time is 00:17 and I hear the gravel crunching under his feet. Not only am I connected to the moon and stars above, but I'm also in close intimate contact with the Santa Claus, who comes to visit me every night. Not down the chimney, but over the railing on the deck in his black boots. He swiftly tackles the hill, with the moon at his back and a pink halo hovering around his head. He slips out of the darkness over the glittering Christmas lights into the candlelight, like a true professional. First his feet, clad in black leather boots, and then his red coat with its white fur trim and black belt.

He's holding my washing from the line in his arms and knocks gently on the window. Then he takes off his hood. The parcel is too big to fit into the boy's boot.

"I have enough time to tell you a long story," he says.

I loosely brush my fingertips against his black trousers, almost imperceptibly at first, but then stroke him hard enough for him to feel me and then harder again. Next I tackle the white cotton hair, tangling it around my finger to make a skein.

I loosen the buckle of his black belt, slide my hand inside, and pause. His skin is warm; I linger on every pause, concentrating on every detail, and then go searching for a warm mouth and eyes. The nocturnal guest's imagination knows no limits, although I feel no need to divulge any of that here.

I suddenly hear what sounds like a faint swish and, at the same moment, the candle on the table extinguishes itself, leaving a lingering spiral of smoke. And, as if that wasn't enough, I see from the total darkness in front of me that the Christmas lights have gone out on the deck. I feel compelled to break the silence and put my visitor's technical expertise to the test:

"Could you help me with the Christmas lights afterwards?"

He's quick to solve the problem; they only needed to be switched back on. And he also relights the candle.

"You probably need some earthing," he says.

"Really?"

"I have to go," he says, "but I'll be back."

As I'm sweeping up the soot from the chimney, along with the other remains of the night, and pick up the clothes scattered around the living room, I look for evidence of his visit and find a tiny stain—sufficient proof to incriminate the right man.

SIXTY-TWO

It seems that no one knows exactly where the flooding came from, but understandably it's the only thing people can talk about in the shop. The village is covered in sand and black sludge, basements are full of puddles, most of the Christmas lights have been smashed to smithereens and garden decorations have been destroyed. Everywhere one goes there are men in orange overalls mopping up, clearing the streets and scooping water out of cellars. The water seems to have flowed down the slope on the eastern side and taken the church with it, although the village itself has been mostly spared.

"We were planning on building a new church anyway," say the men in a positive spirit; "the old one was just a heap of mouldy rubbish that we're well rid of."

The situation is analogous in the two neighbouring villages. Everyone is flabbergasted; nothing is as it should be. It appears that several rivers in the highlands suddenly broke their banks and started to forge new and unpredictable courses in all directions. The area where the locals used to pick blueberries is now completely inundated. The only thing that doesn't seem to have changed is that rivers still flow into the sea, albeit not in the places where they are expected to. People are totally puzzled by the freakish behaviour of their watercourses, which cannot solely be attributed to the incessant rainfall of the past forty days and nights.

The greatest mystery of all is the whale. The most likely scenario seems to be that it was beached and then somehow carried to the car park in front of the savings bank, although it might look as if it had been carried there by the water over the highlands.

Its giant black mass is visible all the way from the chalet, a fully grown whale, probably fifteen metres long. And pregnant, it would later transpire.

"It doesn't matter where she came from," says the man, "we'll carve her up this afternoon and share the meat around."

Other sea animals have been thrown up on dry land here and there: cod, catfish and redfish. The main thing is that the people were spared.

I give Mum a call to tell her to have no worries; we're preparing our return to the city.

"Good job it wasn't worse and no one was hurt."

"Well three dogs are still missing."

"Is it raining?"

"No, Mum, it's cleared up, just like it has in the city, and the whole country it seems, if the weather forecast on the radio is anything to go by."

"Have you sorted out your affairs?"

"Yes, we're clearing things up. We only have the Christmas presents to pack now."

"How's it going with the boy, does he eat well?"

"Yes, he eats well."

"How are you managing to talk to him?"

"Well, it's a world beyond words."

"How are you?"

"Fine, we're going to celebrate Christmas in the city and then I'm going abroad for a few months."

"What, on a job?"

"I can work from anywhere I want, Tumi is coming with me. I've spoken to Auður about it and she approves. She'll be so busy with the baby twins, she's afraid he might be neglected."

"But doesn't he miss his mummy?"

"Probably, but he also wants to see what the world looks like, he wants to visit ruins."

"Are you taking the child to some Arabic country?"

"No, he wants to see the ruins of castles and temples and churches, we're reading some guidebooks at the moment. He wants to see a pear tree, giraffes and golden sand. I can teach him a few things. He's started to read and he knows how to make Icelandic pancakes."

"And to embroider and knit?"

"Yeah, that too."

She sounds happy to hear me and there's a new softness in her voice. She speaks in a low tone with plenty of gaps between her words as she continues:

"I think that relationship was a bit rash. He's not a bad man, but he's not the man for you." She no longer refers to Thorsteinn by name.

There's a silence.

"Well then, Mum, I think I'll say goodbye then."

Another silence.

"Provided you have no objections, I was thinking of leaving some money to charity when I'm gone. I was reading about

253

a school in Bosnia for women badly affected by the war. Of course, you don't read the papers?"

"No, I have no objections."

"No, I didn't think you would. You'll survive, never expected anything less of you. Your brother is the same; he says he has enough too. The triplets just started kindergarten the other day."

"Well then, Mum, we have to tidy up here now. Tumi has just finished knitting socks for his sisters, so we've got to deliver them. We should be in town by tomorrow evening, barring any mishaps."

She suddenly remembers some good news:

"You'll never believe this, some light green shoots have grown out of that plant of yours that I thought was made of silk."

"Right then, Mum, we'll say goodbye for now."

"I won't decorate the tree until you've arrived then."

SIXTY-THREE

This is how the darkest day of the year begins: a new light has filtered through the pallid, rainy sky of the past weeks, and a cloud resembling a crown has formed.

"Like a tooth," says the boy pointing at his gaping mouth.

It must be a sign to herald in the wonderful beginning of the shortest day of the year. Just before noon, the heavens raise their black blanket and the sun horizontally pierces through the window in a narrow pink streak, like the thin line between the drooping eyelids of a sleeping woman. I contemplate myself and the home in the reflection of the window. The Christmas gifts from the co-op are ready and wrapped on the table, and the cards have been decorated and adorned with glitter. Little overlapping handprints are visible on the window, a slew of sticky fingers stamped on the glass. Soon, everything will revert back to normal again: snow drifts, ice, closed mountain roads—once more the country will be as white and odourless as it should be. We sit out on the deck with hot chocolate and our faces tilted towards the first ray of sunshine in two months.

There is actually no need to drive around the whole country, half a circle is more than plenty.

"Three men," says the boy.

"Three men what?"

"Around the table."

He points at a drawing he is completing. In the middle of the table there is a woman who clearly has green eyes and short dark hair.

"My hair has grown," I laugh, I've changed. Now I look at the world through a long fringe.

Santa Claus turns up at midday, dressed in civvies. The dog has been found, unhurt but a nervous wreck. He is carrying an accordion that he asks me to take to the city to be repaired. He'll pick it up fairly soon, he says. I tell him of my plans to travel abroad.

"I don't know for how long," I say.

"I don't want to lose you," he says. "I certainly don't."

"I'll be a bit busy to begin with, then I'll certainly be in touch and look you up."

There's no hurry, plenty of time ahead and vast expanses of sand. Then I add, clearly feeling my heart beat as I say it:

"I need to go on my own first, then we can go somewhere together, if we still want to."

SIXTY-FOUR

As we drive down the side road, I see the whale has been cut open and that her calf is lying there in the car park beside her, all in one piece, two metres long and black just like its mother.

Before setting off, I ask the kid at the petrol station to take a picture of us and, as he carefully hands the camera back to me, he says:

"Did you know that the heartbeat of a whale can be heard from a distance of five kilometres?"

I say I didn't know that.

"Then you probably also didn't know that a whale's heartbeat can disrupt a submarine's communications and prevent a war?"

The turn behind the blind hill comes as a surprise. I'm not driving very fast, but still almost swerve off the road. The car runs on loose gravel and the bay opens up ahead, a long stretch of black, sandy shoreline strewn with seals. The sand is covered with their warm, glistening bodies, flipper rubbing against flipper. They move sluggishly, dozens at a time, as if they had overgrown the straitjackets of their own skin. I pull the handbrake on the side of the road and we get out.

The boy wants to take his shoes off and find a wish stone, whereas I wouldn't mind hugging one of those seals and stroking its earless head.

There is plenty to choose from on the beach, thousands of stones to test one's wishes on, every one you touch, one after another. We sit down. I arrange my stones in a small circle; Tumi assembles his in a small, vertical mound, one on top of the other, making a cairn, erecting a monument.

I have almost completed my circle and dash over to the car one moment to grab my camera. When I come back I see that he has pulled everything off: his hoodie, trousers, leggings, T-shirt and underpants. Stark naked in his snow-white skin, he abandons his clothes in a small bundle in the middle of the sand and charges towards the seals on the black shoreline, heading straight for the surf and sea. He is so white that his torso is almost phosphorescent and fuses with the white of the ocean and the heavens above. His approach triggers a clumsy stampede of seals into the water. I run after him in my bare feet, feeling the sharp shells and cold seaweed under my soles, sludge squishing between my toes and salty water reaching my ankles. I catch up with him in a pool of floating algae, throw my sweater around him and lift his cold little body onto my shoulders. There is black sand between his toes. He strokes my earlobes. I glance swiftly at the ocean before running back again.

"Lots of sea," says the boy in a clear voice.

14:14, says my watch.

West, says the compass in the car.

He is dressed again and sits silently in the back seat, his chin buried in his overalls and the tip of his balaclava barely reaching the window. I fasten his belt.

After slipping an Astor Piazzolla bandoneon disc into the player, I turn on the heater full blast. Then I hand Tumi a sandwich and cocoa milk over my shoulder and pierce the hole with a straw for him. In return he stretches out his clenched hand with a bleeding smile. I unclasp his small fingers, one by one, and finally see his little front milk tooth in the palm of his hand.

FORTY-SEVEN COOKING RECIPES AND ONE KNITTING RECIPE

A WORD OF CAUTION

The following are forty-seven recipes or descriptions of dishes/ beverages and one knitting recipe that are connected to the narrative of *Butterflies in November*. The recipes more or less follow the same order in which they appear in the book. Some of them may make excellent meals, but it should be noted, however, that certain of these dishes may work better on the page than on a plate. Readers are warned that these recipes are, to some extent, fictitious and there is therefore always the risk that they may not be accurate down to the last gram or millilitre. The story also includes references to food that did not go down particularly well with the characters or to dishes that simply failed. No words can be categorical enough to exclude any possibility of misinterpretation and it is therefore up to the reader to find his or her own way. In this context, it is barely worth mentioning that the stuffing of the goose was made up of more than just the words on the page. Similarly, some of the descriptions of the dishes may be too elusive to be interpreted with absolute precision or for any usable recipe to be drawn from them. An example of this is "Not another of those spicy city recipes with beans" (Chapter Thirty-five).

Most of the recipes are conceived for one woman and a child.

The dishes are normally easy to make, and intended to enable the woman to spend as much time as possible with the child. The child can also lend a hand in the cooking. The portions are more often than not designed to leave ample leftovers. In the event of any doubts regarding the recipes or questions on these dishes, the reader is welcome to contact the narrator. It should be pointed out, however, that the narrator is not always responsible for the recipe herself. Examples of this include the snow buntings grilled by foreigners in the highlands and whale steaks. There are many more recipes to be found in the story than those listed here and the narrator will be happy to provide them upon request (e.g. lemon chicken with olives).

It is impossible to determine the exact source of these recipes; some may even have come straight out of the narrator's neighbour's cookery book.

Two of the recipes are designed for funeral receptions, others are conceived for a man and a woman. When a woman cooks for a man or a man for a woman, they generally put more effort into it. In these cases the recipes are also more elaborate. The amount of leftovers will be determined by the state of development of their relationship.

FRIED FISH IN BREADCRUMBS AND ONIONS

Fried haddock in breadcrumbs and onions is a classic Monday dish. However, fish is often fresher in shops on a Tuesday. Naturally, there are a number of alternatives to the traditional halibut and a welcome variation can be pan-fried catfish or brown trout. Catfish is related to wolf-fish but is a darker, savoury fish that reminds some of monkfish. Catfish never fails to catch the eye as it lies on display on the fishmonger's iced steel tray. As most people know, it has beautiful leopard skin which has been used in, among other things, the design of handbags and skirts. Instead of the famous Paxo Golden Crumb pack, you can use home-made breadcrumbs, which are thicker and give the fish a crispier crust. That is because the fish itself does not touch the pan and the fat goes into the breadcrumbs. Fry the onion in a dab of butter in the pan and a splash of olive oil. Remove the onion from the pan when it turns golden brown. Fry both sides of the wolf-fish fillet for a few minutes. The fish should be fried over high heat in a mixture of olive oil and butter until it acquires the colour of a sunny golden shore. Season. Serve with white or barley rice and fresh green salad with tomatoes and cucumber. Make a dressing for the salad with honey, Dijon mustard and olive oil. It is good to mix brown and white rice. Brown rice is a lot slower to cook than normal rice, however, and normally needs to boil for an hour.

THICK WILD GAME SAUCE (WITH GOOSE)

Goose broth, ½ litre of water, salt, pepper, 1 tablespoon of redcurrant jelly, cream. Pour the goose broth into a dripping-pan that will siphon the liquefied fat. Season the sauce according to taste. Since the sauce has to be thick enough to conceal the tread marks of the car tyres left on the run-over bird, it is probably best to use old-fashioned flour to thicken it. Mix a tablespoon of flour with several tablespoons of water and blend it into the broth. Add one tablespoon of redcurrant jelly into the sauce, whip the cream and mix it with the rest before the sauce is presented. The sauce should be the last dish placed on the dining table adorned with candles.

TEA AND BREAD WITH SMOKED SALMON

Tea and bread with smoked salmon is the ideal afternoon snack when someone pops in to see you on the way home from work, for example. Trout is also a perfectly acceptable alternative. Many types of trout can be used: lightly smoked, dung-smoked, birch-smoked, hot-smoked. Many trout breeders have started to do their own smoking at home and you can therefore choose fish from various parts of the country. To add variety, trim some cress over the smoked fish, since cress can be grown in soil or wet cotton on the kitchen window sill all year round.

TEA

Tea can never be praised enough as an afternoon refreshment. All research indicates that green tea is the healthiest beverage one can drink. In some places in the Far East one can spend the whole day in tea houses, while a waiter wanders between guests with a pot of boiling water balanced on a bamboo shoot over his shoulder. People who have lived in

Britain generally like to have cream biscuits with a yellow or pink filling with their afternoon tea. In Iceland one can use *Frón kremkex*, which have a white cream inside. For anyone suffering from insomnia, herbal tea with two to three slices of toast would be preferable.

Green tea: *2 tablespoons of tea leaves, 1 litre of boiled water.* The teapot is heated by rinsing its interior with boiling water. Place the tea leaves in the pot and pour boiling water over them. Steep for 4 minutes. Pour into cups through a tea-strainer.

Herbal tea: August is the best month for gathering herbs. Pick thyme, white dryas, cinquefoil, mint leaves, yarrow and lady's mantle. Dry the herbs. It is a good idea to pre-dry them inside a clean pillow case before placing them on a tray to fully dry them. Boil 1 litre of water in a pot, remove it from the heat and put a fistful of the dried herbs into it (2 tablespoons if the herbs have been finely chopped). Close the lid and allow to brew for 15 minutes. Herbal tea can be reheated several times but not reboiled. It is advisable to read up on the healing properties of the various herbs (e.g. their effect on sore throats, stomach problems and ailing hearts) and experiment with dosages.

SPINACH LASAGNE

Lasagne is generally on the table on Wednesdays. The recipes on the Barilla packet are fairly easy to follow in themselves. Finding the right size of baking pan can be tricky, though. The following is a vegetarian alternative to the traditional minced meat recipe. Pour the oil from a packet of feta cheese into the pan. Fill the pan with spinach and maybe onion and mushrooms, if there happen to be some in the fridge and it tickles your fancy. Cover abundantly with cream and allow to simmer until the spinach leaves have softened. Arrange a base layer of pasta sheets at the bottom of a baking pan and then pour the spinach mix over it, followed by bits of feta cheese. Then repeat this, layer after layer, according to the size of the baking pan and the number of people eating. Finally, sprinkle grated mozzarella over the top layer. Bake in the oven for 30 minutes. Eat with good bread and green salad. This is a very nourishing and relatively simple dish which most people can do, and can be just as appealing to the young as the old.

WILD GOOSE WITH TRIMMINGS AND A RICH, THICK WILD GAME SAUCE

Wild goose can be cooked in a variety of ways with a vast choice of trimmings. The chef cannot always choose the size of the goose, as the case of the run-over goose clearly demonstrates, but ideally the goose should be neither too big nor too fat. It should preferably be rather young, and young geese are generally recognizable from the reddish-pink colour of their feet and beaks, as well as the softness of their bills. The average goose weighs between three and six kilos and feeds between five and ten people. Since part of the goose's fat melts away during cooking, it diminishes by a corresponding volume. This recipe is intended for one man and one woman and one can therefore expect ample leftovers. It is best to leave the goose hanging outside for several days after it has been shot or killed by other means. Collect the goose from your balcony and pluck it without tearing its flesh. Once the goose's feathers have been removed, the beige colour of its skin is revealed with an interesting argyle pattern. It is best to skim over the bird with a Primus blowtorch, e.g. out in the garage where the primus is kept, or alternatively by using the flame of a candle. Grab one of the goose's legs and wings, hold it at a comfortable distance from the flame and then swing it to and fro. When you have finished torching it, cut its neck, wings and legs. Then cut into the bird just above its sternum to scrape out the gizzard and remove the gall, heart and liver. Take the goose's heart, slice it with a sharp knife, rinse out the blood and put it aside for another occasion. The heart can be both roasted with the bird to sharpen the taste of its juice or can be used as part of the stuffing. Then rinse the goose in cold water and wipe it. Once this has been done, you have to decide how to cook it:

1. Icelandic wild goose with apples and prunes roasted in the old-fashioned way. *Wild goose, salt, pepper, apples, prunes, parsley.* Massage the washed goose and season it with salt and pepper, both inside and out, before placing it on the draining board and preparing the stuffing. The stuffing is made with apple wedges, soft, stoneless prunes and chopped parsley. Shove the stuffing into the goose and close the opening with a skewer or by sewing it. Ensure you also close off other holes the stuffing could leak out of, such as the neck cavity. Then place the goose, breast side up, on a roasting pan and fry it for several minutes at high heat. Pour boiling water over the goose and carry on roasting it at a low temperature for 2–3 hours, depending on the bird's age and size. The bird can be turned over while it is being roasted, although it is not necessary. It is customary during roasting to wet the bird with its juices at 15-minute intervals to prevent it from shrivelling or burning. The goose should be eaten in good company and with baked potato wedges, home-cooked

red cabbage, green peas, carrot purée, apple and walnut salad with crème fraîche, a rich, thick sauce and redcurrant jelly.

2. Boiled goose with potatoes and onion stuffing á la Irish. *One goose, salt, pepper. Broth: neck, heart and gizzard of goose, a small onion, a carrot and fresh thyme, parsley, a little celery, 6–7 peppercorns, water. Stuffing: 10 medium-sized potatoes, 7 onions, 6 apples, 50 grams of butter, one tablespoon of chopped parsley, one tablespoon of chopped lemongrass, salt and pepper.* Pluck and torch the goose in the same way as Icelandic wild goose. In Ireland there is an old tradition of hanging onto the feathered wings to dust the dark corners of the house. The smaller feathers went into pillows. Start by preparing the stuffing. Boil potatoes in salted water, and then peel and mash them. Chop the onion and brown it in a pan or pot for 5 minutes, without burning it. Add the sliced apples to the onion in the pan and cook them until they soften. Regularly stir the onion and apple mix. Add the mashed potatoes, parsley, lemongrass, salt and pepper and blend them well together. Allow the stuffing to cool before filling the goose. Clean out the innards of the Irish goose in the same way as the Icelandic one. To make the broth, throw the neck, heart and gizzard into a pot with a small onion, one carrot, thyme, parsley, celery and the peppercorns. Drown them in cold water and allow them to simmer at a low heat for 2 hours. The wings can be added if one wants. Season the washed and dried goose with salt and pepper, both inside and out, and insert the stuffing. Rub sea salt into breast exterior. Place the goose in a big roasting pot, slip it into the oven, add water to the pot, place a lid over it and boil at a moderate temperature for 2–3 hours or for as long as it takes to remove all traces of the accident. Lift the lid off the pot 3–4 times during the boiling and spoon off the fat and juice

and keep in a jar for another occasion. The fat can be kept for a long time in a jar in the fridge and can be put to a variety of uses, e.g. to pour over potatoes in the oven. In the olden days it was considered beneficial to rub the goose fat into the chests of people with respiratory problems. Goose fat was also used to polish kitchen utensils in Irish homes as well as leather garments. Add the potatoes to the goose and allow them to cook with it for an hour. For the last 30 minutes remove the lid from the pot, and turn up the heat to brown the goose. Meanwhile, make the sauce. Filter the broth, add the cooking juices and fat from the goose, taste and season (dilute with water if the broth is too strong) and bring to boiling point again. Thicken the sauce according to taste. Eat the goose with the stuffing, baked potatoes, apple mousse and sauce. While the goose is cooking, use the opportunity to take a stroll around the cemetery.

SLICING ONIONS

Peeling and chopping seven onions can be a daunting task for sensitive souls. The use of swimming goggles is recommended or ski goggles, when available, since the latter are, of course, bigger and work better in many cases. Some people are of the firm belief that holding one's breath during the cutting is an effective antidote. It normally takes less than a minute to peel and chop an onion, but seven onions represent a far greater challenge. There are also those who recommend peeling the onion under a tap of running cold water. If none of these remedies work, it is best to ask the nearest person to you to cut the onion, a man, for example. Although this is by no means a universal law, their emotional make-up is often structured differently, particularly with regard to the thickness of their skin.

CARROT MOUSSE (SIDE DISH WITH GOOSE)

1 kilo of carrots, ½ cup of carrot juice, 1 teaspoon of salt, 2 tablespoons of sugar, 1 cup of cream, ¼ teaspoon of nutmeg. Wash carrots and boil in a pot with as little water as possible. The carrots are cooked when they become soft. Put them into a food processor or mixer, if you happen to have one handy in your home (if not mash the carrots with a fork) with a little bit of carrot juice, cream, salt, sugar and nutmeg. Eat it as a side dish with the wild goose or roasted lamb (see recipes). The same method can be applied for the making of turnip mousse by substituting turnips for the carrots. Or you can even mix the two vegetables to make carrot and turnip mousse.

SUCCULENT REDCURRANT JELLY (SIDE DISH WITH GOOSE)

1–2 shrubs of redcurrant, sugar (60% of the weight of the fruit). If you don't have any redcurrants growing in your garden, you can always negotiate with a neighbour who doesn't make any use of his or her bush—due, for example, to back problems or old age—and bribe them into allowing you to pick the berries in exchange for two succulent jars of redcurrant jelly. The island is littered with unexploited redcurrant bushes, particularly in the older neighbourhoods of towns. One needs to bear in mind that there is considerably more waste in the making of redcurrant jelly than other types of jelly. Pick the redcurrants and rinse them. There is no need to strip the currants from their light green stalks. Place in a big pot. Put on heat for 2–3 minutes and allow to boil or wait for the berries to start bursting. Turn off the heat and let it simmer a while in the pot. Tip the whole lot into the sieve and allow it to drip through. Add sugar (600 grams for each litre of juice). Boil for a few minutes or until it starts to thicken. Skim the froth off and make sure the juice does not boil for too long. The succulent redcurrant jelly is ready when it slides off a silver spoon in long blobs. If there is no silver spoon in the house, a normal spoon will do. Allow to cool and place in small jars. Remember to give your neighbour his/her jars.

SPAGHETTI CARBONARA

Spaghetti, dry or fresh, a packet of bacon (preferably diced), 2 egg yolks, 1 pot of crème fraîche or 1 cup of cream, grated parmesan, olive oil. Boil water in a pot, salt it, throw the pasta in and cook it as instructed on package. Be careful not to over-boil it. Meanwhile, cut or slice the bacon into thin pieces and pan-fry them in a tiny bit of oil. Drain the water from the pasta through a sieve and then throw the pasta back into the pot again. Do not place the pot back over the stove. Mix the two egg yolks with the pasta and toss in the pieces of bacon with the tub of cream. You have to be quick mixing all this together to make sure the egg yolks don't curdle. Sometimes the cheese is added into the pot. Season with freshly ground pepper and eat immediately with parmesan and, on special occasions, with a glass of Umbrian red wine.

OVEN-BAKED PEPPERS

Sliced or whole peppers baked in the oven or grilled are one of the simplest dishes to make, and will normally just cook themselves, with a maximum time of 10–15 minutes. Peppers are rich in iron, beneficial to women, and make a good side dish with fish, meat, other vegetables, rice or as a dish on their own. It is the ideal dish for a woman taking her first steps in the culinary arts. Choose organic peppers and cut each one in four, slicing them lengthwise. Place them on a baking tray or an oven-proof plate, sprinkle them with olive oil and sea salt and bake. You can mix all colours of peppers, yellow, orange, green and red. Red peppers are the sweetest and tastiest, however. You can throw any kind of vegetable into the oven to roast, e.g. sliced vegetable marrow, mushrooms, leeks and aubergines.

CHRISTMAS CAKE WITH RAISINS

When a guest appears unexpectedly, it is a good idea to buy Christmas cake in the nearest bakery, i.e. if guests appear with only ten minutes' warning. That is normally the simplest way to be totally sure of the quality of the cake. Very few working single mothers actually have the time to bake a Christmas cake. The following, however, is a quick recipe. *2½ cups of flour, 3 teaspoons of baking powder, ½ cup of sugar, 1 egg, a few drops of vanilla, 2 cups of milk, 100 grams of butter, 50 grams of raisins.* Mix the flour, baking powder and sugar in a bowl. Mix half of the milk and the egg into the dough. Melt the butter in a pot and mix it with the dough, remainder of the milk and vanilla drops.

Finally, mix in the raisins. Pour into a buttered cake tin and bake for 40 minutes.

SOUR WHALE (FOR BUFFET)

1 kilo of whale blubber, 1 litre of whey. Even though sour whale might be offered on the buffet table of a kindergarten (along with black olives, mozzarella, feta cheese, French goat's cheese, blood pudding, dried fish and mushrooms) in a novel, this isn't a combination I would want to offer any guests of mine. Yet many young children are curious to taste this white whale jelly and it is very easy to make. As is well known, whale blubber is the thick layer of adipose tissue that covers the stomach of the whale and is rich in fat. The main obstacle is the scarcity of these basic ingredients. The method to be used is roughly as follows: wash the whale blubber, place it in a pot and boil it until it becomes tender. Drain it fully using a colander and then cut the blubber into pieces about 2cm thick. Then place it in a container, pour the whey over it and allow it to ferment. Make sure the blubber is completely covered by the whey and note that you may need to add whey from time to time. The blubber can be tasted after 5 days of fermentation in the whey. Keep in a cool place but do not freeze. If the whale blubber is transported between countries, ensure it is kept in a little whey in a receptacle with a good lid.

KRÚTTKEX (CUTIE COOKIES)

There is no guarantee that all of the food items mentioned in this novel can be found on the shelves of a supermarket. One example of this is the episode in which the narrator does a weekend shop for the child in her charge. The items mentioned include, among other things: whey, Superman yogurt, bananas, hopping sausages, children's cheese, Little Rascal bread, milk, kindergarten pâté, letter pasta and Cutie cookies. Some of these products are to be found in stores, others not. However, since fiction can sometimes have a prophetic dimension, one cannot exclude the possibility that some of these products may appear on the market in the future.

PORRIDGE

3 cups of water, 1 cup of organically grown oats, salt. When the water is on the point of boiling in the pot, put in the oats, salt it and mix it once. Remove the porridge from the heat as soon as it boils. That way the porridge stays granular and retains its original form. The porridge can also be cooked starting in cold water, which will make it softer and smoother. The porridge should then be boiled for two minutes and divided equally between two bowls, if both parties have the same appetite. Porridge is eaten with milk, or perhaps with a little cream. In Iceland some people like to substitute the milk with AB milk (a local dairy product produced from pasteurized and homogenized milk) http://www.ms.is/Vorur/Markfaedi-og-baetiefnavorur/AB-vorur/204/default.aspx or *súrmilk* (a type of yogurt made from skimmed milk). In the last century, cold porridge was often mixed with *skyr* (buttermilk) and known as *hræringur* around the country. Many of the people who were sent off into the countryside and had parched mouths at the end of their long journeys have mixed memories of this kind of porridge, which was served with blood pudding. Nowadays, dates, apples and dried apricots are sometimes mixed into the porridge. One can also put green leaves into the porridge to give it a green colour, such as finely chopped lemongrass, boiled Icelandic moss, yarrow, lady's mantle and white dryas. This would make it summer porridge.

RED WINE (ON VARIOUS OCCASIONS)

Some of the characters in the story have a keen fondness for alcohol, although this applies more to the secondary characters than the narrator. Examples of excessive drinking are to be found in various parts of the novel, even from an expectant mother. There are also various references to light wine, liqueurs or stronger spirits such as cognac, but equally often, if not more often, the characters drink water or fresh milk. The journey begins with two bottles of water, for example, and there is one occurrence of three to four glasses of milk being downed by a child in the space of a paragraph. Even though moderate drinking can occasionally help us escape the burdens of existence, it is by no means an established pattern in the narrator's life nor a lifestyle, but rather behaviour that is strictly dictated by narrative necessity. In fact, it would be more accurate to talk about regular exceptions. It may be of symbolic significance that the narrator does not dwell on the potential consequences of inebriation; the fulcrum of the plot lies elsewhere. If one does go too far, however, there are a number of day-after remedies that can be suggested. I will mention only one that remains infallible: a tasty miso soup.

HOME-BREWED CROWBERRY SCHNAPPS IN A JAR

Crowberries (you can also use redcurrant, blackcurrant or various other berries), sugar, pure vodka. Take a large, clean 2-litre jar with a lid and fill half of it with berries. Fill a quarter of the jar with sugar. Fill the remaining quarter of the jar with pure vodka, right up to the brim. Fasten the lid on the jar and place it somewhere safe out of the reach of children, but not under a bed or somewhere else where the jar may be forgotten. Turn the jar over once a day for a period of two months. If you prepare the jar in mid-October, the schnapps will be ready just before Christmas. As soon as the winter solstice dawns, it is ideal to sit out on the deck, well dressed, and to drink two to three shots of this beverage with the celestial vault in full view.

EXTREMELY THICK RICE PUDDING WITH CINNAMON SUGAR

2–3 cups of rice, 2 cups of cold water, 1 teaspoon of salt, ½ cup of raisins, 1 ½ litres of milk, cinnamon. There are a number of rice pudding variants of varying thickness. Thoroughly rinse the rice in cold water. Different types of rice can be used, everything from organic brown rice to the sticky River Rice that was used for a long time. Put 2–3 cups of rice in a pot and pour 1 ½ cups of cold water over it. Salt. Bring it to the boil, reduce the heat to a minimum and cook it until almost all of the water has evaporated, but without allowing the rice to stick together, i.e. about 5 minutes. Allow the child to sprinkle it with raisins. Pour the milk into the pot, bit by bit, and bring to the boil again. Do not place the lid on the pot while the rice is cooking or it will boil over. Boil the rice at low heat until the grains are soft. Turn off the heat and allow it to simmer for 5 minutes, while the milk seeps into the rice. Help the child to mix the cinnamon and sugar in the bowl. Eat with cold milk and cinnamon. It is nice to eat the rice pudding with slices of liver pudding.

SESAME SEED BREAD ROLLS FROM THE BAKERY

Sesame seed bread rolls rapidly fell out of fashion because of the white flour they are made with, but they are regaining popularity again, particularly at weekends. They are ideal for a man and a woman after their second night. The easiest thing to do by far is to buy sesame seed bread rolls in the bakery. They can vary greatly from one bakery to the next. In some places they can be quite dense and soft, whereas in others they have a crispy crust and airy interior, completely empty in fact.

FISH BALLS WITH BOILED POTATOES AND BUTTER

Buy 1 kilo of fresh, fat haddock. Check out the origins of the fish and at least make sure that it was not fished in Fossvogur, but rather in the north or west of the country. Tuesday is normally fish ball day. Ask your fishmonger to personally skin and fillet your selected haddock from the north or west. You can also ask him to mince the fish to save you the trouble—specify whether it is for a woman and a child or for a man, woman, child and mother-in-law—and decide at the same time whether, and if so how many, onions should go into the mincer. It is best to get to the fishmongers before the crowds get in, i.e. before five-thirty. That will also give you time to talk about other things, and, for example, discuss the theoretical differences between the head and tail of the fish and other topics, such as catch quota issues and the pricing of marine products. It is four-thirty and, for the third time, the old woman in front of me in the queue tells the fishmonger, who is cutting some fish for her, in a low voice to take another three centimetres off the tail, after which, in an almost inaudible whisper, she confesses: "Because it's just me at home." Although it can be interesting to ponder who buys what and for how many people, I give very little away about my family status. I confess nothing to the fishmonger and am saved by the child, since I can say I'm buying for two. That way the fishmonger can imagine I'm happily married and that he's selling minced fish to a very enamoured couple. Then I can give the boy the leftovers of the fish balls the next day, while I have tea and toast with tomatoes. Sometimes your personal fishmonger will give you a good recipe for *gellur* or cod tongues. Although I've never really been able to relate to those fleshy triangular muscles behind the cod's chin and under its tongue, when a man passes on a recipe to a woman it creates a certain kind of bond, intimacy even. If I were to divulge too much information and were to reveal, for example, that there were two adults in the house or that my husband is from the west of the country where those cod tongues come from, or that he prefers haddock fried in breadcrumbs or something along those lines, because that was what his mother used to cook for him (the kind of thing women say sometimes), then the fishmonger would probably keep his cod tongue recipe to himself. In the two minutes that he is away operating the mincing machine, I swiftly glance at the rye bread, dry fish, lamb dripping and love balls on display on the glass counter. Seeing my reflection in the glass I brush my fringe aside. *1 kilo of minced haddock with or without onion, 4 tablespoons of flour, 1 tablespoon of potato flour (optional), 1 tablespoon of sea salt, 1 teaspoon of pepper, 2 eggs, 100 millilitres of milk, ½ onion and/or chives.* Mix the minced fish, flour, potato flour and seasoning, also mixing in the eggs and then the milk. Add in the chopped chives as well, if you want. Chives grow in the garden or in a pot on the balcony from April to November. You can also use parsley that will grow all year round in a pot on the kitchen window sill. Heat some olive oil and butter in a pan. Mould the fish balls with the help of a spoon until they assume the shape of little white mice and then fry them in the pan. Quickly remove two half-fried fish balls and place them on a saucer so that you can eat them with Japanese soya sauce, while you finish frying the other balls. The fish balls should be eaten with butter and new potatoes, preferably from the November harvest, if available. The potatoes should be boiled at moderate heat for a short time so that they do not become too soft. Instead of butter, you can use curry sauce on the fish balls. Melt 1 tablespoon of butter in a pot. Add 1 tablespoon of flour and mix together, then add 2 cups of milk and bring to the boil. Meanwhile keep on stirring. Season with Indian curry powder, salt and pepper, and finally add 1 teaspoon of sugar.

LAMB PÂTÉ ON SLICES OF RYE BREAD

2 kilos of lamb meat, salt, pepper, allspice, bay leaves. Classic lamb pâté is made with pretty fat meat. Rinse the meat and let it simmer on a low heat in as little salted water as possible for an hour. Add a few bay leaves and two peeled onions in the last 30 minutes of boiling. At the end of the boiling the meat detaches itself from the bones. Remove the bones and put the meat into the mincer (or mixer) with the onion. Then put the pâté back into the pot and heat it. Season according to taste with, among other things, pepper and allspice. Allow the pâté to cool a while and then transfer to a suitably sized receptacle or freezing-bag. Store in freezer. Eat on slices of rye bread.

HOOCH (FOR PARTIES)

This is obviously a sensitive issue for many law-abiding citizens. The objective is not to encourage the production of hooch or other types of home-brew (with the exception of crowberry schnapps; see recipe above), but just to remind the reader that some drinks are better enjoyed on the page than in the stomach. There is no need to remind you that not only does hooch have a disgusting taste, but it can also cause temporary blackouts and do bodily harm. Five kilos of sugar are required for every 20 litres of water and about 4 tablespoons of yeast. Mix the sugar and yeast in water heated to 25 degrees and leave at a constant temperature for three weeks, e.g. in a windowless boiler room or greenhouse. Then check to see if the liquid has fermented, i.e. whether all the sugar has dissolved, by tasting one drop on the tip of your tongue. The mixture should then be moved to a cool place where it will be allowed to settle. This should kill all germs. The liquid obtained is known as *gambri* (non-distilled hooch) and is normally of a greyish-yellow colour. The *gambri* then needs to be distilled with what is very often home-made distilling equipment. Install the equipment in an appropriate place, e.g. in the guest toilet or in the garage. It will give off a bitter odour that those in the know will not fail to recognize.

A large portion of the liquid evaporates during the distillation process, leaving you with just a few litres of alcohol. Finally, filter the brew through charcoal to purify it and reduce that home-brew taste. Some people improve the taste by adding essences, which they buy in bottles in special home-brew stores.

MEAT-STUFFED CABBAGE ROLLS

1 kilo of fresh sausage meat, 1 head of cabbage, butter (melted), 1½ kilos of potatoes. Buy 1 kilo of fresh sausage meat from the supermarket. Boil the head of cabbage in lightly salted water for 10 minutes or until it starts to soften. Allow it to cool and peel off its leaves. Calculate 4 cabbage leaves per person. Put 2 tablespoons of the sausage meat on each leaf, and then roll and wrap the leaf around the meat to create tidy rolls. Arrange the rolls in a pot with a thick bottom and add water to it. Cook the meat-stuffed cabbage rolls at moderate heat for 20 minutes. Eat the dish with potato purée and melted butter. The potato purée is prepared as follows. Boil the potatoes in water at a moderate heat for 15 minutes. Then drain them, place them back in the pot and mash them. Classic potato purée has 2 cups of milk, 2–3 tablespoons of sugar, a pinch of sea salt and a dab of butter. The sausage meat can also be fried as meat balls in the pan. You then cover the bottom of the pan with water, turn off the heat and place the lid on the pan and leave it to simmer for 5 minutes without any interference. That way the sausage meat begins to swell, doubling its volume, like rising dough. In some cases, the lid of the pan will even rise on its own. The sausage meat balls are then eaten with potato purée, butter and boiled white cabbage.

UNDRINKABLE COFFEE

Undrinkable coffee can be made in a variety of ways. The simplest way is to leave a packet of coffee open in a cupboard with cream biscuits, light bulbs, batteries and teabags for several days. You can also make very thin coffee that is the same colour as tea. Another infallible method is to heat up old coffee, even in a microwave oven.

HAMBURGERS

As anyone driving through the dark days of winter and endless stretches of black sand will realize, the petrol stations and snack bars that are to be found on the circular road around the island are just about the only distractions one comes across. The inevitable therefore happens, i.e. people end up eating junk food: hot dogs that have been simmering in a pot for an entire weekend, or hamburgers, mayonnaise sandwiches, express pizzas, whipped ice creams dipped in chocolate and bags of mixed sweets. This is not in any way an attempt to promote the dietary habits propagated by these establishments, nor the extremely dangerous dyes used to colour wine gums and children's excessive consumption of sugar, to mention but a few examples. The fact that the narrator buys three bars of chocolate for a four-year-old child who is unable to choose which one he wants should not be taken as exemplary behaviour either. In this context it should be pointed out that the narrator has no child of her own and is therefore no expert in raising children. Eating habits are, to some extent, dictated by circumstance, but above all by narrative necessity. The following is a recipe for home-made hamburgers. *200 grams of minced beef, salt, pepper, parsley, chives, 2 wholewheat hamburger buns, 1 tomato, 4 slices of cucumber, 4 leaves of salad (different types can be used: lettuce, rocket salad, scurvy grass and chickweed leaves). Sauce: 1 teaspoon of mayonnaise, 2 teaspoons of milk curd or AB milk, 1 teaspoon of tomato sauce, half a teaspoon of French Dijon mustard.* Mix the chopped parsley and chives with the minced meat and mould two handsome burgers. Salt and pepper. Fry the burgers in some olive oil in a pan or grill in the oven for 10 minutes. Lay out the leaves of salad on the heated bread buns and place the meat on them. Slice the tomato and cucumber and divide them equally between the two burgers. Put one tablespoon of sauce on top and then cover with the top of the bun.

COCOA SOUP WITH RUSK AND WHIPPED CREAM

Many people who have been hospitalized for a short period of one to two days (to have their appendix removed, for example) might have memories of a lukewarm cocoa soup served with a soggy biscuit. However, good cocoa soup is a real treat when, for example, served as a dessert after fried fish on a Tuesday. *2 tablespoons of cocoa, 2 tablespoons of sugar, 2 cups of water, a few drops of vanilla, 1 litre of milk, 1 tablespoon of potato flour, a pinch of salt, rusk, cream.* Mix the cocoa and sugar in the water. Bring to the boil for 5 minutes. Then add milk and bring to the boil again. Mix the potato flour in a tiny bit of cold water and stir into the soup. Allow it to boil. Stir the vanilla drops into the soup last, but do not allow the soup to boil again. Eat the soup with the rusk, which everyone crumbles over their own bowls, allowing the crumbs to float on the surface. Place a dollop of thickly whipped cream on top.

BANANA DESSERT

Bananas are a tasty, nutritious and healthy snack to take on a journey, and suitable to hand to a hungry child over one's shoulder while driving a car. And now that I am getting to know children a bit better, I can tell you that my banana and chocolate milkshake has become one of my travelling companion's favourites. Chuck the banana, vanilla ice cream and chocolate sauce into a mixer or food processor (or mix it by hand) and make a cold banana drink. If there is no freezer in the chalet to store ice cream in, cultured milk can be used instead.

And who doesn't know the following simplest camping dessert recipe in the world? Calculate one banana per person. Make a long incision along the length of the banana with a sharp penknife and stick in 4–5 pieces of dark chocolate. Wrap the bananas in aluminium foil, place them on a cooling grill and allow to bake for a short while. Chocolate bananas can also be eaten with whipped cream. To whip the cream, pour it into a jar or receptacle with a lid (e.g. an empty half-litre Fanta bottle) and shake it to a suitable rhythm, passing it from one person to the next, until the cream thickens. If you have a travel CD player handy you will be able to find some appropriate music. Fetch a bottle of Calvados from your backpack and eat the chocolate banana straight out of its wrapping with a spoon and whipped cream. Captain Morgan rum is not particularly recommended, except for men, who generally hold their drink better. Sit by the entrance of the tent or lie in zipped-together sleeping bags listening to snipes echoing through the night.

MUSHROOM SOUP (LECCINUM SCABRUM)

1 kilo of freshly picked mushrooms (eg. Leccinum scabrum or porcini mushrooms), water, 1 cup of cream, ½ cup of port. Pick 1 kilo of mushrooms, then clean them by brushing off the soil and cutting their stems, before rinsing under running water and drying them. Trim the mushrooms or chop them and fry them in a pan in butter or in a pot with a thick bottom. Season and add a tablespoon of ground thyme if available. Add 2 litres of water and a cube of vegetable broth and cream. Take the pot off the stove and add the port. Serve with fresh bread.

COKE IN A SMALL GLASS BOTTLE

In the 1970s, or at around the time I was born, it was popular to drink Coke from a small glass bottle through a liquorice straw. The method was as follows: uncap the bottle and slide a liquorice straw into the bottle. Ensure the Coke does not foam over the bottle. The skill lies in sucking up the Coke through the straw. There was also a tradition of leaving the liquorice straw steeped in the Coke for a certain period of time, say ten to fifteen minutes, to allow the liquorice to absorb the liquid in the meantime. The liquorice straw would then swell up, giving the Coke a brownish-grey colour and sticky consistency. The liquorice had to be pulled out of the bottle in time, before the straw started to turn to mush and blocked the neck of the bottle.

APPLE PIE FROM GIANT RED APPLES WITH CREAM

The narrator has a vision of giant red apples in a dream. To dream of food is normally a good omen, provided the food is fresh and sufficient for the occasion. The circumstances and individual elements need to be carefully examined, however. Food doesn't have the same taste in the world of dreams as it does in our wakeful state. On the other hand, dream recipes may have something in common with fictitious ones. An example of a fictitious recipe is the apple tart made out of giant red apples. In reality most people would, of course, use green apples to make an apple pie. There are hundreds of variations of apple tart recipes. The following is a very simple and delicious one. *4 giant red apples, 2 cups of peeled almonds, 1 bar of chocolate (100 grams), 1 tablespoon of brown sugar, 1 cup of white sugar, 1 cup of butter, 1 cup of flour.* Peel the apples and slice them into small pieces. Place them at the base of a buttered baking tin. Sprinkle the almonds and chopped chocolate over them, followed by a tablespoon of brown sugar. Mix the flour, sugar and butter so that it turns into a light yellow dough, like marzipan. Roll out the dough with your hands, spreading it over the filling. Press the dough all around the perimeter of the tin. Bake in the oven at 180 degrees for 25 minutes and eat with whipped cream.

GRILLED SNOW BUNTING, HIGHLANDS-STYLE

Please note that the following recipe should not be construed as an incitement to kill small protected feathered birds. It is not unlikely that the foreign hunters targeted the snow buntings because of their lack of familiarity with this species and poor knowledge of local regulations, since as everyone knows snow buntings are a sedentary breed and therefore Icelandic through and through. Overseas, small birds are a popular source of food and often impaled on skewers and then roasted over an open fire. On drizzly November days it is in many ways more suitable to cook small birds in baking trays in the heated electric ovens of highland kitchens. The narrator bears no responsibility for this recipe. *16 snow buntings, 20 pearl onions, salt, pepper, 2 cups of cream, a packet of bacon, mushrooms, 8 slices of white bread, milk, garlic, parsley.* Start by plucking the birds. First cut the wings, necks and legs. The necks, if there are any, can be used for the juice. Next cut the skin under the sternum and peel it off like a coat. Then make an incision under the wing bone and extract the innards, gizzard, heart and liver. Put the hearts aside. Rinse the birds, salt and pepper them, both inside and out, and line them up on the draining board while you prepare the filling. Fry the small pieces of bacon and finely cut hearts in butter for 10 minutes. The hearts will give the broth a strong taste. Before frying them, though, make a small incision in each heart to drain the blood from it. Add the chopped mushrooms and garlic. Immerse the slices of white bread, devoid of their crust, in milk. Mix the bacon, hearts, mushrooms, garlic, wet bread, chopped parsley and other spices and stuff the filling into the small birds. Peel the pearl onions and fry them with the birds in butter in the pan for 10 minutes. Brown the birds on all sides. Arrange the birds, side by side, in the baking tray, pour cream on them and bake for 40 minutes. Sixteen snow buntings can easily fit into the average-size baking tray. Eat them with stuffing, green salad and macaroni.

ICELANDIC MEAT SOUP

It should be noted that the contents of this soup will vary according to whether it is made in the summer or winter and the availability of vegetables in any given place or time. *1 kilo of lamb meat (shoulder or leg), 2½ litres of water, 2 tablespoons of salt, 1 teaspoon of pepper, ½ cup rice (it is good to use brown rice, which you will need to pre-boil, however), 4 tablespoons of oats or barley, 4 tablespoons of dry soup herbs, 1 big turnip or 2 small ones, 10 small potatoes, preferably unpeeled, 5 carrots, 1–2 onions or one leek. Celery can also be used (both stalk and leaves), fresh spinach, garden dock, green cabbage, broccoli and whatever other vegetable happens to be handy in each case.* Rinse the meat, cut it into rather small pieces and put it into a pot. Cover with water, salt it, close the lid and boil for 15 minutes. Lift the lid and skim off the froth. Add water to the pot and then the various vegetables, according to the cooking time of each one. Be careful not to overcook the vegetables. Boil it all together until it fuses. It is good to throw some thyme into the soup and some chopped mint, which grows wild in many parts of Iceland and is particularly good with lamb, since it reduces that farm shed taste.

SHEEP'S HEAD JELLY

After torching the sheep's heads, brush them with an abrasive brush to wash away the soot. Next place the heads in lukewarm water and scrub them well, both internally and externally, making sure that you scrape the eyes and ears. Arrange the black heads together in a big pot, salt them and pour water over them, without necessarily covering them. When the pot comes to the boil, brown froth should ooze out of the heads. Seal the pot and boil the heads at a moderate heat for an hour or until the meat loosens from the bone. De-bone the meat and place it in a tin (e.g. Christmas cake tin). Remove the eyeballs, although it is a question of taste whether the eyes and ears should be left in the jelly. Pour a little broth over it to ensure it glues together better. Store under light pressure in the fridge overnight, then turn it upside down and cut it into slices. Sheep's head jelly is more often than not eaten with turnip mousse or boiled potatoes and white milk sauce.

PEPPER COOKIES WITH ICING SUGAR

The baking of pepper cookies in close collaboration with a child is a permanent feature in any household with a kid in the lead-up to Christmas. *150 grams of sugar, 250 grams of syrup, ½ teaspoon of pepper, 2 teaspoons of ginger, 2 teaspoons of cinnamon, ½ teaspoon of cloves, 125 grams of butter, 1 egg, 2 teaspoons of baking soda, 400 grams of flour.* Mix the sugar, syrup and butter and bring to simmering point. Mix in the baking soda with all the spices, pepper, ginger, cinnamon and cloves. Then add the egg and flour. Keep 1–2 cups of flour to knead the dough. Knead the dough on the table with the child. Roll out the dough and let the child cut out the shapes him/herself (Santa Clauses, Christmas trees, bells, angels and reindeer) and decorate the cookies with the icing. Icing: 125 grams of icing sugar and 1–1½ egg whites mixed well together. Colour according to taste.

HOT COCOA

2 tablespoons of cocoa, 2 tablespoons of sugar, ½ cup of water, ½ litre of milk. Mix cocoa and sugar in a pot of water. Heat and stir until boiling point. Add the milk and bring to the boil again.

HOT CHOCOLATE FROM REAL CHOCOLATE TABLETS

2 tablets (200 grams) of chocolate, 2 cups of water, 1 litre of fresh milk, a pinch of salt. Break the chocolate over a pot and pour water over it. Heat and stir until the chocolate has melted. Add the milk and bring to the boil. Add a pinch of salt. It is good to drink boiling hot with whipped cream in a country house on a cold and rainy day. You can also pour the hot chocolate into a flask and take it with an extra cup on a visit to an old people's home.

KLEINUR (TWISTED DOUGHNUTS)

500 grams of flour, 2 teaspoons of baking powder, 1 ½ teaspoons of soda powder, 75 grams of margarine, ½ cup sugar, 1 egg, 2 cups of cultured milk. Mix the baking and soda powder with the flour in a bowl. Add the mashed margarine, egg, milk and sugar. Knead the dough and then flatten it out with a rolling pin into rather thick pieces, i.e. up to 1 cm thick. Sprinkle the table with flour before flattening out the dough. Cut the dough into strips of about 4 cm in width. Then cut those into pieces of about 8 cm in length. Cut a small slit in the middle of each piece of dough (future twisted doughnut) and gently pull one end through the slit to make the twists in the doughnuts. Arrange the doughnuts side by side on a tray and leave them there while you heat the oil in a pot. Immerse the doughnuts in the fat and then fish them out again with a perforated spatula when they turn to a brownish colour. Deposit them on fat-absorbent paper, e.g. newspapers, and then move them to an old-fashioned floral bowl or heirloom, even.

Skonsur (thick Icelandic pancakes)

4 cups of flour, 1 teaspoon of baking powder, 1 teaspoon of sodium bicarbonate, 1 egg, milk as required. Ensure the dough is not too thin. Fry on a skillet at medium heat.

Four-tiered mayonnaise sandwich cake (for funeral receptions)

(Estimated 200 mourners in the church and 80 mourners at the funeral reception.) *5 loaves of white bread, egg, "salmon petals" and parsley for decorating purposes.*
  Prawn salad: 7 hard-boiled eggs, 500 grams of prawns, mayonnaise.
Salmon salad: 7 hard-boiled eggs, 1 fillet of smoked salmon, mayonnaise.
Tuna fish salad: 7 hard-boiled eggs, canned tuna fish, mayonnaise.
  Buy 5 loaves of white bread and cut off the crusts. Cut the bread lengthwise into four slices that will make up the four tiers or layers of the sandwich cake. Choose an adequately sized plate for the cake and place the bottom tier on it. You can make the prawn salad by mixing the prawns and chopped hard-boiled eggs with the mayonnaise or a mixture of mayonnaise and crème fraîche or mixture of crème fraîche and fermented AB milk. Salmon and tuna fish salads are prepared in the same manner, except that instead of using prawns you use finely

chopped smoked salmon or mashed tuna fish out of a can. If you like you can add flavour to the mayonnaise salads with a touch of Dijon mustard and herbal salts. Spread the bottom tier with prawn salad and place the next tier of bread on top of it, over which you then spread salmon salad. The tuna fish salad goes on the top tier of the cake. Finally spread a thin layer of mayonnaise over the top of the cake (the sides too if you like) and decorate it with slices of boiled egg and "salmon petals". You can also use icing bags to adorn the rim of the cake with mayonnaise puffs, as if you were decorating a cream cake. Chop the parsley and stick a parsley shoot into the salmon petal. The sandwich cake is cut into large slices like a big cream cake. Even though the slicing of this cake may seem a little daunting at first, experience has shown that guests at funeral receptions normally manage the task with surprising skill and without the need for assistance from relatives.

SUSHI (FOR FUNERAL RECEPTIONS)

(Estimated 200 mourners in the church and 80 mourners at the funeral reception. Only some of the mourners are likely to eat sushi, however, which is why alternative dishes should be offered, e.g. see mayonnaise sandwich cake recipe above.) *1 kilo of sushi rice, 25 seaweed sheets (each roll is cut into 7 pieces, which makes 175 pieces), 1 cucumber, 1 avocado, three types of raw fish, e.g. salmon, halibut or cod, trout or salmon roe (jars are OK), wasabi (available in ready-made tubes or as powder in jars to be diluted in water), sesame seeds (approx. 1 teaspoon for each sheet of seaweed), pickled ginger, Japanese soya sauce.*

Rinse the rice until the water is almost transparent—about ten times is recommended. Boil the sushi rice, carefully following the instructions on the packet. While the rice is boiling, chop the vegetables and raw fish into very thin strips. Spread out the seaweed sheets and coat four-fifths of each sheet with a thin layer of compressed rice. Sprinkle a teaspoon of sesame seeds over the rice. Garnish with fine strips of vegetable and raw fish. Spread a very thin layer of wasabi paste on the edges of the seaweed sheets and then roll them tightly together, as if you were making a Swiss roll. Slice the roll into reasonably sized morsels with a sharp knife. Put the morsels into a bowl with Japanese soya sauce and eat with pink pickled ginger.

HORSE SAUSAGE MEAT WITH BOILED POTATOES AND WHITE SAUCE

This is a dish that the narrator managed to botch; she therefore does not recommend it. *8 centimetres of horse sausage meat, 2 potatoes, 1 tablespoon of margarine, 2 tablespoons of flour, 1 cup of milk, salt, sugar.* Boil the meat in water for 10 minutes. Allow the potatoes to boil for an excessively long time or at too high a temperature so that they will be overdone and crumble when you try to peel them. To make the white sauce, melt the margarine in a pot with flour and dilute with milk. Add a pinch of salt and sugar. Cook at a moderate heat in an uncovered pot for 5 minutes, stirring from time to time. The sauce should be white, sticky and glistening, preferably without any clots and too much taste. Serve lukewarm.

OVEN-ROASTED LAMB

1 leg of lamb, rosemary, salt, pepper. The meat should be quite muscular and not too fat. If the raw material is good, it is difficult to go wrong with oven-roasted lamb. It is best to use meat that has not been frozen, otherwise it will need to thaw in the fridge for five days and then on the kitchen table for a few hours before being cooked. Turn the meat and remove any fat, if there is any. Brush a drizzle of olive oil on the meat and season with salt, pepper and fresh rosemary. Once upon a time, rosemary used to be included in a bride's bouquet of flowers because it was believed to provide protection against heart aches. Slip the meat into the oven at a very high heat for 10 minutes. Then move the meat to the bottom of the oven and roast it at a very low heat for up to two hours—but no more than half an hour if the meat has been de-boned. If you like you can put 1 cup of water into the baking tray to get more broth out of the meat. A tablespoon of soya sauce in the sauce pot sharpens the taste. If the sauce fails you can always save it by adding a teaspoon of cinnamon sugar. Eat with traditional side dishes for lamb: caramel potatoes, red cabbage and redcurrant jelly. While you are browning the potatoes, you can also fry slices of lightly boiled turnip in the sugar as well. Drink with a cocktail of malt and orangeade.

CORRECTLY BOILED EGGS

The art of boiling eggs for the correct amount of time is not quite as simple as some people seem to imagine—confident as one may be who hasn't ended up either boiling en egg for too long, making the outer layer of the yolk turn purple, or for too little, making the white of the egg ooze out between one's fingers. Why not use an egg-timer then, some might ask? The use of a sandglass requires one's undivided attention; you can't just leave it to go and check on a child, for example, or to empty a washing machine. One might as well be staring at the second hand of a watch. If you are feeling insecure about your grasp of the passage of time, scrambled eggs would make a safer option.

HALIBUT SOUP

3 good pieces of halibut with bones (salmon can be used instead). Ask your fishmonger to give you the bones, cuts and heads from the halibut or salmon to use in the broth. 1 litre of water, 1 litre of whey, 4 bay leaves, 4–8 peppercorns, 2 teaspoons of sea salt, 7 prunes, ½ cup of raisins, 3 egg yolks, 3 tablespoons of sugar (you can also use syrup), cream. Put the fish heads and bones in a pot with the bay leaves, peppercorns, sea salt, 1 litre of water and 1 litre of whey. Boil for one hour to get a good broth. Filter it through a sieve and pour the clear broth back into the pot. Bring to the boil again and immerse the pieces of fish in the nice broth. Add 7 prunes and half a cup of raisins and cook them slowly with the fish for a few minutes. Take the pieces of fish out of the broth, wrap them in aluminium foil and put them in the oven at moderate heat, while you finish making the soup. Whisk 3 egg yolks and 3 tablespoons of sugar and pour the mixture into the broth. Bring the soup to simmering point again, without, however, allowing it to boil. Whip the cream and, at the moment of serving the soup, put 1 tablespoon in each bowl. Eat with hot pieces of fish, freshly boiled potatoes and a good cucumber salad.

SILVER TEA

Boil water. Fill one-third of a glass with cold milk and then fill the other two-thirds with boiled water. Flavour with honey. Drink after dinner, with a child who has put on his/her pyjamas, just before brushing his/her teeth. Discuss the events of the day and plan the next day together over silver tea. (Silver tea is not to be confused with priest tea, which is basically a Melrose teabag with a shot of schnapps or hooch and 1 teaspoon of sugar.)

WHALE STEAK

This is another example of a dish prepared by secondary characters, for which the narrator bears limited liability (also see grilled snow bunting, highlands-style). In any case, the passing-on of this whale steak recipe should not in itself be interpreted as a reflection of the narrator's stand on whale-hunting. It should be pointed out that the meat in question is from a so-called "drift whale", that is to say a whale that has been beached by providence and not hunted. In fact the provenance of the whale remains a total mystery, since it could just as well have come from over the highlands as the lagoon. It is, nonetheless, an undeniable fact that every now and then one of two things can happen: a sizeable sei whale or baleen whale will get washed up on the shores of a small community without warning or a small porpoise will get entangled in a fishing boat's net without any hope of being revived, despite the efforts of the crew. This recipe is conceived for four to six people. If you need to feed a higher number than this or indeed the population of an entire village, increase the portions accordingly. As a result, a whole whale may be required. *1 piece of whale meat, salt, pepper, 2 cups of cream.* In the past, whale meat used to be left steeped in milk overnight to kill that liver oil taste. Then the meat was generally boiled in a pot for several hours, after being briefly sautéed in margarine. The following is a more modern method in which the meat is handled in a similar way to beef. Cut the whale meat into long, thin slices, removing the nerves and fat if necessary. Pan-fry the meat in olive oil, seasoning it with salt and freshly ground pepper. Remove the meat from the pan while you make cream sauce from the broth with cream. Lower the heat under the sauce, taste and add pepper if needed. Then neatly place the meat in the pan with the sauce. Eat with the side dishes of your choice, e.g. lightly boiled vegetables, carrots, broccoli and cauliflower.

Lummur (Icelandic Pancakes)

Rice pudding leftovers, (approximately 2 cups), 1 cup of flour, 2 eggs, ½ teaspoon of salt, ½ teaspoon of soda powder, 1 tablespoon of brown sugar, 1 ½ cups of milk, frying butter. Mix everything together in a bowl, adding the milk last. Melt butter in a pan. A four-year-old can make *lummur* with very little assistance when he/she is, for example, recovering from being drenched in a puddle. Place your assistant on a safe stool by the cooker, tie an apron around him and allow him to place the floating dough on the hot pan with a small ladle. If you hold the handle of the pan for the child and make sure he/she doesn't burn him/herself, the child can easily flip the pancakes with a spatula and then fish them out when they have been browned and place them on a plate. Allow the child to sugar the *lummur*. *Lummur* can also be eaten with syrup or jam. It is a good idea to make *lummur* and hot chocolate while the child's boots are drying by the oven.

KNITTING BABY SOCKS

This recipe is designed for one baby. In the event of there being twins, two pairs will need to be knitted. The older siblings are expected to knit the socks. Help the child cast 44 stitches on a circular number 3 knitting needle. Allow the child to choose the colour of the yarn. Teach the child to knit in 8-centimetre-long loops and narrow rows (folded over) knitting into the front and back of the stitch alternately. It could take several weeks to knit each row if the child is learning to knit for the first time. The remainder of the sock is knitted back and forth in the garter stitch. When this point is reached, it is a good idea to find some good person with some experience in knitting socks for infants who might be willing to teach the skill to a child. The child can then work on the project every day and knit several stitches from time to time, while the supervisor helps him/her not to lose his/her thread. Allow the garter stitch to start from the centre and behind. Help the child to knit 1 centimetre. Place the first and last stitch in the row to one side while you continue to knit the middle garter stitch and knit a total of 4 centimetres. Now load all the stitches back onto the needle and knit a 3-centimetre top for the sock. Then slip the first and last stitches off the needle and start to knit the sole. Knit an additional 9 centimetres. Slip off all stitches. Weave in the ends of the sock for the child and bend the tops of the sides.

PUSHKIN PRESS

Pushkin Press was founded in 1997. Having first rediscovered European classics of the twentieth century, Pushkin now publishes novels, essays, memoirs, children's books, and everything from timeless classics to the urgent and contemporary.

Pushkin Paper books, like this one, represent exciting, high-quality writing from around the world. Pushkin publishes widely acclaimed, brilliant authors such as Stefan Zweig, Marcel Aymé, Antal Szerb, Paul Morand and Yasushi Inoue, as well as some of the most exciting contemporary and often prize-winning writers, including Andrés Neuman, Edith Pearlman and Ryu Murakami.

Pushkin Press publishes the world's best stories, to be read and read again.

*

FRIEDRICH TORBERG *Young Gerber*
MARK TWAIN *The Jumping Frog and Other Sketches*
ELLEN ULLMAN *By Blood*
Close to the Machine
The Bug
LOUISE DE VILMORIN *Madame de*
ERNST WEISS *Franziska*
Jarmila
EDITH WHARTON *Glimpses of the Moon*
FLORIAN ZELLER *Artificial Snow*
Julien Parme
Lovers or Something Like It
The Fascination of Evil
STEFAN ZWEIG *Amok and Other Stories*
Beware of Pity
Burning Secret
Casanova: A Study in Self-Portraiture
A Chess Story
The Collected Stories of Stefan Zweig
Confusion
Fear
The Governess and Other Stories
Journey into the Past
Letter from an Unknown Woman and Other Stories
Magellan
Marie Antoinette
Mary Stuart
Mental Healers: Mesmer, Eddy, Freud
Selected Stories
Shooting Stars: Ten Historical Miniatures
The Struggle with the Daemon: Hölderlin, Kleist, Nietzsche
Twilight and Moonbeam Alley
The World of Yesterday
Wondrak and Other Stories